Breathe

Breathe

Book 1 in the Fielding Series

by Kimberley Ash

TEA ROSE
PUBLISHING

Dedication

For Donn, of course. And always.

Author's Note

People have phobias about all kinds of things. Sometimes, unfortunately, these phobias spring from traumatic experiences. Please be aware that this book contains recollections of past sexual assault, and a scene including a mugging and attempted sexual assault. If something similar has happened to you, call 800-656-HOPE. You don't have to go through this alone.

Chapter 1

Somewhere beyond the lights, someone probably had a camera pointed at him.

On a normal day, Kane wasn't bothered by this; on a normal day, he encouraged it. But not tonight. Not while he stood, alone, watching his second building this week collapse into a pile of charred beams and wet ash. The smell in his nostrils was that of the day his father had died: the smell of grief and fear and helplessness.

The site manager puffed over to him, a short, round man, perspiring despite the winds coming off Lake Michigan. "There's nothing else to see, Mr. Fielding. Let me get you some coffee."

Kane's jacket wasn't thick enough for this October night in Grand Rapids; he could feel the contrast between his freezing back and the heat still coming off the doused building. "You're right, Art," he said. But he didn't look at the man, and he didn't move.

"I am sorry, Mr. Fielding." The site manager shifted his feet. "Is it true that the Chicago fire was arson?"

"Yep." That news would have drawn the cameras here. The press would perk up at the word, look up his company. They'd find out about the explosion thirteen years ago that had killed his father. Swoop down to see what fresh hell Fielding Paper was going through. The presence of the camera-friendly president would help.

He'd been trained to analyze the way he looked when the photographers were around, because Kane, to quote his public relations director, was hot, and that was good for business. His messy dark-brown hair, hardly touched since he'd been woken four hours and a three-hour drive ago, was his trademark. His dark clothes were calculated decisions, worn to emphasize his height. He had deep-set, brooding dark eyes and a chiseled jaw, and all that crap that made his PR man rub his hands with glee—and Kane blush if he caught a description of himself in print.

But he was grateful. These tools had kept Fielding Paper in the news—and the gossip columns—for years. So sure, on the outside it was business as usual. But he hoped to God the camera didn't have a long enough lens to pick up the muscle clenching and unclenching in his jaw.

The site manager looked at him more closely. "At least no one got hurt," Art said encouragingly. "And most of the lumber is saved."

Kane worked to keep his face impassive. He could give a crap right now about the lumber. "Yeah," he said again, and then, because Art seemed to be looking for conversation, "Maybe the security cameras picked up something."

"Uh..." Art shifted again. Kane's own feet were cold, and Art had been out here for hours before him. "Everything shut down when the electric was cut."

"But the backup generator would have—"

"He killed that, too."

"*Shit!*" He spat the word so loudly Art jumped. So much for not looking as if this was getting to him. Kane wondered if he was far enough away from the firefighters to light a cigarette. Then he remembered the cameras and tapped his numb fingers against his thigh instead.

There was a surprisingly delicate *whump*, and another corner of the building collapsed.

"The forest is good, too," Art reminded him. Kane had had the trees to their left planted after his father died. They were still several years from maturity.

That had been one of his first acts as CEO. One of the crazy decisions of a twenty-two-year-old, numb with grief, fresh out of college, desperate to save his family's business. "Buy American," he'd touted to any news channel and TV show that would have him. "Buy Fielding Paper." He'd planted acres in the US and given land back to the villages in Central America. The goodwill had been priceless.

People *liked* him, goddammit! Why was someone setting fire to his mills?

The manager was hovering uncertainly, his breath visible in little puffs. The Fielding family history seemed just as visible.

But he had to get them all back on track. He couldn't let this get worse than it was. "Thanks, Art," he said, rolling his frozen shoulders and smiling down at the man. "I'll take that coffee. And hey." He made an effort to shrug off the fear. "Happy Halloween."

♦

Several hours later, behind the podium at the local town hall hastily commandeered for this small press conference, Kane was more in his element. His quick phone call with Leo Palmer, his PR director, had solidified the story they needed to tell. He was very good at giving the press what they wanted.

He stood with his hands on either side of the podium, looking into the cameras or catching the eye of each reporter there.

"Will you rebuild?" they asked.

"Of course," he reassured them. "We have a commitment to this area that spans decades."

"What do the workers do now?"

"We'll find them shifts at other plants if we can."

"What if you can't?"

He looked appropriately serious. "We take care of our own." Whatever that meant. "I'm just glad no one got hurt."

"Didn't you have security cameras? Can you get any leads?"

"I'll have to leave those questions for the fire chief and the police," he said, sweeping a hand behind him where the men in uniform were standing. "But I want to emphasize that the fire was not the fault of the employees. It's all too easy to set fire to a lumber mill if someone really wants to. We spend a lot of time and energy reducing fire risk, but it can't be eliminated altogether."

"Who do you think did it?"

Kane gave a magnificent, all-encompassing shrug. Fielding Paper were the good guys. He couldn't have any enemies. "Just someone with a fixation for setting fire to things, I guess."

He put one hand in his pocket and slouched to indicate that he was relaxed and confident in everyone's ability to fix this problem. "Our reputation means that people won't settle for less than Fielding Paper," he said, leaning more heavily on his Boston accent, as it was part of his image, part of the centuries-old story of the company. "I'm happy to say that we'll have no problem delivering on our orders." *Don't worry*, his body language said, *I got this*. Never mind that in his head a voice was hammering *what if, what if, what if... What if there's another one... What if I can't fix things this time... What if the next time someone dies?*

Someone with a sly edge to her voice said, "On a different subject, are you dating anyone we know?"

Kane grinned at her and said, "Why? Are you offering?" The crowd laughed. The reporter held his look and grinned back. To Kane, this showed that he'd succeeded; if they'd moved on to his social life, they had stopped worrying about the future of his company. If he could convince them, maybe he could convince himself.

Chapter 2

Ellen really didn't want to be here.

She sat on the hard black leather couch, her skirt pulled determinedly below her knees, and tried not to let the receptionist see that her toe was tapping the air with impatience. She had far too much to do today to spend it on a sales call.

The receptionist was almost exactly what Ellen would have expected of a company run by a man with a reputation like Kane Fielding's. She was beautifully dressed and coiffed, with perfect nails painted a professional pink and lipstick to match. The only surprising thing about her was that she was in her sixties, not a *barely out of college* girl like the ones Fielding was always seen with. This woman had greeted Ellen perfectly politely and asked if she could get her a drink before Ellen had even sat down. Ellen had said no, just as politely, and then glowered at her from the couch, disliking her even more because there was nothing to dislike.

Ellen had to be here, because whatever her opinion of its owner, Fielding Paper was one of the largest companies in Boston, and the Rosette hotel wanted to have exclusive rights to Fielding conferences. So when her friend Lucía Jimenez, the conferences' manager at Fielding, had called to suggest she come in "for a couple of minutes" to leave a brochure, Ellen couldn't say no. But she'd been here for fifteen minutes already; the morning was ticking by, and she had a gala for fifteen hundred people to organize that would influence the rest of her career.

After another five minutes, the receptionist—Gloria, according to her nameplate—apologized to Ellen for the wait. Ellen wondered what would happen if she threw her shoe at the woman.

"That's quite all right," she said instead.

"I just love your accent," said Gloria. "You're English?"

"Yes." The accent was an advantage in her work, one she hadn't had back in London. "But I've been here for about four years now."

"Well, you still sound pure English to me."

Too bloody right. Ellen wasn't about to mess with a good sales tool. She gave Gloria a small smile and tried not to sigh with impatience.

The heavy glass entrance doors opened, and the atmosphere seemed to sharpen. A tall, broad-shouldered man with dark hair that brushed his shirt collar backed into the room, carrying a black overnight bag. He wore a rumpled dark suit and had a wool coat in his other hand. He turned to face the receptionist, his back still to Ellen. Gloria came around her desk to meet him.

"Hi, Gloria," the man said, dropping his coat on the floor and putting out his arm.

"Kane, you poor thing!" the receptionist replied, tucking herself under the arm for a hug. "You look pooped. When did you get back? You should have gone straight home!"

For a second it looked as though she was holding him up. His shoulders were hunched, and he dropped the bag without looking to see where it fell.

"Just thought I'd check in," he said.

"You smell like a forest," Gloria said, wrinkling her nose.

His laugh was cracked and harsh. "Yeah, after a wildfire." He ran his hand through his hair. "Guess I need a shower. I slept hard in Chicago last night. Had to hustle to make my flight this morning."

"So go *home*," Gloria insisted. She untucked herself and shook the arm that had hugged her. "You drove from Chicago to Grand Rapids and back again in one day? No wonder you overslept."

Ellen couldn't stop staring. This woman was acting like his governess, not his employee. What kind of company was this? And was this really the great, all-powerful, crooks-a-finger-and-gets-any-woman-he-wants Kane Fielding? He looked almost normal, standing there, silently asking for a little sympathy before getting back to real life. He still had his back to Ellen, so she couldn't see the famous smile or the dark deep-set eyes; she only saw the hunched shoulders and heard the exhaustion in his voice.

"I will, I will," he was promising. "I just want to give Leo a debriefing." He hugged Gloria again quickly, let her go, and began to walk to the inner doors.

Ellen watched him turn to face her and freeze. For a second, the dark eyes still held worry and strain. But then that hundred-kilowatt smile spread over his face. "I'm sorry," he said. "I would never have turned my back on you if I'd known you were there. Kane Fielding." He held out his hand.

Heck. She felt the pink begin to creep into her cheeks. Not that she followed the tabloids or anything—okay, she did, but only when she was getting pedicures, so it didn't count—but he was even finer in real life. Ellen had automatically stood when he came over, and even though she was taller than many men she knew, she had to look up to meet his dark-brown eyes. His hair looked just messy enough to be messed up some more. His broad shoulders fit the line of his suit exactly. But what was really undoing her was the way he'd talked to Gloria—the warmth, the fatigue in his voice, and the tension that still lingered around his eyes. Wasn't he invincible? And didn't he treat women like Kleenex? Use once and discard?

She had to be imagining it. He represented everything she hated about men. Her surreptitious perusal of the tabloids proved it. "Ellen Hunter, from the Rosette," she said stiffly and shook his hand.

A ping went up her arm. Her breath caught in her throat. *What was that?* If she didn't know better, she would have said it was arousal. But no, it was probably fear. That was a feeling she knew well. She dropped his hand and gripped her portfolio case more tightly. She'd gotten used to the occasional wash of fear threatening to overtake her whenever a man stood too close or made his interest clear. She was good at swallowing it, ignoring it, telling herself she'd never be afraid again. And she wasn't, until the next time.

"The hotel?" he said. "One of the best in town. Impressive." He was standing a perfectly respectable distance away, and his smile, while wide, was professional. He didn't look anywhere but at her face. But a wicked glint in his eyes showed he wasn't just talking about the hotel.

This was the kind of attention she hated. She knew she was attractive in a standard kind of way—thin, blond, blue-eyed, etcetera—but she couldn't stand it when men noticed her. She tended to dress conservatively for that reason, keeping her hair pulled back, wearing boxy jackets and skirts that her friend Penny had called "Sister Mary Margaret length." She still got more attention than she wanted, but she couldn't do much about it, other than use the ice-queen role she easily slipped into these days.

"We think so," she answered firmly. "That's what I'm here to talk to your conferences' manager about, anyway."

As if summoned by her title, Lucía appeared, pushing through the inner glass doors in a hurry, her thick dark curls spilling down her back. "I'm so sorry," she was saying before she'd even focused on Ellen. "This conference call—" Then she noticed Fielding. "Kane!" she exclaimed, and Ellen watched, fascinated, as Lucía's harassed frown turned to a sweet smile. "We didn't think you'd come in today."

"Just checking in," he said again.

"Hmm." Lucía unabashedly looked him over. "You must be tired," she said.

"I'm fine," he said. But Lucía didn't look like she believed it any more than Gloria had. What was *wrong* with these women?

Lucía apparently decided to drop it. She moved to hug Ellen. "I *am* sorry to keep you waiting, hon. I know you're busy right now."

"That's all right," Ellen said. "Shall we?" She nodded toward the doors.

She wished Fielding would go away. Why didn't he give his debriefing, or whatever it was? But he just stood there, smiling at the two of them.

"Why don't you use my office?" he said. "You can spread out on the conference table."

Okay, he *had* to know what that had sounded like. Bloody man, couldn't even have a simple conversation without that gleam in his eye. Gorgeous deep-set eyes, x-raying her from under straight brows, with that lock of hair falling over them. Not that she was looking.

Maybe she *had* been reading too many tabloids. He wasn't even that famous, for God's sake. Just another spoiled brat who'd had everything handed to him and who'd happened to catch the eye of an actress a few years ago. He'd been trading on that publicity ever since.

Lucía was already saying, "That's great, thanks, Kane. Better than that hole you call a conference room, anyway," and Fielding was holding out an arm to usher Ellen through the doors, saying to Lucía, "Hey, does or does not your office have a window? Well, then you can't complain when the conference room doesn't," and Ellen had no choice but to follow Lucía through.

The office spaces looked around a hundred years old. The walls were lined with dark wood paneling. The desks were old-fashioned wooden ones. The only signs of the twenty-first century were the large touchscreens on the computers.

The three or four secretaries outside the other offices greeted Fielding with surprise, and more pleasure than Ellen thought appropriate. She couldn't see his face as he replied, but she could just bet he was flashing that come-hither smile at them. His own secretary, a pretty blonde with shoulder-length hair that had a wave in it Ellen envied, was the only one who didn't adjust something as he approached. In fact, she looked quite stern.

"Hi, Anna," he said warmly, and there he was again, being all *nice*.

"What are you doing—?" But then she saw that Lucía and Ellen were with him.

"This is Ms. Hunter," he explained. "She's going to use my office to present..." He frowned and turned to her. "Which hotel was it again?"

"Boy, do you need coffee," said Lucía.

"Boy, do I. Lots and lots of coffee." For a second Ellen saw the exhaustion hit him again. He scrubbed one hand through his hair, and there were gray shadows around his eyes.

Anna tutted but obviously didn't want to say anything else in front of an outsider. "Go on in. I'll get the coffee," she said.

"Thanks," Fielding said and put out his hand to guide Ellen into his office.

She had to pass quite close to him when she got to the door. *Dammit, dammit, dammit.* His height and the dark suit or the smell of him or something... Her legs began to feel odd. This was not good. Unanticipated wobbles about the knees were not permitted; they were, in fact, beginning to send licks of fear into her stomach. *No. I am* not *going to do this again, feel like this again.*

All it took was one memory of Edward, so contained and collected right up until he wasn't, to bring her back to herself. The barriers once again clanging into place, her cheeks perfectly cool, she was able to move to the conference table at one end of Fielding's corner office and take her book out of her briefcase.

The office looked out over the mix of old and new buildings that made up downtown Boston and was just as old-fashioned as the rest of the building—dark mahogany and leather, with heavy furniture that had no idea mid-century modern was back. Had this all belonged to Fielding's grandfather? *Great*-grandfather?

Fielding pulled out the chair at the head of the table for her and sat on one side, with his back to the window. Lucía sat opposite him. Ellen turned the artist-size binder to face them and began. "Well, as Mr. Fielding said—"

"Kane," he said.

What a ridiculous name. He sounds like a soap opera character. She gave him a tight smile and continued. "The Rosette *is* the best hotel in Boston. We've had our five stars for more than thirty years and not one, but two of our restaurants are Michelin-rated. You won't find a more prestigious location for your conferences in the entire state. I'd go as far as to say the entire East Coast."

She showed them the range of meeting rooms, the added facilities that the Rosette gave their clients, the newspaper articles that showed the cachet that came with the name.

"I don't know," Fielding said slowly, but his eyes lit up. "You guys might be too fancy for us millworkers."

She looked at his custom suit, at the expensive furniture they were sitting on. She thought of the news and videos she'd researched from the last few years, where Fielding's face appeared, relentlessly perfect—apart from the hair, and even that looked premeditated—reminding everyone of the quality that his company could produce because it was all American-made. His family probably hadn't worked in a mill in all the ten generations it had owned this company.

"Mr. Fielding, I don't have to tell you about the value of image." She hoped her intrinsic dislike of his public persona didn't trickle into her voice. "Fielding stationery is known for its quality. You work very hard to keep it that way. We can help with that."

"Yeah," he said, leaning back in his chair and tapping one finger on the table, "you don't have to tell me about image."

What did that mean? He sounded almost irritated, as if he didn't like the constant attention.

No way. No one was that good an actor. She went on. "Your clients will appreciate being put up in the Rosette when they come to town, and we can host anything from an intimate meeting for five to…" She turned to the last page, where a large room with high ceilings and spectacular chandeliers was decorated for a banquet. "A ball fit for a queen."

Fielding stopped tapping the table. His gaze centered on her. "The Queen's Ball? That's you? I mean…" He waved a hand, seeming to apologize silently for his slowness. "I know, it's the Rosette. But…" He looked at her again as if he'd only just noticed her. "You run it."

The Queen's Ball was the corporate event of the fall season. The Rosette partnered with a local foundation, charged huge prices per plate, and raised thousands for charity. Thousands more were spent on the food and decorations. Every penny was Ellen's responsibility.

Fielding had attended all four years that she had run the ball. Each time he'd had a different hot chick on his arm.

Not that Ellen had paid attention.

"Haven't you seen her there?" Lucía asked him.

"I—" He still held Ellen with those dark eyes. Her barriers shuddered. "I'm surprised I don't remember you," he said.

She wasn't. She'd developed such a dislike of him that she'd made a point of avoiding him as much as possible at the event. The only time he might have seen her was when she welcomed the chairman of the hotel and the charity at the beginning of the night, and she was on a stage dozens of feet away.

"Well," she said, "there are fifteen hundred other people there."

"Still," he said, "I should have remembered you."

Her inner ice castle shook again, and she wasn't sure if it was from fear or... something else. That one speech was the worst part of her whole year. She had to dress to be noticed that night, to show the hotel in its best light, to put on her best Queen's accent, to let man after man look at her, to shake hands and allow those hands to move occasionally to her elbow or her back...

Anna appeared with the coffee tray. Fielding stood up, and even though the corner of the table was between him and Ellen, he suddenly seemed to take up so much space that she instinctively cringed. She tried to recover, to relax, but he had already noticed.

The scene froze. Fielding's smile had finally gone; he was frowning at her. Ellen was trying to look back at him with her usual expression of cold disdain, while holding the arms of her chair in a death grip. Anna and Lucía looked between the two of them, evidently sensing that something had happened.

Fielding moved first, giving a small shake of his head, and took the tray. "Thanks, Anna," he said, again with that more-than-boss-to-secretary burr in his voice. Anna left, closing the door behind her. Ellen wanted to tell her to leave it open, but that would mean admitting she was afraid, which she refused to do. This was just a business meeting, and she was safe. *Safe,* she reminded herself. She was suddenly so grateful for Lucía's presence she gave her a smile, which Lucía returned with a slightly confused one of her own.

Fielding poured coffee for her and Lucía, then made himself a cup which he drank, black, almost in one gulp. He did the same with the second. He had to be burning the crap out of his throat.

Ellen put milk and sugar into her own coffee and drank it, feeling that she was missing something. Why was he so tired? Why was everyone so concerned about him?

With his third cup in hand, Fielding went over to his desk and leaned against it. She couldn't help noticing how long his legs were and how his thighs strained against the fabric of his trousers.

Now she burned her mouth on her own coffee.

"Let's get to the numbers," Lucía said, snapping Ellen out of her catalog of Fielding's body. Ellen pulled out another piece of paper and went over the costs. He stayed by his desk, listening but not coming any closer.

"That's a lot of money to commit to one place," Lucía said when she'd finished.

"To commit to peace of mind? You know we can handle any event you throw at us."

"I know *you* can handle it, but how long before you get transferred out of the country, and poor old Fielding Paper disappears into your rearview mirror?"

This was true. Lucía knew that Ellen's visa was up in four months. To continue on the career path she'd been working on for ten years, she needed to move to other Rosette hotels, other continents.

"You're leaving?" Fielding said. He'd put down his coffee and one hand was playing with a cigarette lighter, while the other tapped out a beat on his thigh. *He's late for his next cigarette.* She was pleased to find that he had at least one fault. But then why had he smelled so damn good when she got close to him?

Focus, Ellen! Her career was all she had to work toward these days, and to move up the ladder, she had to go. The fact that the idea of leaving Boston dropped a lead weight into her stomach whenever she thought of it was irrelevant. "Yes. But our department, and my replacement, will make the transition seamless," she added, mentally crossing her fingers. She didn't know if her boss had begun looking for her replacement yet.

"I'm taking that into account," Lucía said in a warning tone. She stood up. "Anything else?"

Ellen shook her head. "I'll leave you this price list and some brochures you can send around if you'd like," she said and began gathering her papers. Fielding hadn't moved. He had his back to the windows and looked even more hooded and tired in the shadows cast by the weak fall sun.

When she couldn't think of an excuse not to, she went up to him. "Thank you for the opportunity," she said, holding her hand out, bracing herself.

He stood up, putting his weight back on his feet, and shook her hand. This time she didn't pull away—didn't feel she could, with Lucía watching—and the jolt that went up her arm at his proximity, at the way his hair brushed against his shirt collar, sent the heat rushing to her cheeks. He wasn't smiling, for once, but watching her closely.

"It was... interesting to meet you, Ms. Hunter," he said.

"Likewise," she said, trying to keep her voice firm.

She was aware of exactly when his fingers wrapped around hers, and when, after a much longer pause than the first time, they pulled away.

Chapter 3

Lucía walked her out past Gloria, who gave her a big smile, to the elevators. By the time they reached them, Ellen had the blushing back under control. It was the first time in years that she'd needed to do that. "Thank you for seeing me," she said.

"It was good to see you somewhere other than the gym," Lucía answered. "But to be honest, I don't know if we'll have a deal here. With you not staying on, it might be too unpredictable. And we don't need any more unpredictable."

Ellen frowned. What did she mean? But she focused on the job at hand. "Come and meet the rest of the department," she said. "You'll see."

"Well," said Lucía, "I'll think about it." Then her dark eyes brightened. "I think the boss is on your side, though."

"Oh God." The flush raced back into her cheeks.

Now Lucía was grinning. "Yeah, thought so. For a second there I felt like I wasn't even in the room."

Stupid blushing. Two minutes with Play-the-Field Fielding and she reddened up like a traffic light. "Look," she said, lowering her voice, "I know you're always trying to tell me he's a good person, but look at his social life. Don't you find it just a little reprehensible?"

The elevator arrived, and Lucía got on with Ellen. "He's not twirling a mustache and tying those women to railroad tracks, Ellen," she said as they went down. "I assume—not that I think about it because, eww, he's my boss—that they know what they're doing. Have a little faith in your fellow females, hon. We can't all get by on tea and a good book." She squeezed Ellen's hand to take the sting out of the jab.

Ellen could say nothing to contradict her, since that pretty much had been the extent of her social life for the last four years. She stuck her tongue out instead. "Not just tea and books. Tom Hardy movies too." The blush in her cheeks hit radiation levels. "I can't believe I just said that."

Lucía cracked a laugh that echoed around the elevator cab. "Ooh, she likes 'em rough around the edges, huh? I never would have guessed!"

"Stop laughing. You tell anyone I said that, and I'll..."

"Oh, *m'ija*." The elevator stopped at the ground floor, and Lucía walked out of the main doors with her. "I won't, but damn, it's the first time I've seen you riled up about *anything*. Maybe you should ask yourself why that is."

Ellen opened her mouth to give some form of denial, but Lucía had blown her a kiss and was already back inside the building.

♦

Kane remained standing in front of his desk for a minute after Ellen left. *What the hell was that?* Why had she looked at him like she needed to wipe him off her shoes, as if she wanted to kiss him, and as if she was afraid of him? When had he started ogling women in his office? Had she been able to tell? What had her presentation been about again?

Where the hell were his cigarettes?

Given his family's history, disassembling the smoke detector in his office was not an option, so he'd gotten in the habit of thanking his great-grandfather for buying a building whose windows opened, and leaning out like a schoolboy, looking down ten floors to the noise of downtown below while he smoked.

Perched on the sill, he was soothed by the sounds of his native city. With a clearer head, he could decide that he'd enjoyed looking at her. That was all it was. Her face looked carved from ivory, but those lips... When she forgot to keep them pinched tight he could see himself... There he went again.

And the blushing. What was the point of all the ice-queen daggers she'd thrown at him when she'd spent half the meeting warming him up with those rosy cheeks?

No big deal; she'd just been a nice distraction. Looking at her had been a hell of a lot more fun than the thoughts that were rapidly crowding back into his head—the memories of the first fire, the shudders of fear that there might be more fires, more damage to the company. To an employee.

Think about something else.

But why had she cringed away from him like that? All he'd done was stand up. She'd seemed happier when he moved far from her, so he hadn't tried to go back to his place at the conference table. But her whole body had still been rigid when she came to shake his hand. What was that about?

Ah, forget it. You're never going to figure it out on the sleep you've had recently. She's Lucia's problem now anyway.

But the line of her calves and the sweep of her hair remained his problem.

He brought the coffee tray out to Anna. Thank God for Anna. Ever since he'd hired her, she'd helped him to keep the office atmosphere light. With the trouble the company had been in when he took over, he'd needed to make jokes and tease the managers just to make it through the days. It had become a habit he, and his employees, were happy to continue now that things were better.

Had been better...

While Anna took the tray to the kitchen, he looked through the stack of messages for him on her desk. Three were from the insurance company. One was from Leo, his communications director. The rest were from managers at other mills.

"Don't look at those now," Anna said behind him. "Go home, go on. There's nothing that won't wait till tomorrow."

"Tomorrow's Saturday." But they both knew with this kind of incident, there was no such thing as a weekend.

"Okay, whatever. But for now, go home. You kinda look like shit, you know."

"Gee, thanks. I'll just talk to Leo real quick."

"How about you talk to Leo *tomorrow*," she insisted.

"How about I've got three hundred workers with nowhere to work today? How about a union that's going to bill me overtime for the extra shifts wherever I put them?" he retorted, more harshly than he'd meant to.

"I get it, Kane, but you can–"

"I don't know if you do," he said. "Second fire in a week, Anna. Did you see the papers this morning?" He waved vaguely toward the lobby and the outside world. "'History Comes Back to Haunt Fielding Paper,' they said."

"Who cares what they say? No one was hurt. You're insured. You can rebuild."

He sighed. He shouldn't have said anything. "Yes. Yes, we will. But I still need Leo." He got his cigarettes out of his jacket pocket.

"You can't smoke in–" Anna began.

"I *know*." He stuck one between his teeth anyway and walked over to Leo's office.

◆

"Did anyone cooperate on this piece in the *Globe*?"

Leo was a tall man, almost as tall as Kane, with unexpectedly black hair for his age, and a face just lined enough to look rugged. He was the same age as Kane's father would have been. Apart from Kane himself, Leo was the company's best spokesman. "Not that I've been able to find out so far," he said, "but I don't think they needed any cooperation. Most of the information in it is general, from our annual reports and the police, sources like that. Like the newspapers." Leo smiled. "In PR terms, you come out looking good. You being there made a big difference to them. Shows you care."

"I do care, for Christ's sake." Kane felt around his pockets for his cigarettes and then remembered he already had one in his mouth that he wasn't allowed to light. It made his scowl even deeper.

Fielding Paper meant everything to him; it always had. Even before his father had died, Kane had known he would take over one day, that his family looked to him to continue the company that had been doing business in Massachusetts since Colonial times. Robert had delighted in bringing Kane to work with him, showing him all the different parts of the business, especially Robert's favorite part, the science—the ratio of cotton to linen fiber, the levels of iron and copper in the water, the most efficient ways to reclaim that water.

The sick tragedy of it was that Robert's experimentation with the science of paper-making had killed him, in the end, when a boiler he was working on had exploded.

Kane had been twenty-two, about to graduate from college, with no worries beyond where to find the next keg and how to get rid of his roommate so he could have a girl over, when he'd gotten the call.

And then he'd been shown the finances. Robert, it turned out, was a loyal Fielding but a poor businessman. There had been too much tinkering and not enough modernizing. They weren't producing enough paper to make a profit. The board had told him this and then looked at him in a gray wave of silence, waiting for him to agree to sell what they could, to let someone else worry about the inefficient mills and all the employees who relied on him.

Sitting at the end of that conference table, Kane could have been in a different universe from these old men and women who'd been friends with his father but apparently didn't feel the loyalty to the business that Robert had. He'd begged for a few days to think about a sale and stumbled out of the room.

Leo had been with the company since Robert's time. Kane was grateful to him for his faith when Kane went back and told the board he wasn't going to sell. Half of them resigned, but not Leo.

Leo's loyalty had been rewarded: Kane had had to let more people go than he expected, and had gone hat-in-hand to every wealthy friend of his father's to raise the money he needed, but within a few years of converting half their plants to recycled paper, and the most intense PR work Leo had ever done, Kane was able to hire almost everyone back, and the profit-sharing plan the company had for its employees had taken off. Fielding Paper was a stable force in an ever-changing industry.

Until now.

"I know you care, Kane," Leo said, "but it doesn't hurt to remind the public. The article talks about the inspections you do each year..."

"Didn't do a very good job on this one, did I?" Kane muttered.

"It's not your responsibility," Leo said, but Kane just glared at him.

It was all his responsibility. He had four sisters and three nephews to manage trust funds for. He'd had his mother to console and encourage, until she, too, had died a couple of years after his father. He had thousands of employees and an industry that was always telling him to streamline, which would mean closing mills that had stood in some towns for two hundred years. Of course it was his responsibility. Who else was going to do it?

"Oh, for pity's sake, Kane," Leo finally snapped. "Let's go back to your office if you're just going to fidget a hole in my chair."

He hadn't realized he'd been fidgeting. But he was happy to go back to his window.

"At least it happened at night," said Leo from a seat on the other side of Kane's desk. "I mean, maybe whoever's doing this isn't a homicidal maniac. Maybe he's just a pyromaniac with delusions of grandeur. No one was in the building to get hurt."

"Yeah." Kane scrubbed his hand through his hair, risking dropping ashes into it. *Next time, next time, next time,* hammered through him.

Leo was looking as sympathetic as Anna, and Kane didn't want his sympathy. He knew that people were remembering thirteen years ago—hell, the media was probably pulling archive photos of Kane's first-ever press conference in time for the evening news. He hated thinking of it, hated the vulnerability he'd shown. He'd been too young. He'd spent the next decade trying to make everyone forget that.

He came away from the window, stubbing out the cigarette in the Bruins ashtray his youngest sister had given him. "You really don't think this is affecting our image?"

She'd been digging at him when she'd mentioned his image. He could tell. But her dislike didn't mesh with the other signals she'd given off.

Focus.

"Not right now, anyway. Most of our calls have been from the press, not from customers. Our sales people in the Midwest dealt with the problem as soon as it happened. You'd need a few more fires to affect production in Fielding Paper. So go home, okay? I'll deal with any calls that come in."

"Okay, I'm going, I'm going. See you tomorrow."

♦

But he didn't go. He set up a conference call with the site managers in the North-Central division for the following morning. He talked to the insurance companies about loss prevention and sent emails to give people the right phone number to call. He called his COO about security cameras. At every mill. Many locations didn't have them; they relied on motion detectors and fences, or the fact that most of the equipment and product was too big to steal. He sat in a fog of self-reproach for twenty minutes, kicking himself for not having the cameras installed in the first place. He called his CFO about cash flow. He smoked several cigarettes.

When Anna came in and pointedly cleared her throat, he was at the window again, and nearly fell out of it. "Don't do that to me," he gasped, clutching his heart.

"Yeah, like me making you jump is any worse for your heart than what you're doing to it. You've been here three hours past the time you said you were going to go home. Go home." She grabbed the pack of cigarettes from his desk and made to crush it in her fist. "Or the Marlboros get it."

Unhappy with how much the idea of losing that pack bothered him, Kane got off the sill and picked up his jacket. "See you tomorrow," he echoed, snatching the cigarettes from her.

She laughed, and he walked away from her up the hall. At the lobby doors, however, he glanced back to see if she was still watching, then slipped past and knocked on Lucía's door.

"Hey," Lucía said, looking up from her desk.

"Hi." He leaned in the doorway. "So what do you think about using the Rosette?"

"I don't know," she said, picking up the brochure Ellen had left with her. "I'll have to have the other hotels come in to present as well. But the Rosette's the best corporate hotel in town, and the discount she's giving me is unbelievable. If we go with them exclusively, of course." She chewed her lip for a moment. "I like Ellen. She's wicked smart; speaks five languages or something. And of course she's an incredible event planner."

"If she does the Queen's Ball, I believe it." He was still surprised he didn't remember her from previous years. Then again, he wasn't such an asshole that he'd ogle another woman when he had a date right next to him.

"It's next weekend. You're going, right?" Lucía said.

Crap. So much for putting Ellen out of his mind.

Gloria had a cab waiting for him when he got out to the street. He was tired enough to sleep the weekend through, but as the taxi pulled away, instead of telling the driver to take him home, he found himself saying, "The Rosette."

Chapter 4

The fifteen-minute walk back to her office helped Ellen to calm down. On the third floor of the Rosette's flagship nineteenth-century building, right above the conference rooms and event spaces she was in charge of, she truly did feel safe. She had set definite rules here, and after one or two false starts, the men she worked with followed them. She'd never had any trouble with her own boss, but some of the other men had asked her out when she'd first come to the hotel, and she'd had to make it abundantly clear that she was not on the menu.

She stopped briefly at her boss's office. "How did it go?" Jon said.

Jon was officially safe. A small, intense man, with short brown hair and a well-trimmed beard, Jon had pulled himself up from valet to marketing director and had nothing less than the chairmanship in his sights. Ellen had met his wife and their children, and Jon's ambition was all for them. He was the only man she was really comfortable around.

"With Lucía? Okay." She didn't want to mention that her impending transfer had put a damper on Lucía's enthusiasm. Since she'd just spent fifteen minutes telling herself to forget him, she also didn't mention Kane Fielding. "She thought our numbers were a little high."

"Only okay? What else does she want?"

"To meet the rest of the department. I'll follow up with her." It was true, even if it wasn't the answer to his question.

"By the way, Claire Holland was looking for you."

"Oh. Yippee."

Claire was the HR manager for the hotel, and despite being English like Ellen, the two had never been friends. The hotel usually only kept its international employees in one place for two years. Jon had petitioned to keep Ellen on for another two, after she'd produced a Queen's Ball more glamorous and sophisticated than he could ever have managed. Claire had taken the extra paperwork involved as a personal affront. "She wants to make sure I'm really going this time," Ellen added with a wry smile.

"And are you?"

"Yes," she said heartily, though she found it hard to meet Jon's eye. "Onward and upward, as they say."

Jon sighed. He'd suggested last month that when he went for a promotion, she should take over the marketing department. Ellen had clamped down on the leap in her heart at that idea and given him her excellent reasons for going.

Jon gave her a slightly more focused glance. "You all right? Did you get lunch yet?"

"Oh, no, not yet." She didn't want to think about what Jon was reading in her face. "I'll get something now. Let me know if you think of anything else I need to do for the ball."

Her afternoon was spent on the phone, working on the minutiae of the event. Every decision made and small crisis averted calmed her, helped her get back to her own reality. With so many details, and only one week to go, she was almost, *almost*, able to put Kane Fielding and his intense stare out of her mind.

Bill Cohen, the operations manager for the hotel, called to tell her his department had found forty chairs that needed repair or replacement, and that he was dealing with it. She thanked him in what she hoped was a repressive tone. Bill was older and more old-fashioned and loved to tease her about her lack of social life. He couldn't be convinced that the subject made Ellen uncomfortable, if not downright mad.

Her tone didn't even make a dent. "So does CinderEllen have a date for the ball?" he asked in a jovial voice that had her gritting her teeth.

"CinderEllen's going to be too busy to take anyone to the ball," she said. Bill laughed and hung up. She made a mental note to put him as far from her table as possible on the night.

She was just thinking she would need one more cup of tea to get her through the last couple of hours of the day, when the phone rang. It was reception, which was bizarre. She didn't know anyone who wouldn't use the business entrance at the back of the hotel if they wanted to meet with her.

"Ms. Hunter?" came her best friend's voice.

"Penny? What's with the Ms.–?"

"I have a Mr. Fielding here to see you," Penny interrupted. Ellen could hear the repressed scream of excitement in her voice. Penny knew full well who Kane Fielding was, spent most of her days defending him to Ellen–well, not defending, exactly, just implying that she herself would not throw him out of bed for eating crackers. If he stood in front of Penny much longer, he probably wouldn't even make it up to the offices.

Much easier to think about Penny's reaction than admitting that her own breathing had just shortened and the blood had–dammit–rushed back to her cheeks. What was he doing here? Had she left something at his office? No, that was ridiculous. He'd never come himself to return it. Did he have a question about the presentation? He could have picked up the phone. Could he possibly want to take her up on the invitation to meet the rest of the department? At four o'clock on a Friday with no appointment? He had to be out of his mind.

Or was he here... for her?

No. It couldn't be that. Apart from a couple of vague innuendos, he'd been nothing but professional. And she wasn't even his type. He preferred bubbly blondes with large chests who could gaze up at him with puppy-dog eyes. Kind of like Penny.

Yeah, like Kane Fielding would be interested in you.

She looked down at her own lack of assets, gave a snort of laughter, and remembered that Penny was waiting for an answer. "Well, I suppose you'd better send him up."

"Certainly; I'll do that!" came Penny's voice, the epitome of enthusiastic American customer service. Knowing that Penny was going to grill her for every detail as soon as work was over, Ellen smoothed her skirt and made sure her jacket was firmly buttoned before going to the office lobby.

He came through the doors, all six-foot-whatever of him, in the same slightly rumpled suit that showed off those shoulders and that white shirt that still looked so good against the skin of his neck. Whatever calm she'd gained from laughing at herself fled.

Not safe. He was definitely not safe.

Think about your job. Are you going to let fear take over again? If that's what this feeling is?

So she put out her hand. "Mr. Fielding," she said, bracing herself for the jolt, which came right on schedule. Maybe it had been too long since she'd had human contact.

Male contact.

Oh, help.

"Ms. Hunter," he said, his hand still in hers. He wasn't smiling at her and didn't seem to feel the need to break eye contact.

And this close, she caught a hint of his cologne. *Gloria was right,* she thought faintly. *He does smell like a forest.*

Ellen caved first, turning her head away toward her office. "Won't you come through?" Penny wasn't the only one who could roll out the banalities.

This time when he went through the door, she made sure to stand well back, but once inside, he took up far too much space in the small office. "Do sit down," she said, sounding like her mother, and only when he was seated, making her guest chair look small and flimsy, did she come around to sit behind her desk.

"So," she said, moving her mousepad a little farther in front of her, "was there something else you wanted to know about our proposal?"

"No," he said. The hard stare without the smile was more disturbing than the hundred-kilowatt attack. She surreptitiously pushed a pen and pencil to join the mousepad. "I want to take you to the Queen's Ball."

"*What?*" She'd been *right?* "No," she said instinctively. Then, because she thought she might be going mad, she said, "What?" again.

One side of his mouth quirked up. "I was hoping you would allow me to take you to the Queen's Ball."

The language may have been more flowery, but it was no more comprehensible. Her cheeks at Defcon 3, her answer was firm. "Of course you can't," she said. No matter what tiny part of her trembled with a "yes."

"Why 'of course'?" He didn't look concerned, just curious. He was resting one wrist on her desk, tapping the wood with a finger while he watched her.

He's so damn cocky; he must do this every flipping day. She came out of the trance and began to get angry. She was just another woman, just another chance to get his jollies.

But she couldn't show him this. Casting about among all the reasons she could not, would not go anywhere with him, she hit upon the safest one. "You're a client."

"Not yet. And anyway, that would be Lucía, not me."

His tie was loosened, and his top button was undone. If she cared to look, she'd see the slow pulse of his heart at the hollow of his throat. *Don't look.*

"It amounts to the same thing." She took another pen out of the holder and held it in front of her as if it were imperative she write down their conversation.

"I hate to tell you, but if you're leaving in four months, Lucía probably won't use the hotel."

"Oh." Now she was getting it. Her anger flamed higher. "So if I don't agree to go out with you, we don't get the account?" She'd half risen from her chair without realizing.

"No!" His eyes widened, and finally he looked away from her for a second, giving a rueful laugh. "Jeez, you really don't think much of me, do you?"

So he had noticed. *Way to piss off a potential client, Ellen.* But then, if he wasn't a potential client, why the hell was he here?

She sat down and tried something else. "And I'm working at the ball. It's not a social occasion for me."

"I understand," he said. "I guess what I really want is to get to know you before then, take you out for dinner this weekend. Then at the ball I can just sit back and watch you work."

He could do that without going as her date, but she was more incensed by his easy assumption that one dinner would make her desperate to be in his presence again. To touch him again…

God, this was infuriating! She was so confused around him she didn't know what to say. But the easiest emotion to bring to the surface was anger. So with a voice that trembled more than she'd like, but held on to some of the cold disdain she'd worked so hard for, she said, "The answer is still no. To dinner and the ball." Then, because she couldn't ignore her upbringing altogether, she added stiffly, "Thank you."

She had now arranged three pens, a pencil, a stapler, and her tape dispenser in front of her. Kane's eyes dropped to them, her pathetic instinctive shield. "Okay," he said. "I apologize."

"What?" He'd left her gaping again. It wasn't just his looks that left her feeling so off-kilter around him.

"I was trying to ask you out, not make you uncomfortable."

"I'm not uncomfortable," she said, though her teeth were beginning to hurt from how tightly wound she was. "I just don't want to have dinner with you."

"Yeah, I got that," he said with another one-sided smile. But he didn't stand up. He was still giving her that assessing look.

"Right, well," she said, standing herself. "I expect you have a lot to do."

He came to his feet slowly. If she didn't know better, she'd have said he was trying to avoid startling her the way he had in his office. Damn, why had she cringed away from him? She never showed weakness; it was a habit she'd gotten very good at in four years.

She waited for him to move to the door, but he just stood there, taking up too much space again. "That's a wicked cool accent you've got, by the way," he said, and she could have sworn he broadened his own. "Can you sharpen knives with it?" He pronounced it *shahpen*.

"No, just cut down overblown egos," she flashed back. *Oh, crap.* "Sorry," she said automatically, then bit her lip. She shouldn't be apologizing to him. Her friends always told her she said sorry too much. But she made one last heroic effort to keep her snark under control.

"That's all right," he said, and there was the face that riled her up so much in the magazines. The man who assumed every woman in the vicinity would give a limb to be seen with him. "See, even when you're insulting me, your accent still makes it sound like a compliment."

Ellen snapped in a way she hadn't since college, since before Edward. Her fists clenched beside her, and her cheeks burned. Hang the account. Hang Lucía for being late this morning. Hang this man and all men like him. "You just can't stop, can you? What is it, some kind of knee-jerk reaction for you? See woman, ask woman out?"

"You consider yourself just any woman?" he said, still smiling, still unflappable.

"I'm not the kind of woman you'd be interested in." Oh yeah, this account was flying right out of that window. And the problem was, telling him what she really thought of him filled her up with a righteous anger that felt good. Penny would be thrilled; she was always saying Ellen was too buttoned up.

"How do you know what—"

"Because you make no secret of it!" She could feel the flush in her cheeks, knew she'd regret it later, but, like him, she just couldn't stop. "Don't you date women based on how much exposure they'll give you?"

"How much exposure *they* give *me*," he said evenly, folding his arms. He seemed calm, but the look he sent her showed that she was finally getting somewhere. "So," he continued, "you know all about me based on a few clickbait headlines?"

Damn. He had her there. But— "No. And you don't know anything about me. If you did, you'd know I have absolutely no interest in your paltry idea of a relationship." She could feel herself shaking a little. It was time to get him out of there. "I have to get back to work," she said, letting off one last shot. "You know, work? It's what your employees do while you're off getting your picture taken."

That did the trick. All traces of amusement were gone. His dark eyes were boring into her so hard she caught her breath. "Yeah, I know work," he said. "You mean, work like trying to figure out who the hell's setting fire to my buildings? Surprisingly, that *is* taking up a lot of my time."

Oh, shit.

She remembered now. She'd hardly looked at the news for days, with the planning for the Queen's Ball taking up all her attention. She'd done her research on the company last week. A few days ago, she'd heard something about a fire in Chicago but hadn't connected the name of the company to her meeting with Lucía or with the laughing, shallow man in the tabloids. "Right, of course," she stammered and broke the eye contact. Now she really had killed the account. See, this was why she shouldn't ever let herself lose it. "I... I didn't..."

"It's fine," he said curtly.

She was a complete harpy. When she was younger, she'd had a temper. But having a temper meant losing control. And now look what had happened, the first time she'd let out the demon in years. And for what? Just some playboy she never had to see again. No matter how much she wanted to run her fingers over the pulse in his neck.

He turned around and opened the door to the office himself. Ellen had to follow him out to the stairs. Seeing his back, the creases in his suit jacket, reminded her of that morning. The exhaustion made sense now, the worry, the pain she'd seen in his eyes.

At the top of the stairs, he turned around. "You don't have to show me out," he said, and his face had cleared. God, he smelled good. Ridiculous. She could smell cigarettes on him. She hated people who smoked. She couldn't possibly want to lean in.

He didn't hold out his hand to shake. "Goodbye, Ellen."

A warmth that she didn't recognize bloomed in her chest when he said her name.

Chapter 5

One short cab ride later, Kane could finally escape into his apartment. He leaned on the closed door for a second, allowing himself to relax for the first time. His eyes became more shadowed, lines of worry more defined between his brows. His bag stayed by the front door, a leather heap of memories he didn't want to deal with yet.

He was officially crazy. Only someone certifiably insane could have gone and tried to scale the wall that Ellen Hunter had put up around herself. She could make a guy feel like an unwashed barbarian with one lift of her patrician eyebrow.

Man, had she read him wrong. Or rather, she hadn't read him at all. She acted as if she were above that kind of thing but hated him because of an image the press had fed her. He must have imagined the way her eyes darkened when she'd met him.

He had a corner apartment in a new high-rise building on the harbor. The place was light-filled and white, with deep purples and grays in the furnishings, chosen for him by an ex-girlfriend. The kitchen had those shiny white cabinets they called "European-style," though when his first-generation Italian brother-in-law had seen them, he'd said they hurt his eyes.

Up here, on the twenty-second floor, he could hear no noise from the city; nobody was anywhere close enough to look in his windows. And even though he loved to bring women back here, he also loved it when he could shut everyone out and be himself.

What did it matter whether or not she made snap judgments about him? With the fires to deal with, he had no time for flirting, no time for anything personal. He knew his position: it was to keep this business running for whichever of his family members ended up taking over. No one else could do it. He'd been the CEO for more than a decade, and only now was one of his siblings joining the company. He couldn't wait for Megan to graduate college and get started, but he was afraid if there were any more fires, she might not have a company to come to.

At the refrigerator, he checked the date on the milk and picked a bottle of water instead. The cool air billowing around him made him think of the cold night spent watching the fire near the lake. He stayed there for a moment, trying to erase his fear from that night.

Fear... heat... cold...

He was thinking about Ellen again. He slammed the door. He wasn't going to do that anymore; hadn't he decided already?

Since he hadn't eaten since that morning, he microwaved two of the frozen dinners one of his sisters must have left behind during a "Kane isn't taking care of himself" phase. Then, sitting stretched out in the corner of his enormous sectional couch—we'll have a lot of fun on this, the ex-girlfriend had said, and they had—he lit a cigarette and watched the smoke drift up. He may have a sore throat coming on. He had smoked a lot lately. He wasn't a heavy smoker, and a pack a day was a lot for him, but the last two days had been so draining, he'd needed this crutch more than usual. His mind went back over the fire, the destruction...

The flames blurred his vision. He jerked himself upright and put out the cigarette before he started his own fire. He was unutterably happy to leave his clothes in a heap on the floor and collapse into bed.

♦

Hours later, he was awakened by the telephone. Instantly on alert, he picked it up fast.

"Kane! Paul."

"Shit, Paul." He collapsed back into bed. "You scared the hell out of me. I'm half-asleep here."

"What are you doing sleeping on a Friday night, buddy?" Paul was a record producer and always knew where a lot of pop and movie stars hung out when they were in Boston. He'd brought Kane along to a party a couple of years ago, and Kane had caught the eye of Didi Ravello, an actress in her forties with the body of a twenty-year-old, none of it, Kane soon found out, surgically achieved. He, and the entertainment industry, had never looked back. It was thanks to Paul that Kane had made it into both *Rolling Stone* and *Entertainment Weekly* in the same month.

"Just saw you on TV," Paul said.

Kane groaned, putting out a hand for his cigarettes. "Oh, great."

"Dude, you couldn't have asked for better coverage. You know how many girls want to meet you tonight? It's the hair, I swear to God. If I didn't know you better, I'd say you had a stylist standing behind the camera in Grand Rapids."

So he'd been right about the camera. "It was too dark to see anything except the fire."

"Yeah, man, lighting. You are literally a hot mess right now. Lit up all those angles and cheekbones and whatnot."

Kane shook his head. Paul could, and often did, turn anyone into a commodity. Until now, Kane had found it funny. "What do you mean, tonight?"

"Stephanie Seton's launch party? The new studio?"

Damn. And Kane had told Stephanie personally that he'd go. He really did like her photographs, which for this show were black-and-white celebrity shots, juxtaposed with homeless people photographed in the exact same clothes and locations. His girlfriend at the time had been one of the celebrity models and had raved about the shoot, and he and Stephanie had stayed friends after the girlfriend had gone off to her next movie.

"Sorry, I... You know, a little distracted here." After the last few days, it would be nice to get back in the swing of things. "Are you picking me up?"

"I'll have the car get you first, then me. He'll be there in half an hour. Do you, in your comatose state, remember Cassandra?"

A sweet girl he'd met two weeks ago at Paul's studio. She'd been recording her first album. Mostly Kane remembered that she was trying not to look terrified by the hype surrounding her amazing voice. It had been before the first fire, and therefore a lifetime ago.

"Yeah, sure."

"Well, she's told me specifically she's hoping to see you there tonight."

Ordinarily, this would be perfect. He could have set his clock by how quickly he could get the nubile Cassandra back to this very bed. But tonight... Tonight he was tired. He had too much to worry about to be all charming and seductive. And it crossed his mind that Cassandra was barely twenty-two, which meant he was too old for her.

What? Where did that come from?

He knew exactly where. God, could he please get Ellen Hunter and her judgmental glare out of his mind? What the hell did she know about his life?

Anyway, he'd promised Stephanie, and it wasn't like he had to be up all night. He could go for a couple of hours. "Okay, Paul; see you in a little while."

"Me, Cassandra, and probably a half dozen Fielding-loving fans."

Kane hung up on him and got into the shower. Then he pulled on black jeans, a gray T-shirt, and an ancient pair of boots that had just the right amount of wear. As he picked up his jacket and keys, he turned around and looked at his apartment, at the huge sectional and the giant bed just visible through the bedroom door, covered with pillows solely used to aid in positioning. Jeez, was anything in this place not geared at seduction? Was that all he ever focused on?

Okay, now he might really hate that woman.

◆

The launch was tasteful and warm, the focus on the formerly homeless people and their stories, not on the celebrities. Stephanie, a tiny woman with very short black hair and enormous green eyes, barely came up to Kane's chest, but had more energy than anyone else in the room. He found a group that included some agents, managers, Steph's wife, and a wall to lean against, and let them talk around him. They asked how he was doing after the fires but didn't press him for details, which he appreciated.

Too soon Paul brought the lovely Cassandra to him. At once she made it clear that she would consider a liaison between them a great boost to her career. She stood close to him, put her hand on his arm, laughed at his—to him rather feeble—jokes. Everything that signaled loud and proud what Kane would normally be quite happy to receive.

Eventually he had to pull her aside—making her eyes light up—and confess that he was just too beat to do her justice. He was probably causing bodily harm to his reputation by admitting that, but it was all he had to give tonight. Cassandra gave up with a good grace, and Paul, while raising his eyebrows to the stratosphere behind her back, good-naturedly led her away to someone more interesting. Kane took the opportunity to make his excuses to Steph and went home; he knew they'd all seen the footage on TV, and he used how he had looked then to get one more night alone before his life got back in bed with him.

Chapter 6

Ellen worked until after seven, until the people on the street below stopped going home from work and started going out to extend the Halloween spirit into the weekend. When she got downstairs, she turned into the lobby, instead of taking the back entrance to the parking lot. She had never liked that quiet, unfrequented passageway; the brightness of the lobby and the people in it made her feel a whole lot safer, and Kane Fielding's visit had made her even more jumpy.

The lobby was very busy. People were coming down dressed to go out or coming back from a day of sightseeing with tired and cranky kids. New arrivals clogged all the pathways with suitcases while bellhops waited for direction. She looked over to the front desk. For some reason Penny was by herself, trying to cope with everyone. Without saying a word, Ellen stepped behind the counter, flicked on a monitor, and turned her best customer-service smile on the person in front of her. She'd started her career in reception at the Rosette in London; Penny had shown her the systems soon after they'd met.

After fifteen minutes or so they got a chance to say a couple of words. "Where's Francesca?" Ellen asked, scanning in a keycard.

"Sick," Penny said quickly before she told a couple in perfect Portuguese the arrangements for having their room cleaned.

It was another hour before they could say any more. "What kind of sick?" Ellen said.

"Looked like the flu, nose like Rudolph and a voice like Joan Rivers. She was putting off the customers. Ugh, *finally*, guys." The receptionists from the next shift had come in, and the pressure lifted a little. Penny waved to a man who had been in the reading area for the last half hour. Ellen picked up her bag and followed her into the back room.

"Second date?" Ellen guessed. Penny was a cute, petite blonde with short hair and a mouth born to pout. She ran with her assets, channeling fifties pinup models, with scarlet lipstick, shirts that were just on the business side of tight, and a large flower of some kind usually pinned to her chest. In fact, if you didn't know her, you'd think that she was off to a Halloween party as a blond Betty Boop. She loved to love men and was constantly trying to convince Ellen to let her guard down.

"Third, if we're counting," Penny answered with an appealing leer. "He's an accountant with a real 'head' for 'figures.'" She struck a pose and then turned to her mirror, ignoring Ellen's groan. "But don't change the subject. What the hell was—"

Ellen's cell phone rang. Gratefully, she picked it up. "It's Francesca. Hey, Francesca. Sorry you're ill."

"OMG, Elena, I'm as white as a shit." Francesca's Italian accent hadn't softened in her two years of living in Boston. "But my nose, it is red like Penny's mouth." She sounded god-awful, and Ellen told her so. "Yes, precisely," she said. "I have to ask you a favor, my love. Can you please help me? I know it is short notice, but I am *disperata*."

"All right; what do you need?" Ellen asked. Penny raised her eyebrows while penciling them in at the same time. Ellen could never figure out how she did that.

"I have the dog of my brother to stay with me. He is a big giant of a furball, and he is jumping all over my apartment. I cannot take him out to walk him; my head will fall off if I get off the couch. I know is a lot to ask but please would you come and take him out tonight?"

Ellen had precisely no plans for tonight. Or almost any night. "Of course; don't worry. I'm just leaving work now. I'll be there in twenty minutes."

"You are still at work?"

"Yes!" Penny called over from the mirror. "Saving my hide when you deserted me!"

Ellen had held out the phone. When she put it back to her ear, Francesca said, "She is late for her accountant, I know. Thank you, *cara*, thank you a million. He is a good dog. I will lend you sneakers."

That didn't sound good, but Ellen had promised, so she could only say goodbye and hang up.

Penny was done prepping. She looked ready for a photo shoot. Ellen was aware that she hadn't paid any attention to her hair or face all day. "So come on," Penny said, looking at Ellen in the mirror.

"Oh no, Pen, I don't want to make you late for your date," Ellen said, wide-eyed.

"Screw him. Come on. Details. How does Kane Fielding—oh my God, just the name—know you? What did he want?"

"Believe it or not, because I don't, he asked me to go to the Queen's Ball with him."

Penny jumped over to her and slapped her on the arm. "No, he *didn't!*"

"Yes, he *did.*" Ellen aimed a slap back, but Penny moved out of range. "And I told him to shove off."

"No, you *didn't,*" Penny echoed on a breath.

"Honestly, Pen. I know you think he's a god and all, but I don't think I've met a more egotistical brat in my life."

"Are you *nuts?*" Penny's face was one big O of amazement. "You, not even you, could turn down that incredible hunk of meat."

"Uh, yes, I could, and it was quite easy, actually," she added, crossing her fingers behind her back. "He was an ass, Penny, I'm telling you."

Penny smoothed her stockings and checked her lipstick again. "And what an ass. My God, I'd—"

"I know, cut off your feet to get horizontal with him. You said, many times." Ellen put on her coat.

Penny assessed her, her big blue eyes narrowed. "I'll tell you something, Miss Supposedly-Can't-Stand-the-Man. In all the time I've known you, the *only* person who's gotten *any* reaction from you is Play-the-Field Fielding."

"Horsewhip."

"I can see it now!" Penny yelped, pointing at her. "You're excited!"

"God's sake, Penny, I just told you I turned him down, didn't I? If I was interested in him, would I not have said yes?"

"I don't know. You might be out of practice. Scratch that. I know you're out of practice." Penny sighed. "Weren't you even a little bit curious?"

Ellen willed her cheeks not to answer that question. "Go and have fun with your accountant."

"Oh God, one of these days, Ellen," was all Penny said before they stepped out of the back room and she had to smile up at her date.

Ellen followed them through the front door and turned right, toward the car park. As she began to enter the relatively dark parking area, she automatically took her keys out of her purse and arranged them so they poked through between her knuckles—an instant knuckle-duster. Her other hand held her little flashlight that doubled as pepper spray. She approached her car, crouched down, and looked under it, then looked under the ones next to it. All clear. She peeked in the back window, shined her flashlight in, then opened the door and got in, throwing her handbag on the passenger seat as her other hand locked the door.

She started the car quickly and backed out, relaxing with the familiar feeling of safety she always got in her car. Having a car in the middle of the city was a pointless expense, but not to Ellen. Late-night cabs and subways held too many dangers. She needed this cage like she needed three locks on her apartment door.

She parked in the lot of Francesca's building, took all her precautions in reverse, and went to meet the dog, who was barking before Ellen got to the door.

Francesca opened her door a crack. "Do not come near me, *cara*."

"It's okay. I had my flu jab."

"Ugh, don't remind me. I meant to get it but... Here, I have sneakers, and here is the leash and look out because here is Cabo on the end of the leash." Cabo squeezed out of the door and tried to give Ellen a stand-up hug.

He was a Bernese mountain dog with a big smile and obviously a lot of love to give. Ellen decided against the sneakers, as her heels weren't too high, and she was only planning on walking him around the block. This, she soon found out, was a mistake; for Cabo, apparently every walk was really a run, and the Halloween revelers drove him wild. Ellen's shoulder was soon complaining from pulling him back; he seemed to want to personally examine every fancy costume they passed. She decided to increase the walk to a good ten blocks to try and use up some of his energy, but he just got happier and bouncier the more ghouls and pirates they met.

The partygoers were building up outside the bars; despite the chill of the air, people didn't seem to mind being there. The drinking crowds would normally have made Ellen extremely nervous, despite the self-defense classes she continued to take at the gym with Lucía, but Cabo was a wonderful deterrent. No one looked at her. They were laughing at him while making sure he didn't slobber over their costumes. *I should get a dog. Why didn't I think of that before? Something big and hairy that scares people off.*

For no good reason whatsoever, an image of Kane Fielding's hair curling that little bit over his collar flashed through her mind. She stopped dead in the street at the heat that suddenly went through her body; Cabo, miraculously, stopped too. Only when someone behind her bumped into her did she set off again, cursing herself all the way down the street.

Back at Francesca's place, Ellen feared for her friend's sanity, with a dog as big as Cabo bouncing around her flat. She knocked on the door again. "Francesca, let me take him this weekend. I don't have anything else going on, and you're ill."

"That is too much to ask of you," came Francesca's muffled voice through the door. "He is so big and—"

"And he likes to test rotator cuffs, I know. There's no way you can take care of him in your state. Get his food and bowls and whatever."

"You are sure you are available?" Francesca asked as she opened the door to hand Ellen boxes and bowls. "No Halloween parties to go to?"

Definitely not. Crowds and drunken men and the anonymity of masks. No.

She had to make a couple of trips to her car to get the dog's stuff in it. Each time she brought Cabo with her. Francesca said, "Ellen, you are such a good friend. I will never, never forget—" And she gave an almighty sneeze. "Ow, my sinuses! Okay, I got to go. I'll take you out for lunch when I'm better."

Ellen waved her off and took a happy Cabo back to her car.

By the time she finally got back to her flat, one arm was numb from keeping the dog in the back seat the whole way. He seemed to think the front seat was the only way to travel. Once she was in her front door, she closed and triple-locked it. Now, she was really safe. The cold, set face she put on for work relaxed.

She set up Cabo's bed in the living room and was relieved that he knew what "bed" meant and went there obediently. In the tiny kitchen area, flicking on the television and throwing her shoes toward her bedroom nook on the way, she made the quickest meal she could think of: baked beans on toast with grated cheese—English cheddar, of course—over the top. She rationalized it by adding a carrot on the side and telling herself that most of the food groups were represented.

She lived in overstuffed, rather messy surroundings, with shelves packed with books, and lots of throw rugs and pillows for spending nights in with a DVD. The required pictures of her family were arranged on the shelves. A spider plant that she'd been given three years ago was on the windowsill, along with seven or eight pots of baby spider plants that the darn thing kept sprouting. All the colors in her flat were muted, soft greens and creams. Here she didn't have to explain why she ordered baked beans from England instead of eating the brand that looked exactly the same in the supermarket, or why putting water in a microwave to make tea was so disgusting. She could listen to the British news on the internet and try and convince herself that not much had changed over there since she'd come to America. She could invite in only a select few friends and relatives, and keep the rest out.

For about the forty thousandth time, she contrasted her life now with the one she'd given up when she'd left England. Had she given it up? Or had Edward taken it from her? She'd been devoted to him, ready to commit her whole future to him... until the night he'd become someone else. Someone who'd cursed at her, beaten her. Raped her, if she was going to get technical about the term.

Perhaps it was her fault. He had said it was. Even now, the memory of his words, his weight on her, mocked her trust in him and made her flinch back into the couch cushions. She should have known him better. And if Edward could hide a dark side so well, why not other men?

She took her empty plate into the kitchen to snap out of the memory. She was here now; she had made a cocoon of safety for herself, and she liked it. She was good at her job and respected for it, whatever her reasons had been for coming to it. And she had unexpectedly fallen in love with Boston—with its age and its history and its respect for its old buildings and spaces, and with the Charles drawing everyone to its banks every time the sun came out.

Pulling on a pair of boots and making sure she was holding the pepper spray, Ellen went out to the car to get Cabo's food. When she got back the second time, the ten o'clock news was on. The newscaster began to speak of the fire in Grand Rapids. The reporter on site showed the impressive spectacle of twenty fire trucks surrounding the inferno that had been a Fielding lumber mill. He said that the fire had blazed until four o'clock Thursday morning, and that Kane Fielding had stayed until the end.

They showed him standing by the ruin. The image held Ellen in place. He was very still, not looking anywhere but at the mess that had been the mill, his jaw set, mouth tight, eyes hidden in shadow. This was the man who'd come into the lobby: tired and carrying a huge burden.

Then his face came up again, while the voiceover told of the press conference he'd held on Thursday afternoon. Now, he looked more like he had in her office. His thick hair fell attractively over his forehead, and when he brushed it away, his deep-set animal eyes were even more noticeable. But when he said, "It's all too easy to set a fire in a lumber mill if you really want to," fine lines appeared, bracketing his mouth and making him look older than the thirty-five years the papers said he was.

There were no leads. When some of the press had gone to the Grand Rapids site the day before the fire, to ask about precautions, the site manager had explained that they had safety systems all over the plant, and that since Mr. Fielding came every year to inspect them himself, they were all in perfect working order. She looked at Kane's face while the other man spoke; he looked furious about something.

Ellen, sitting in a pool of soft light from the lamp beside her, a warm throw blanket covering her and protecting her in her safe, structured little world, felt that disturbing side of her again, that reached toward him instead of sensibly running the other way.

But when a female journalist asked him, "Are you dating anyone we know?" he looked at the woman with a grin that chased the clouds from his face and made even Ellen's breath quicken, and answered, "Why, are you offering?" which won him a laugh from his audience. Ellen switched off the television, thankful for the reminder that he was a chauvinist pig. He couldn't even keep his mind on this serious matter for one moment. It just went to show how throwaway his offer to her was, and how it didn't matter how melty that feeling in her stomach was when she remembered his eyes, or his hair falling over his forehead.

Chapter 7

Kane was only on his second mile, but the sweat was already pouring off him, despite the cool day. His breath was fogging in front of him in embarrassingly short gasps. He'd wanted to do the full seven-mile circuit of the Charles, going down as far as the business school and crossing over into Cambridge. But now he didn't know if he was even going to make it past BU. He really had been smoking too much, and with so many hours traveling or in the office, he was off his usual schedule.

Running was the only exercise he could stand. It came with the bonus that when he ran, he was almost invisible, especially when he wore his Sox cap. He could give in to the rhythm of his feet hitting the pavement, focus on the simple problems like getting enough oxygen to his muscles, without wondering if someone was going to take his picture.

But today was not the soothing break he'd planned. He'd woken up this Sunday after a frustrating Saturday spent half at work and half arguing with his heavily pregnant sister, whose useless husband had skipped out again. The conversation had gone around in the same circles as usual, with Thea convinced Kane would kill Gabriel if he found him this time, and Kane unable to categorically promise her he wouldn't.

His feet were hitting the ground so hard his teeth were rattling. He eased up a bit, saw the first bridge, and told himself he'd take a break when he got there. His lungs screamed in protest. Two women running in the opposite direction gave him a smile as they passed, and he didn't even have the energy to do more than give a quick, polite smile back.

And the fires! They made him so freaking mad he was surprised his feet weren't thumping right through the concrete. This was *his* company, goddammit; they were *his* mills and factories and printers and warehouses. *His* new equipment that had taken him three years to persuade the board to buy. *His* dream to convert entirely to recycled or sustainable raw materials within twenty years. *His* employees who'd come back to the company gladly.

Dragging a company into the twenty-first century was one thing; having a nameless, faceless threat attack it from the outside scared the hell out of him.

He let out a low growl that startled a family going past him. He had stopped at the BU bridge without realizing it. He tried to smile at them, hands out—*I'm harmless*—and it occurred to him that he really wanted a cigarette. Instead, he pushed his baseball cap off his head and scraped his hands through his sweaty hair. He found himself vaguely wondering if he was being watched, and if so, if he had the right proportion of sweat to leg muscle and messy hair going on. The press coverage of the last few days was obviously making him twitchy.

He wasn't exactly vain; he just paid attention to the way he looked because he was always looked *at*. He knew his looks made him as good a salesperson for the company as Leo or any of the rest of the team. When he'd started dating Didi and suddenly found his picture showing up in the entertainment—rather than the business—pages, he took the added publicity as a bonus. He knew that in those pictures he was merely the sideshow: the prop in a tux with a killer smile, there to make the star look even better. The Boston papers had loved it, singing their hometown hottie's—he had cringed at that one—praises and seeking him out at any function he went to. As long as it kept the name of Fielding Paper in people's minds, he was fine with it.

But the fires were generating a new kind of publicity, a new reason to take his picture. And he was worried because he didn't know if he could control the game this time.

He looked north, up the river, to the next bridge. He couldn't face going farther away from home. Maybe he would just go back and sleep for the rest of the day. Maybe his eldest sister, Cat, hadn't left messages on his cell, giving him a hard time for his argument with

Thea, or for some other damn thing. Picking up his baseball cap, turning his back on the curve in the river, on the fading leaves—peak fall foliage had come and gone without him noticing—he began to jog back along the path to the Esplanade. *To the Clamshell, you lazy bastard,* he told himself. *At least to there.*

Despite the cold, there was a lot of activity along the Charles: families taking their kids to the playgrounds one last time before winter locked them all in their homes, young couples from the trendiest parts of Back Bay leaning against each other on picnic blankets, reading, or working on laptops, people chasing dogs around, illegally off-leash. Some of the dogs came up to say hi to him, which gave him another excuse to slow down, to pet them.

Lifting his eyes from a black and tan shepherd mutt with one eye, his gaze was caught by a huge shaggy dog that appeared to be trying to climb up its owner. The owner, who was in a long padded coat and hood, despite the temperature hovering around fifty, was holding a stick above her head and laughing at the dog, who looked like it would break its back if it leaped off the ground one more time. Its paws knocked her back a couple of steps; the long leash she was using on him tangled up her legs, and down she went.

He took a step toward her, to help her. Then her hood fell off as the dog jumped on her to get the stick. Kane's mouth went dry, and his stomach turned over, like it did when he thought about fire. He'd seen that shade of blond just two days ago and had been telling himself to forget about it ever since.

No way, man. She's already made it clear she doesn't want you anywhere near her.

Yeah, but why *was* that?

Not your problem, remember? Remember her looking down her perfect British nose at your social life?

But when she got mad, she was even more fascinating.

And you don't have the time to date anyone right now. Just keep on running, buddy.

But of course, just as he had done on Friday, he walked toward her, not away.

She was untangling herself, which was difficult as the dog kept jumping around her. Kane crouched down next to her. "Need some help?"

The sun was behind him, making her squint as she looked up. "No, thanks, I—" Then she recognized him. Her eyes went very wide. "Oh, no," she breathed. She pulled with more urgency on the leash around her legs, which just tangled her up more. Also, the dog had the stick and was trying to run off with it, which wasn't helping.

Kane took off his baseball cap to see her better. Damn, she was even more striking out here, with a dark-red scarf bringing out a reddish tint in her hair, and her cheeks a little pink in the breeze. As he watched, they got pinker; she was looking at him as if she'd been caught doing something wrong.

The dog pulled at her legs again, swinging them into his knees. "Cabo, no!" she gasped. But Kane was inclined to thank the dog. She was wearing a great pair of knee-high boots, which he could see better now.

"May I?" he asked, indicating the leash.

"Um," she said. But she let go of it, so Kane started at her ankles, unwinding what he could while touching her as little as possible. Leaning over her, he could hear her breathing, taut and uneven. Jeez, was he that terrifying?

Cabo found a little slack in the leash and used it to launch himself at Kane, who went down in a mass of fur and legs and stick. Ellen's legs, again, went with them, kicking him in the thigh this time.

"Oh, sorry!" she said helplessly.

He wanted to tell her it wasn't her fault, but with the full weight of the dog on him—this Cabo had to be part yeti, he weighed so much—he had no breath for talking. All he could do was try and stop the stick from poking him in the eye. Once he'd wrestled it out of Cabo's mouth, the dog hopped off him and sat, grinning, waiting for him to throw it. Kane sat up again, rubbed at his bruised ribs, and noticed that Ellen's legs were beside his now; a row of rivets on her boots was a cool line against him.

This time he unbuckled Cabo's leash from his collar—"You're not allowed to—!" she began—and kept hold of him while he fed the free end of the leash through her legs and finally got her untangled. Silently she handed him another, shorter leash, and he got Cabo hooked up again. Ellen coiled the long leash and put it down on her other side.

Kane didn't want to move, now that he was this close to her. She had every opportunity to move away from him, but all she was doing was staring at him, her cheeks still flushed, still looking mortified. Just to show how trustworthy he was, Kane moved so he was no longer touching her and leaned back on his hands, one of which still held Cabo's leash. The cold grass was beginning to prickle at his bare legs.

They sat quietly for a moment. She seemed to wrestle internally with something. Cabo got bored and lay down on Kane's other side. Then she burst out, "Mr. Fielding, I hope my—what I said the other day—didn't reflect on the hotel." And before he could reply, she added, "I'm not usually—I mean ever—that... tactless."

He noticed that she didn't apologize for what she'd said; she just regretted saying it out loud. But he said, "Ellen, I think we've moved beyond last names. I'm sure Emily Post has something about what to call the guy your dog just attacked."

"He's not my dog," she said irrelevantly. "I'm watching him for a friend."

"Okay, *a* dog. And you may be surprised to know that I can keep my business and my... overactive social life completely separate." She put a hand up to cover her flushed cheek, then moved it again to unzip her coat. She was obviously getting hot and bothered around him, but was it in a good or a bad way?

Those blue eyes looked even bluer against the red of her scarf. And he could see that her pupils were definitely dilated.

You don't have time for this.

Just look at her.

She isn't your usual diversion.

I just want her to... to trust me.

Don't do it. You don't have time. You don't know what the hell you're doing.

"See, the problem is," he said, surprising himself even as he said it, "I've been trying not to think about you all weekend." That made her take in a fast breath. "And failing," he added.

Was it his imagination, or did she give a tiny, answering nod? Her eyes were dilated, her lips full. They were only a couple of feet apart; she smelled of flowers. He bet if he buried his face in her hair, it would smell incredible.

"Ellen," he said, and she closed her eyes and opened them again. "Have dinner with me tonight."

"There's no *point*," she said, almost desperately.

"No point in good conversation? In a good meal with a beautiful woman?"

She squirmed under the compliment. "No point, when I can*not* be a part of the life you lead."

"Have dinner with me, and I'll tell you about the life I lead. And you can tell me about your life. That's how it works." She was already shaking her head. "Besides, I prefer being judged *after* people have spent time with me."

Now she put both hands to her cheeks. "Oh, I did do that, didn't I?" she said, her eyes wide in dismay. He waited. "But I'm leaving. The country. In four months."

"All the better. No pressure, no strings. It's just dinner, Ellen. You'll survive."

She closed her eyes again. "All right, then."

It wasn't the resounding "yay" he was looking for, but he'd take it. "Where?"

"Do you know Carpenter's?"

It was a very good steak restaurant on Boylston, with sports on five different TVs in the bar. Not what he would have imagined for her. "Sure. I'll pick you up, what, seven thirty?"

"No," she said quickly. "I'll meet you there. Seven thirty."

She really didn't trust him at all. "If that makes you feel"—he nearly said "safer" but changed it—"better."

She put her hood back up and squinted at him from its fur lining. Fear, desire, mistrust, longing. He'd never wanted to get to know a woman more.

Ellen stood up; Kane and Cabo followed suit. "'Bye, Cabo," Kane said to the dog, who was already pulling her away from him. "Seven thirty," he called to her, taking in her wide blue eyes and her blond hair escaping from the hood and spilling onto the red scarf.

Chapter 8

As Ellen walked down Boylston, in her fourth choice of outfit, two voices were warring in her head. The first said, *What the hell were you thinking, saying yes to this? Once again, Ellen, you led with your libido, which you didn't even know you still had. This is a loss of control, and it's scary. He's scary. Get in there, make an excuse, and get out again.*

The second said, *Okay, you can do this. It doesn't matter how badly your thighs quiver when he says your name; you are in full control of your reactions, and you will not for one second show him that he's been getting to you. You will not sigh, like you just did, and you will not think about what you could see of his legs today, of those strong, hard muscles, and the hair on his thighs...*

Oh God.

She raised her chin, thought cooling thoughts, and gripped her pepper spray in her pocket. Then she saw him standing under the streetlamp outside the restaurant, his head down, hands in his pockets, and let all her breath out in a rush. Well, that just wasn't fair.

He was wearing dark jeans and a dark-green tweed jacket, and—bloody hell—another white shirt. His hair was falling over his forehead and brushing his collar as usual, and it looked even better next to the precise fit of his clothes. Ellen set her jaw against the melting feeling she was getting in her chest. *Why* did he have to be in a white shirt again? *Why* did she react to him when he was so clearly not safe?

She walked closer, and he looked up. His eyes were hidden by the shadow from the streetlight; for a split second, his face looked so forbidding she wondered if he'd thought twice about asking her out. But then he broke into a smile that was warm and genuine, and he came over to meet her.

"Hi," he said. "Thanks for coming."

"Hello," she answered, giving a tight smile of her own. *Remember. Control.*

Kane nodded, for some reason, and said, "Shall we?" Ellen let him usher her into the restaurant, and if she noticed like mad when his hand grazed her shoulder as he helped her with her coat, she gritted her teeth and ignored it. *And you're paying your half of the bill. That way it's not a date.*

As they went through the door, a man came from behind the bar, greeted Kane by name, introduced himself as Joe, the owner, and led them to a table at the front, in the window. "Is this okay?" Kane said to her. "It's a little close to the bar, but I thought you'd feel—I thought you'd prefer it."

She did prefer it. The last thing she wanted tonight was to be in some cozy corner with him. But she hated that he knew that she had a... preference for being out in the open. *You showed too much the other day; this is what comes of losing control.* Anyway, surely Kane Fielding would have liked nothing better than a cozy corner booth where shoulders could touch and legs could tangle under the table...

"Ellen?"

"What? Oh, yes, it's fine." And she sat down before he or Joe could pull out her chair. *Don't start thinking he's considerate. He does this stuff to get to his version of the end of the evening; remember that.*

The bar was noisy, with a different game on each TV and music thumping from somewhere behind her. But the public space was worth it, and when the guitar solo from Aerosmith's "Walk on Water" pealed out of the speaker behind her head, she hardly even winced.

Joe was back with the menus and wine list. Kane indicated that Ellen should take the wine list, but she hadn't lived in Boston for four years without learning a little something about etiquette. She shook her head and said to Joe, "I'll have a Sam Adams Oktoberfest, please."

Kane smiled at Joe. "Beauty *and* brains. I'll have the same."

As Joe disappeared, she said, "You don't have to keep doing that. In fact, I'd rather you didn't." Best to start as she meant to go on.

"Do what?" He looked completely at ease, leaning back in his chair, one elbow hooked over the back, his other hand on the table, rolling a fork between his fingers.

Stop staring at his hands. "The cheesy compliments." *Dang it. Why can't I say one single thing to him without putting my foot in my mouth?*

Still, it was a cheesy compliment.

"Hey, lady," he drawled. "You think that was bad? I've been doing it so long I got the cheese and the crackers and a nice cabernet to go with 'em."

Now, *that* was the Kane Fielding she'd expected. She wasn't crazy. She glared at him, but he just said, "In fact, let's get them all out of the way at once, 'cause, you know, I have a quota." He began counting on his fingers. "Your hair is incredible in this light, like raw honey. That cream coat you were wearing"–he gestured behind him to the coat check–"makes your skin glow. And you might think that shirt is loose enough to hide you, but it doesn't; it just hints enough to drive a guy crazy. Face it, Ellen," he finished, holding down her menu when she tried to use it to cover her face, "you're beautiful, and any man who doesn't tell you that several times a day is a moron."

She was so uncomfortable. And so warm. She pulled on the menu, but his hand stayed put. "I'm not..." she began. "I'm not trying to... I'm not asking for that kind of attention."

He ducked his head to get in her line of sight. "Why not? Own it."

"Like you do?" she shot back. What was it with him getting under her skin like that? When had she ever thought she could stay professional around him?

He grinned. "Yeah, sure. Like I do. You can't do anything about it, you know. I don't care how hard you tie your hair back in the office or how much you scowl at me."

"Can we *please* talk about *anything* else?"

"Okay. I'm sorry." He let go of her menu. "Something about you. Brings out the divil in me, as my useless brother-in-law would say."

The beers came. Ellen would have liked to find out more about the useless brother-in-law, but that would imply she was interested in

Kane's private life. Which she wasn't. She took two big gulps of her beer before she could stop herself.

Kane was watching her. When he opened his mouth, she almost flinched. But all he said was, "What do you like to eat here?"

She ordered the lamb chops. He got swordfish. Ellen raised her eyebrows. *Don't say it.* But she said it. "You know, this is a steakhouse." Maybe he wasn't the only one with the devil in him.

"I know it," he said. Even when she was being bratty, he smiled at her. "I've been on the road a lot these last few days. Ate a lot of junk food."

"Hence the running."

"Well, the running is supposed to be a regular thing. I usually go down there later at night during the week, but this week…"

She now remembered, not the press conference, but the Kane she'd seen watching the fire, the Kane coming into the office, tired and worried and being sweet to his receptionist. She thought of the ever-so-quick glance she'd had at his Wiki page, of losing his father so horribly, and taking over the company while still so young. And now someone was setting more fires, possibly endangering more people. It had to be bothering him.

This was a much more dangerous path to go down. If she started feeling sorry for him, she would start thinking of him as human.

He had picked up the fork again and was making it shake back and forth between his fingers. Was he thinking about the fires as well? Or did he just need a cigarette? After a second he focused on her again, saw her watching him, and gave that slow smile. *Bloody man,* she thought, and *ohh.*

"So tell me," he said, sitting up straighter. "What brought you to Boston?"

That was an easy question; she had the edited version finely honed. "The hotel likes to move its employees around, get us used to different cultures. I'd worked at the London site for a few years. It was time."

"So why Boston?"

Edward's cool, blond, arrogant face, smirking at her across her parents' dining table, swam into her mind, making her take another sip of beer. *Because it was the first available job, and I had to get out of there.* "The history," she half lied. "You don't get much older than Boston in this country." She looked at him, her mouth twisting. "And the accent."

"What accent?" He smiled.

Ellen had to laugh at that. "Well, quite. I'm kind of a student of them. One of these days I'm going to take a road trip across the country and just listen." Well, she'd planned to do that. Somehow four years had slid right by her, and now she was out of time.

"Lucía said you speak five languages."

Ellen lowered her eyes and began picking at the label on her beer. So he'd asked Lucía about her? What had Lucía said? *What do you care, Ellen? This is not high school. And it's six languages, actually.* Aloud, she said, "I'm getting rusty. I started on reception at the Rosette in London before I moved to events and conferences, and there aren't many languages required in this job."

"My brother-in-law's Italian," he said. "He's taught me a few phrases."

"Let me guess, to impress the ladies?"

His smile quirked up. "Not enough to impress you, I'd guess."

"Obviously."

Their waiter brought their food, and Ellen was completely distracted. The garlic-rosemary sauce on her lamb chops smelled like pure heaven. She was suddenly so hungry it was all she could do not to pick up a chop in her hands and go at it with her teeth. She kept herself in check, however, and got the first piece eaten with minimal ecstatic moaning. Kane, she saw with no surprise, ate the American way, cutting his pieces and then switching his fork to his right hand to eat. Penny called her way the "shovel approach," and tonight she might live up to the term.

After a few minutes, Kane broke the silence. "Good?" was all he said.

"Really good," she had to admit, aware that she was at risk of dripping juices.

He laughed a little. "That's the nicest thing you've said all night."

As swept up in the flavors and the pleasure of plain good food as she was, she said, "Maybe if you were covered in this gravy and served up next to this pile of mashed potatoes, I'd say something nice to you too."

Kane laughed out loud. "Deal!" he shouted, making her blush scarlet and a few heads at the bar turn around. Kane couldn't stop laughing, and Ellen couldn't stop blushing. She was going to lock the memory of tonight up in a vault as soon as she got out of here and never refer to it again.

"All I was trying to say was–" But he waved her away and held his sides. With what little dignity she had left, she worked on her food, until Kane finally stopped laughing.

"I'm sorry," he said, ostentatiously mopping his brow. "You just–surprised yourself–so much!"

"Don't start again," she begged. "Eat your fish." And to give him something else to think about, she said, "And tell me about your useless Italian brother-in-law."

"Oh, he's not the useless one." Kane took a drink. "He's fine. My sister's the pain in the ass in that marriage."

Ellen frowned. "Can you start again?"

Kane settled back in his chair and counted on his fingers. "I've got four sisters. Cat's the oldest, older than me. She's married to Antonio. I have twin nephews."

"Me too." Lordy, how could she possibly have something in common with this man?

"How long before you could tell them apart?" She grimaced. "Yeah, I know, right?" he said. "Then Thea... She's the one with the useless husband. Worthless piece of–Anyway." He cleared his throat and glanced over at the bar. "Then Sam, she's an archaeologist. Wicked smart, wastes her time moving dirt from one place to another with tiny brushes. Then Megan. The caboose." He smiled then, a clear, uncomplicated smile that showed how much he loved his baby sister. "She's just finishing up college, then she's going to come work for me."

Four sisters. It explained why he was so comfortable around women. Perhaps it also explained why intelligent women like Lucía continued to work for him. *Oh no. Don't start liking him.*

"Oh, and there's Carl. I met him in college. I would say he's my brother, but the way my sister Sam looks at him…"

"Bit dangerous, isn't it? You having a brother?" She opened her eyes wide at him, wondering if he had any ability to laugh at himself. At that name.

He rolled his eyes and picked up his beer bottle. "Yeah, yeah. It's *K-a-n-e*, not *C-a-i-n*. And it's my grandmother's maiden name, if you care. And Carl could and would kick my ass if he thought I needed it." He took a drink. "Luckily for me, he lives in New York, so I don't get to piss him off much."

He sounded wistful. Maybe having a houseful of women had disadvantages as well.

He frowned, losing himself for a moment in picking the label off his bottle. Then he shook himself and said, "Whoa, sorry. So tell me about your family."

No, she supposed he wouldn't want to give her a glimpse of how he really felt about anything. She recognized it because she was fighting against the same thing.

She told him about her brother, Adam, and her parents, whom she Skyped with religiously. And then she heard herself saying, "Mum asks me the same questions every week. 'How's work? How's the flat? Been anywhere nice? Met any new friends? Met anyone English?' Meaning a man. 'Cause God forbid I date a Yank."

"Yeah, that would be awful," he said, widening his eyes.

Would it, though? The thought came unbidden. Her cheeks threatened a blush. "Well, they'd rather I come home and marry…" She stopped dead at the image of Edward that charged into her mind. "Someone like them," she finished, her throat a little tight. "Someone with the classic British stiff upper lip and all that, don't you know." Good, okay. She'd covered up that pause, hadn't she?

He didn't seem to have noticed. "Good thing none of that stiff upper lip thing rubbed off on you," he said, deadpan.

She threw a piece of bread at him just as Joe came up to offer dessert. Ellen ordered the flourless chocolate cake. Kane just got coffee. "You can't do that to me," she protested.

"I told you, I—"

"Oh, come on," she said, aware that she was almost begging, that she'd forgotten all about the cool, collected self she'd been determined to portray. "I'm not going to enjoy dessert if you're over there sipping a measly cup of coffee."

He grinned. "I don't think I've 'sipped' anything in my life. And watching you eat chocolate cake sounds like a whole lot of fun." Ellen blushed again; she was really going to have to do something about this constant reddening of her cheeks. Hadn't somebody invented a pill? "But okay. I'll have the cheesecake."

When the waiter was gone, Kane fell silent again. It occurred to her that being flippant about her parents was not exactly tactful around someone who'd lost both of his. There she went again; any and all breeding she'd acquired simply evaporated around him.

"It must be hard," he said finally. "Not being home. When do you go back?"

It was quite easy not to go home, in fact. Grateful for the change of subject, she said, "Thanksgiving. I have to get on with ordering my tickets."

"I mean, when do you go back for good? When are you done with all the jobs in other countries?"

"Oh." How long was long enough before she could go back and live in a world that included Edward? Her mother and his were still very good friends. He wasn't married, she knew. When she saw him at the events she couldn't avoid, he purposely came over, stood too close, loudly talked to his mother about Ellen being "the one who got away," and then gave her such a predatory look that she shivered now. "Um, not for a while," she said.

He hadn't missed that shiver. He was watching her. Reading her. Apart from his fingers tapping the table—no longer having a fork to play with—he was very still.

Desperate to get out of the spotlight, she said the first thing that came into her head. "Why do you smoke?"

"How do you know I do?" he asked, surprised.

She indicated his tapping fingers. She almost said, "And I could smell them on you," but even the idea of the smell of him shortened her breath. She couldn't get the words out.

He looked at his hand as if he'd never seen it before. "Because apparently," he said, "I'm more addicted to them than I thought."

She got her breath back. "Yes, but why start in the first place? Haven't you—" She broke off, and her face fell in horror.

"Had enough of fire?" Kane said with a wry smile.

"Oh shit," she said, putting her hand to her mouth. "I—I didn't—" Crap, could she say *one sentence* to him tonight without making a complete arse of herself?

"It's okay," he said. He thought for a moment, while Ellen tried to bring the temperature in her cheeks down. He said, "I guess it's a kind of fire I can control."

He looked so serious for a moment; she couldn't imagine why she'd ever seen him as shallow. "I'm sorry," she said from behind her hand.

"You can make it up to me," he said as the waiter reappeared with their desserts. "Eat your cake. And, Ellen," he added, when they were alone again, "if you want to keep up the stiff upper lip thing, you might want to quit blushing so adorably."

And you might want to stop saying my name.

See, all I had to do was say no when he asked me to dinner. That was all I had to do. She could have taken Cabo back to a mostly cured Francesca and taken up *her* offer of dinner instead. But he'd said her name, and she'd turned to mush. Was even this incredible chocolate experience on her plate worth the humiliation?

She'd finished half of it before she could look at him again, but he was looking out the window, his dessert hardly touched, his expression serious. She followed his gaze, but only saw the debris from yesterday's ticker tape parade. Then she saw a makeshift memorial from the Boston marathon bombing attached to the lamppost across from them: two faded red shirts tied into a cross and pinned to a board with "Boston Strong" written over it. Some flowers lay at its foot.

She looked at Kane again. He caught the slight movement of her head and focused on her. "Are you all done?" he said, still not smiling. She nodded. Joe appeared as if by magic with their bill, which Kane paid. She let him guide her out of her seat, into her coat, and out the door.

The air had gotten a lot colder; Ellen held her collar closed and wished she'd brought gloves. Kane looked as if the cold wouldn't dare bother him.

Ellen nodded at the memorial and said, "Did you know someone?"

"I think almost everyone knew someone," he said. "But yes, I did. An old girlfriend from high school. We used to run together. She lost her foot."

"I'm so sorry," she said and put her hand on his arm. "It was bad enough for me as an outsider. It must have been devastating for you." She hesitated, and then said, "Kane," which was the first time she'd used his first name. "I'm sorry about your father."

He nodded. Somehow, she was standing in front of him, looking up at him, once more aware of how much taller than her he was. And how good he smelled. She took in a breath and swayed closer.

"You know," he said, inches from her. "I don't... talk about my family a whole lot. Especially not Thea and Gabe. There are a lot of people who'd like that kind of information."

"What information?" she said and smiled. "I told you; I'm not about to go looking for publicity."

She wasn't sure what she was doing, but when he quietly said her name, frowning a little, she didn't back away. He seemed to close the gap very, very slowly, until Ellen, drunk on his height and scent and the sound of his voice, kissed him.

Chapter 9

It was a light kiss, her lips only brushing his before he pulled away a little, but she could swear light flashed behind her closed eyes. Then the feel of his arms, strong against her back, and the wool of his jacket, and the stubble on his chin, that brushed her hand where it still clutched her coat to her, made Ellen's heart rate double, and she fell into a panic attack out of all proportion. Her eyes flew open, and she saw him smile. *Now I've done it. Now he'll think he's entitled to more than a good night kiss and–*

She pushed hard on him with the hand at her collar, which made him choke and put his hand to his neck, releasing her from the circle of his arms. Ellen took a few steps away from him; if the street hadn't been busy with the last of the weekend's dinner-goers, she would have broken into a run.

"Ellen," he said a little hoarsely, putting out his hand to stop her. But she dodged him and had made it a few steps farther before his longer legs caught up. He got a hold of her arm and pulled her around to face him. "What–"

She didn't know what kind of face she turned on him, but it made him drop her arm as if it had burned him.

"Shit, Ellen," he said. "I don't–"

She started shaking. "Just let me go," she said; it came out as a plea.

"Let me at least get you a cab."

"No."

She continued to walk away from him, hoping he couldn't see her knees wobbling or hear her heart pounding in her throat.

At the corner of the street, she risked a quick look over her shoulder. But he was still standing where she'd left him, watching her go.

◆

It took a lot of concealer to cover the dark rings around her eyes the next morning. She wished she hadn't given Cabo back; he had been a nice solid presence in her apartment. Without him, she had nothing to distract her from how bad she looked, how little sleep she'd had. She was already late, and fighting through the rush-hour traffic didn't help her edginess. *You've got five days to make the Queen's Ball the best yet,* she told herself over and over in the car, *so you'll get your pick of transfers. Stop jumping at every movement, stop feeling like shit at the idea of leaving, and stop remembering.*

She hoped Penny wouldn't notice anything wrong when she walked past reception, but her friend was onto her from the minute she walked through the doors. "Hi," Ellen said, keeping a few feet away from the desk.

Penny excused herself from the man she was helping and, as decorously as possible, raced over to the end of the desk. "Hi, yourself," she said, keeping her voice low. "So how was your date?"

Ellen looked up, eyes wide. Penny wasn't smiling, for once. After telling Penny what an ass Kane had been on Friday, she hadn't been able to confess that she'd agreed to dinner with him. "How did you know?"

Penny said nothing, just reached under the desk and pulled out that morning's *Herald,* open to somewhere in the middle, and a quarter-page shot of Kane kissing her. Reaching up to him, her hair had fallen back from her face; she was easily recognizable. Kane was always easy to place, with his height and his hair.

"Setting his own flame," said the byline below the picture. "Kane Fielding takes some time off from fighting fires to start one of his own under new squeeze Ellen Hunter, an employee of the Boston Rosette Hotel. Looks like Kane'll be getting a discount on a room pretty soon."

The flash of light. That I thought was my own fireworks. A quiver of fury ran through her, so strong that she visibly swayed. She focused on Penny for a moment, then spun around and walked right back out of the hotel, the newspaper still clutched in her hand.

She didn't remember much of the walk between their buildings, the ride in the elevator to the top floor, or her sweep past Gloria without even a nod. When she strode past Anna's office, though, Anna said, "Miss—hey, wait a minute—" But Ellen was already opening the door to Kane's office.

◆

"You're an arrogant, self-serving little shit," she said loudly, the door banging back against the wall.

Kane looked up from the inspector's report of the Grand Rapids fire, which he'd been too distracted to read anyway. Ellen was striding the few steps from the door to his desk, her coat falling open to show a blouse with small beads running around the neckline. When she slammed her hand down on the desk, he got an involuntary shot straight down her cleavage. He made himself look up at her face; this was not a moment to get sidetracked.

"What the *fuck* were you thinking?" she shouted and threw the crumpled newspaper at him. Anna was at the door, mouth open, apparently too horrified to speak. He could imagine heads popping up over the top of their monitors behind her.

"I am *not*," Ellen continued, "one of those little bimbos you use to further your reputation!"

Kane peered around Ellen and made "go away" motions with his hand. Anna scowled at Ellen's back but retreated and mercifully closed the door.

Ellen's cheeks were red, her hair falling into her eyes. She was only a couple of feet from him across the desk. This was the most animated he'd seen her, the most beautiful. Certainly the most pissed. And it was all his fault. Anna had brought him the paper with his coffee.

"I suppose your little friend Joe called your buddy the journalist and told him where we were. I suppose you've done this kind of shit before, and those little tramps lap up the publicity–"

"Not tramps–" he tried.

"Don't–say–one–word to me!" she snapped back. "Do you understand that I have a *career*, and that you have probably just destroyed it? I've been working for ten years to get where I am, and your fucking ego has swept it all away in one photograph!"

She took a breath; her shirt shifted, and the beads rattled. He didn't mean to do it, but the sound made him look down.

"Look at *me*!" she shouted and shoved at the closest thing to her: his inbox. Focusing on it, she picked a handful of papers off the top. "I"–she threw the first sheets at him–"have to host a party"–another shower of papers landed on him–"for half of Boston *this weekend.*" He put up a hand to stop the next pile from hitting him in the face. Now out of ammo, she leaned across the desk. "You get me feeling all sorry for you, and then you take advantage and you think I'm just going to roll over and help you further your revolting reputation and I am *not having it.*"

She seemed to realize she was closer to him than she usually allowed, and she straightened up and tugged her hair to the side, out of her eyes. The beads chimed again, and Kane could smell her flowery scent.

She'd stopped talking. Yelling. He thought maybe he could speak now. "Yes, it's my fault," he began.

"I know it is, you attention-seeking piece of shit!"

"Jesus, Ellen. Of course I didn't know the camera was there. I'm not that bad." He wanted to point out that *she* had kissed *him*, that he'd been holding back as much as possible because he'd wanted her to be sure. But perhaps this wasn't the moment.

That one brief kiss had taken up more of his dreams last night than all the passionate clinches he'd been in in his life, and not just because of his bruised windpipe. The brush of her lips against his had haunted him almost as much as her reaction afterward–the panic he'd seen in her eyes, the fear in her voice.

"I just mean, because of my"–he sighed, hating that she'd been right about it—"social life. Joe called me this morning; he swears he didn't know anything about it, and I believe him. We go way back. It must have been one of the waitstaff or someone at the bar who heard us talking. I guess they found you on the Rosette website." He scraped his hand through his hair in frustration.

"Stop rearranging your hair," she snapped. "And don't even *think* about lighting that around me."

He looked down, surprised to see a cigarette in his hand. "Didn't even realize I got it out," he said distantly, but now that she'd mentioned it, he wanted nothing except to go open that window and smoke the damn thing. He adjusted his position instead, stretching his legs under the desk. "And I don't 'rearrange' my hair."

"Oh, please," she said in the same scornful tone. "Your whole life is based on how good something makes you look. Leering at your plastic secretaries—"

"Hey—"

"When's the last time you got a haircut? Always ready for a photo op, aren't you? I saw the press conference the other day. Couldn't go three minutes without coming on to someone."

"For God's sake, Ellen." He finally had to fight back. "First of all, Anna was a NICU nurse for five years before she came here. She finally couldn't handle losing the babies she couldn't save. I'm sure the others are just as valuable to society, and I don't *leer* at any of them. Second of all, you really think so little of me that you believe I'd hook up with that journalist? Based on one flirting comment in a room full of people?" He tapped the filter end of the cigarette on the desk. "I'm trying to show our customers that our supply chain is just fine and they don't have to look anywhere else for their paper. I *had* to sound like I wasn't bothered by it, or by anything. You think I have *time* for a social life right now? And third." He glanced at the door and lowered his voice a little. "Do you understand that I own a business here?"

"Yeah," she snorted, folding her arms tightly, "like a child *owns* a toy train."

"No." And now he was mad. He'd screwed with her life, he admitted it, but she wasn't going to malign his commitment to the company. He leaned forward. "Like a tenth-generation Fielding owns a business that's putting one sister through college and has just started growing trust funds for three more who only have him to rely on. Like a family who knows how many *other* families rely on us, in an industry that's going through so many changes; anything smaller than International Paper has folded long ago. Like a guy who knows that an accident of birth gave him one damn thing that sets us apart from the competitors, that makes people remember us when they decide whose paper to choose, and so yeah, I run with it."

Her arms were by her sides now. She'd lost most of the rigid fury that had kept her standing.

"And I'd appreciate it if you *didn't* go paying me back by telling that to anyone." Fuck it. He was having that cigarette. He stood up, shedding all the paper she'd thrown at him, and went to the window.

While he opened it, she said in a smaller voice, "Of course I wouldn't tell anyone. I told you I wouldn't."

"Of course nothing, Ellen. I don't know a damn thing about you, remember?" He blew smoke out of the window and looked back at her. "Guess I won't get to find out."

Her chin lifted. "Guess you won't."

She turned for the door. "One more thing," Kane said. When she turned back, he took the opportunity to fix her face in his mind, since he wouldn't be seeing her this close again. Her hair was still disheveled, but with highlights showing from the light coming in the window. Her coat was half off one shoulder, showing more of those beads that would make him crazy if he let them, and the creamy skin over her collarbone.

He'd looked at her from here only three days ago, yet he felt like her eyes had been bothering him for half his life. "I'm sorry I scared you."

Ellen's mouth fell open. Her throat worked for a moment, but then she just turned back around and walked out. He heard her say, "Sorry, Anna," and her steps as she walked away down the hallway.

In half a second Anna was in the room. "So that's that," he said.

"Good riddance," said Anna.

Chapter 10

The next morning, Ellen was standing over a conference room table, with a seating chart and a list of fifteen hundred names in front of her. Three hours and four cups of tea later, she had them all wrangled into position. Half an hour later she was back, after some intel that the ex-wife of one of the CEOs was marrying one of the other CEOs, and so they definitely could *not* be at the same table, which meant that his entire party of six had to be put somewhere else. Then it was changing the name of one of the lead counsels for another company, who'd suddenly been given bed rest for the last three months of her pregnancy. Her female replacement, Ellen had been told in fervent tones over the phone, had a wife and two children in Brooklyn and would not appreciate being seated next to the notoriously homophobic director of a large hospital.

Then there was the tricky question of where to put the CEO of Fielding Paper and guest.

By three o'clock she'd lost all ability to focus on the little slips of paper. When Penny found her, she was flopped in one of the chairs, trying to make her back as horizontal as possible.

"Why don't you just lie on the floor?" Penny suggested. "No one will see you there."

"Oh, right. Like Bill Cohen wouldn't get fodder for years from finding me on the floor of the conference room."

"Point." Penny held out a bag. "I thought maybe you'd forgotten to eat."

"Do two Snickers bars and a handful of Skittles count as lunch? Actually, as breakfast, second breakfast, and lunch? No? Okay, what did you bring me?"

They cleared a corner and ate together; Penny's shift had had her working through lunch that day as well.

"How was the gym?" Penny asked once they had a few bites in them.

Ellen stopped chewing. "Appalling. I nearly knocked Lucía out."

"*Ouch.*"

"It was terrible. I'm lucky she didn't lose a tooth. I forgot to pull the punch." Ellen grabbed at her hair and pulled it to the side so hard she turned her head. "How do I forget to pull the punch?"

"Little distracted, maybe?" Penny shook her chip bag out. "Little focused on a certain hottie–"

"Oh God, *don't* call him that, Pen, it makes him sound like a kid from a boy band."

"Okay, a certain walking orgasm–"

"Oh yes, that's much better," Ellen said with high sarcasm.

"–who you insist you can't stand but who gets you more worked up than I've seen you in four years."

"I *can't* stand him! He admits his whole lifestyle is geared toward getting cameras to take pictures of him!"

"You ever stop to think *why* he does that?"

He'd told her. She didn't tell Penny. "It doesn't matter why. He's a public figure, in this town anyway. Now maybe in other places as well because of the fires. I couldn't bear to live that kind of life."

"Really? Don't you think he might be worth it?" Ellen opened her mouth to say no, but hesitated too long. Penny took out her phone. "Have you seen that first press conference?"

"Yes, and he was being his usual–"

"Not the one from the other day. The *first* one. After his father died."

"God, no, and I don't want to. No, don't look it up–" But Penny was already searching for it on her phone. "I don't want to know, Pen. What if that picture screws up my job?"

"Did you talk to Jon?" Penny asked, waiting for the video to load.

"Yes. He says it's no big deal. But how am I going to face everyone at the ball on Saturday, with what they wrote under the photo ringing in my ears?"

"It's the *Herald*, Ellen; your guests aren't exactly that paper's target audience. Here."

Twenty-two-year-old Kane was gorgeous. And devastated. Seeing him like this, Ellen realized that the Kane she knew had a hardness to his face that was missing here. Kane's throat closed up several times while he talked: when he said that the mill that had killed his father wouldn't be rebuilt; when he apologized for the jobs that would be lost, and how determined he was that they'd hire everyone back when they could; when he talked about how many years he'd hoped to learn from his father, that were now gone.

Then the press had asked him question after question about the fire and the unions and the employees and what was going to close and what was going to stay open, and he stood there and took it all, while he got paler and paler. When it was over, he still remembered to help his mother carefully out of her chair.

Penny said, "My friends and I had crushes on him for months after this."

Yes, he was a teenager's dream, with all that tragedy surrounding him, and those dark eyes and slightly hollow cheeks.

"Well," Ellen gave one last feeble effort, "he dines out on it now."

Penny let out a growl of impatience. "Half his board resigned, Ellen. They didn't want to work for a kid right out of college. They wanted his family to sell, but he wouldn't. He knew if anyone else took it over, the mills would all be gone within five years." She gestured to the still of him. "Why are you so against him?"

Ellen looked at her sandwich wrapper, now twisted into a rope in her hands, then up at Penny. "'Cause I'm a judgmental bitch?"

Penny laughed. "Well, yeah, you have been a little," she said.

Ellen put her head into her hands, tugging on her hair. "I've been *such* a bitch," she said.

"One thing I know about guys," Penny said, gathering up the remains of their lunch. "They can't resist a pretty face. And an *apologetic* pretty face, oh mama."

♦

She had so much to do. She should be inspecting the carpet of the ballroom for weird and funky stains from the annual conference of chemical biologists, or biological chemists, or whoever it had been. She should be checking the roster for reception for Saturday night, to make sure Penny was on, because she'd said if she wasn't, she would be coming for Ellen in her sleep. She should be making an appointment to get her hair done for the ball. She should be contacting bloody Claire Holland with her top three location requests. She certainly should *not* be sitting on this bench for the third night in a row, bundled in the warmest coat and gloves she had, pepper spray in one hand and keys poking between the knuckles of the other, waiting for someone who might not come.

She was going to have to give up after tonight. Tomorrow was Friday; she would be up most of the night, getting everything into the ballroom and making sure it looked right. She couldn't skip out on that.

It was nine o'clock; she would give herself one more hour. She hid her face as much as possible in her scarf and looked beyond the light from the streetlamp above her.

It was ridiculous to imagine that she already knew which outline was his in the dark, but she was standing before he got into the pool of light.

He slowed down as soon as he saw her. She pushed her hood off and pulled down the scarf so he could see it was her. Her heart was lodged in her throat, or she would have said his name.

Kane stopped altogether, still several feet away from her. "What are you doing out here?" he said, his voice quiet but carrying in the cold air. "It's so late."

Aware that she was changing many things about herself with each step, she walked up to him, dropping her pepper spray and keys into her pocket as she did so. "I couldn't call you through Anna," she said. He was in a sweatshirt this time, and he still smelled delicious to her. "And I couldn't think of any other way to see you."

Even sitting here, alone, in the dark, had broken her self-imposed rules. And she had been afraid. She'd been on high alert for every minute of those two hours a night. But this was more important: standing in front of him, accepting that looking up into his eyes was about the most exciting thing she could do, that the heat coming off him was curling into her chest and making her want to lean into him, to be the one to push that forelock of hair out of his eyes.

She needed to apologize. Everyone made fun of her for how easily she said sorry. But she just stood and looked at him and breathed him in, and inside she trembled with how badly she wanted to kiss him.

Instead, she said, "Can I buy you dinner?"

"Now?" He looked down at himself.

With his head down, his hair was right in front of her. She lifted up one hand to touch it, but he'd already raised his eyes back to her. "Just..." she said, leaving her hand in midair. "Just to a pub, nothing fancy. I... I meant to pay for half the other day. So I owe you." *For more than a meal.*

"All right," he said, still looking at her very hard. Then he took her hand and tucked it through his arm. "All right?"

"Uh-huh," she answered, giddy with the pleasure of letting herself be next to him. They walked a few steps out of the light, toward the street. This was the first time in four years that she'd been completely alone with a man, the first time in forever that a man had made her legs feel like noodles just from the smell of him.

In for a penny, in for a pound. She turned to face him. As Kane gave her a puzzled smile, she reached up and pulled his mouth down to hers.

His hair was damp under her fingers, his skin cool in the November air, but his lips were warm and soft, and Ellen moved hers slowly over them, learning him.

She opened her eyes—she hadn't realized she'd closed them—and he was looking at her, his dark eyes and obnoxiously thick lashes an inch from her. One of his arms went around her waist, but the other rested on her arm, as if he was about to push her away.

Put your arms around me, she begged silently. Every bone and muscle strained to be held. It had been so long... She hadn't realized how much she'd missed the simple pleasure of being enveloped in a strong man's arms.

She was even more dizzy now; he smelled sweaty and foresty, and she could give two shits that he smoked because somehow the scent of him altogether went straight to her gut. She put both hands in his hair and kissed him again, and now Kane got with the program and wrapped his arms around her, which made her legs buckle with relief. The heat of his tongue against hers made her shiver, and she turned her head to deepen the kiss, while Kane groaned and braced her against the full length of him, leaning back against a tree.

This wasn't the kind of kiss she remembered having with Edward, or any of the handful of men she'd gone out with before him. She was hot from her feet to the top of her head; her cheeks were on fire as she pressed herself more closely into him. She forgot that he was not safe, or maybe she remembered, and that was what made him so exciting. She forgot that she was the epitome of poise and calm, that she hated being around men, that she had eliminated passion from her life because it led to a lack of control. She was in control despite the passion, and when she changed the kiss, Kane followed. When she grazed her fingernails against the back of his neck, she made him groan again, and her fire flamed higher.

A few minutes, or a century or two, later, Kane slowly broke off the kiss. "Look at you," he said, running a finger down her cheek, giving her a sweet smile that made her melt even more.

She blushed some more, aware, now that there was a tiny gap between them, how well she'd glued herself to him. When she backed up and put her weight on her own feet, Kane took her arm in his again and they began walking, though they were much closer now than before.

But when they reached the crossing, she thought, *Don't make it so easy for yourself*, and pulled away. "I shouldn't have said all those things I said." There was something in her throat. Shame, probably. "And I shouldn't have chopped you in the neck like that."

Kane laughed loud enough to echo down the street and tucked his arm around her more closely. "Ellen, honey, it is not even funny how thoroughly you are forgiven. Come buy me a burger."

Chapter 11

Kane was glad he'd walked to the hotel when he passed the line of cars stretching down the street, despite the army of valets taking keys. The Rosette was sparkling, with all lights blazing and a red carpet out front. He could swear even the buttons on the valets' jackets shone more brightly tonight.

The lobby was packed with tuxedos and evening dresses. He could see over most of the heads of the crowd making their way into the ballroom ahead, past reception, where the girl who'd called Ellen for him that first day, the one who seemed to be channeling Betty Boop, was handing out room cards. He let himself be funneled past her into the ballroom and gave his habitual slow smile to the waitress who handed him a glass of champagne. She blushed, and he thought, *Ah, crap, that's no fun anymore.*

The woman whose blushes he really wanted to see was running this show, and Kane didn't expect to get to talk to her for a while. He would have to content himself with the memory of their evening together, two nights ago. Of Ellen, demolishing her burger and taking tugs on her beer bottle that made him squirm. Of their conversation, which had no agenda and went off into rambling stories of their siblings and hometowns. And of Ellen finally, finally, giving him a smile that didn't hide anything, that told him she was glad to be in his company. He wouldn't be able to talk to her much tonight, but she'd put him at her table. So he could look at her and plan their next date and not think too hard about that warm, languid feeling he got around her that he usually associated with really good sex.

The ballroom was huge, at least half the size of a football field. The musicians at one end were playing big band tunes. The colors in the room were all creams and blues—the windows were draped in great swathes of blue fabric, and the tables had crisp cream tablecloths over more blue. Silverware and candelabra and crystal chandeliers were everywhere, directing the flattering light onto the guests.

He found his name card and walked toward the table, taking his time as he met friends and colleagues on the way. He tried not to look as though the only person he really wanted to see was the hostess.

Ten days since the Grand Rapids fire with no new incidents, and Kane could finally begin to relax. It was frustrating as hell to be forced to let someone else deal with the problem, but the FBI had made it clear that if they needed anything from him, they'd call. They hadn't called. Kane wasn't used to letting someone else do the work. The fact that he had almost no idea how to find an arsonist in a country of three hundred million people was beside the point. Well, now he had something else–someone else–to focus on. Who knew? Maybe he did have time for a social life after all.

The main sponsor of the ball was already at Kane's table. He liked Barton Laing, who had a Boston elite attitude of service and modesty. The Laing family's wealth had founded one of the biggest children's charities in the country, but his name was tucked away in an unobtrusive list of directors, and his table was just one of the many on the ballroom floor. Although Kane's family had never scaled the lofty heights of the Laings, Barton's and Kane's parents had been friends.

Barton was a big man with sandy hair that still wasn't going gray, even in his sixties. He was also rather deaf. He stood up, with a little difficulty, when Kane approached him, shook his hand heartily, and gripped his arm.

"Might have known they'd put your ugly mug at my table." Barton smiled.

"Wouldn't miss it," Kane answered.

"You remember my son Darren?" said Barton.

"Yes," Kane said, surprised but putting out his hand. He hadn't seen Barton's son at this kind of event before. "How are ya, Darren?"

"Oh, hi, Kane," Darren said, his voice a little nasal. Darren was three years younger than Kane, but still looked about fifteen years old, as if he'd never quite got over his gangly teenage years. He blinked a lot as he shook Kane's hand, and Kane noticed that his rather large nose was red at the tip. Sure enough, as soon as he let go of Kane's hand, he fished a handkerchief out of his pocket and blew his nose loudly. He looked as if his tux had been made for someone fatter and shorter, which, knowing Barton's ability to pay for custom, couldn't be true. Poor Darren, Kane thought, which was the same thing he'd thought twenty years ago when they'd been at high school together. Kane, king of the world as he'd been then, had tried to be nice to the awkward kid he'd been seeing at barbecues for years, but really, Darren just couldn't get out of his own way. Kane wondered what Ellen would think of his so-called altruism.

Jon Mayhew was also there, with his wife, Deborah. It was Jon's friendship with Barton that had inspired the idea for the fundraiser five years ago. Bill Cohen, whom Kane knew slightly, shook hands. Jon introduced him to the chairman of the hotel chain and his wife. Kane practiced not trying to elicit blushes from the women. Failed, but still, he'd tried.

There was no sign of Ellen.

The waiter took his order. The other tables were filling up until only a few people still stood talking. The band was playing "Don't Get Around Much Anymore;" the waitstaff were beginning to gather at the doors to the kitchen, and she still hadn't appeared.

Jon caught his eye and grinned at him. Kane realized he'd been looking anywhere but at the people at his table. Deborah was on his other side, so he started talking to her and the chairman's wife next to her.

The band finished the song. In the hush Ellen walked onto the stage. It nearly killed him, but he made himself respond to Deborah's last comment before turning to follow everyone else's gaze.

Even in this room full of bright ballgowns and twinkling jewelry, Ellen stood out. Where the skirt of her gown was a simple gold that fell to the floor in soft folds, the formfitting bodice was encrusted with jewels of every color. Every time she shifted even a little, they reflected the light. The dress was guaranteed to draw everyone's eyes to her, though her hair, piled on top of her head with just a few pieces coming down around her face, and her face itself, were enough to do that.

And she'd told him she didn't like being looked at? She was in the wrong business.

She stood at the 1940s-style microphone and welcomed everyone, thanked them for coming, and introduced the chairman, who Kane hadn't noticed had left the table along with Barton. That was all she did. But Kane was so blown away by her, the chairman and Barton could have been sending designer handbags to the starving for all he heard of their speech.

Finally, the three of them made their way back to the table, while everyone politely applauded and the band picked up again. Even then it took them a little while to reach him; people were stopping Ellen to talk to her. He recognized the all-business, set smile on her face and her rigid manner, composed but with an icy edge. It was such a contrast to the last time he'd seen her, the goodnight kiss they'd shared when he'd walked her home, the flush in her cheeks, the softness in her lips and her body...

Somehow, she'd gotten to their table. Barton introduced Darren, who gave the table a mighty jolt with his knees as he stood up. Now he was too close to Ellen for politeness. "Hi," he panted with embarrassment. "God. Hi." Ellen shook his hand with a tight smile Kane was beginning to know well and looked very happy to turn from the kid.

And finally, she was in front of him.

"Hi," she said, the hard smile she'd had for Darren relaxing. Even in that one word he could hear the relief in her voice, and though Darren was obviously not a threat to anyone, Kane could have sung. Ellen sat down next to him, her flowery perfume delicately scenting the air.

Unfortunately, Darren seemed to feel that the only way to cover his faux pas was to start talking, so he leaned around his father—not an easy task—and asked Ellen where she was from, so she had to turn her back on Kane.

As the appetizers came around, Darren monopolized her, saying asinine things like, "Went to England once. It rained the whole time. How do you stand it?" Ellen just ate her salad and kept on smiling politely. Kane took it out on a slice of pear, then remembered his manners. Joining in the conversation on his side of the table, he tried not to eavesdrop on what was happening on his other side.

The main course came; the filets had been cooked to order, no mean feat with this many people to feed. That's what you got for your thousand bucks, he guessed, and he noticed that when Ellen got hers, she stopped being nice to Darren and concentrated on her plate.

Now that she was finally facing front again, he said, "Good?"

She smiled at him, remembering, and blushed a little. "Really good."

"Not too much gravy?"

"All right, that's enough." She laughed quietly. "I'm working."

Her head was always lifting to look over at her bosses, both Jon and the chairman. Sometimes they would call over to her to ask for statistics, money raised, attendees, which companies hadn't come. But even when they were talking to each other, she never kept them out of her sight for long. No wonder she was so tense next to him.

She only ate one of her filets before she was on her feet; he caught her flowery scent as she made to walk behind his chair. "Where are you going?" asked Darren.

"I have to check on my guests," she said with an apologetic smile that Kane knew she didn't mean. As she turned away, he could have sworn he felt her hand press briefly onto his back. He tried not to watch her walk between the tables, lean over slightly to talk to people, murmur requests to the waitstaff. She was so poised and classy and beautiful, he hoped he wasn't sitting there with his mouth open. The chairman started to circulate as well. Darren was draining one of the bottles of wine into his glass.

The band began to play more noisily, and Jon stood with Deborah to start the dancing. When the other men didn't come back to the table, Kane automatically asked the chairman's wife to join him. She was very short and plump, held him very close, and from her grins and flirty looks, had a whale of a time. Halfway through they were interrupted by her husband. Kane said all the appropriate things and handed her over.

When Kane got back to the table, Darren was still there, looking morose and halfway through another bottle, and Ellen had not returned. Given Darren's body-mass index, Kane spent most of his time trying not to look as though he was keeping the alcohol out of the man's reach. Ellen didn't need a drunk and sick guest at her table.

Darren blew his nose again. "Damn allergies." He was allergic to one tasteful flower arrangement three feet away from him? Poor kid. "So," he said, his hangdog expression looking more hopeful, "you think Ellen would dance with me? Think I should pull the sponsor card?"

"God, no," Kane said at once. Jeez, how uncouth was this kid going to be before the night was out? "I'm sure she'll dance with you. If she's not too busy." Dammit. There was feeling sorry for Darren and there was being an idiot. He didn't want Ellen to dance with anyone but him. "I guess you won't know until you ask." Kane, you're an idiot.

"Okay," Darren said, apparently feeling like Kane's suggestion was a command and rising to his not-real-steady feet.

"Wait, not right this–" But when he followed Darren's gaze, he saw that Ellen was coming back to their table. "Ms. Hunter," Darren said–though Ellen was the same age as him–"will you dance with me?"

Ellen looked at him, her face completely frozen. Then her eyes flickered, just once, to Kane, before she said, "Certainly. Thank you, Mr. Laing."

"Oh, let the woman eat, boy!" boomed the chairman from across the table. Sure enough, the desserts were being served, small mounds of chocolate lava cake so rich they were almost black, next to equally perfect mounds of vanilla ice cream.

"Thanks, Mr. Stephanopoulos," said Ellen. "It really would be a sin not to eat this hot," and she sat down. Kane liked to think she was sitting a little closer to him than to Darren, but her discomfort was rolling off her in icy waves. Although she was overreacting to Darren's awkward offer, Kane wanted to help her.

"Tony," he said abruptly when they were mostly finished with the dessert, "isn't one of the perks of being the chairman that you get the first dance with the hostess?"

"Sounds good to me," said Tony Stephanopoulos, raising his thick black eyebrows at Ellen. "If Ms. Hunter would do me the honor?"

Ellen's smile was more genuine now, and she allowed the chairman to lead her away. Kane followed them with his eyes until he was satisfied that Tony was keeping a professional distance from her on the dance floor, then he went outside for a cigarette.

But he didn't get there. He couldn't even get out of the ballroom for ten minutes because he was waylaid by friends and colleagues, all keen to ask how the investigation was going. He was thankful that no one mentioned the photograph of him and Ellen that had appeared in the paper, though he was sure some of them gave him a harder stare or a brighter smile than usual or had an extra emphasis to their voice when they asked him how he was. That could have been because of the fires, but it was also likely that by pushing himself into Ellen's life and onto her table tonight, he'd all but confirmed the insinuations in the newspaper.

He cringed. Was that photograph on Ellen's mind? Or had the million other things she'd probably had to deal with today pushed it to the side? He only had a precarious hold on her attention as it was; he hoped that nothing like that happened again, or she might just run for good.

Once he was finally able to leave the room, he was halfway across the lobby when someone else called his name. He looked over at reception; it was that Betty Boop girl, coming out from behind the desk to meet him. His teeth clenched instantly. Was there another fire?

"Hello, Mr. Fielding," she said, giving him a big smile that did not indicate bad news. "I'm Penny Mahoney. I'm a friend of Ellen's."

She was wearing a shiny black blouse that fit her exactly, with a large white flower with lots of petals above one ample breast. Not that he was looking, but the flower did make it hard not to. "Nice to meet you, Penny."

"How's it going in there?"

"Great. She did a great job." He didn't really know how to describe these things. "Everyone's enjoying themselves."

"Cool," she said. "Nice tux, by the way." She backed off to give him an appraising, impersonal sweep of her eyes. "Is that the one you wore to the Skies are Blue premiere with Sarah St. Clair?"

You've got no one to blame but yourself, buddy. "Probably," he said, trying to shake off the piece-of-meat feeling.

"Well." She held out one tiny hand to shake. When he did, she pulled him closer and gave him a full-beam smile. "I just wanted to meet you, and to tell you that I have quite a few jars at home, glass ones, all different sizes, and that if you do anything to hurt her, or even upset her just a little bit, I will remove your testicles myself with some kind of blunt instrument, I haven't decided which yet, maybe a butter knife, and then I will put them in the appropriately sized jar, and hand them back to you. 'Kay?"

For the second time that night he was left speechless. This was what getting Ellen in his life had done to him. Threats and promises and gold hair and skin and a simple touch on his back that he could still feel an hour later, all in one night.

Penny let go of his hand and went back to the reception desk as if nothing had happened. Kane decided he'd been away from Ellen long enough and returned to the ballroom.

Darren had gotten Ellen onto the dance floor. He had one hand in the middle of her back and the other was in hers, but he kept moving his hands, as if he couldn't figure out where to put them. Kane could see that her arm muscles were flexed, holding him off her as much as possible.

Jon Mayhew appeared at his side. They watched Ellen and Darren for a few seconds. Kane could only focus on the flexing of Ellen's arm, the set look of her face.

When he made a sound in his throat as Darren once again moved his hand around Ellen's back, Jon laughed.

Kane rounded on him. "I'm glad you think this is funny."

Jon stopped laughing, but he still looked at him as if he knew a joke that Kane wasn't part of. "You can see she's uncomfortable," Kane continued, getting mad. "Why don't you go and rescue her?"

Jon did laugh again at that. "You think she needs rescuing?" He nodded at the couple. "Yep, there she goes."

Ellen and Darren had sprung apart, Darren looking mortified, Ellen overly apologetic.

"Oh, I'm so sorry!" Kane heard her say as he and Jon moved toward her. "I'm just not used to wearing heels this high." Darren was favoring one foot. "I think I'd be safer sitting down," she said and stalked away from him in the direction of their table.

Jon raised an eyebrow at Kane. Kane glared back. Okay, okay, he'd made assumptions that were total bullshit. Jon had known Ellen a hell of a lot longer than he had. But what would anyone else have thought, considering how she reacted around men?

"I'm just telling you for your own safety," Jon went on. "She takes self-defense and boxing classes." He put out a hand to guide Kane back to their table. "You might want to wear a cup for a few weeks."

A few weeks? Would she let Kane stick around that long? How was he, who'd been careful to show that his commitment to the company and his family did not extend to his social life, going to convince Ellen that she should trust him? And why was it important that she did?

Ellen was sitting at the table, holding her wineglass as if it was the only thing keeping her upright. When Kane sat down, she looked up warily but saw it was him and smiled. Well, it was a start. Kane cast a look at Jon across the table. Take that, sucka. "How are you doing?" he asked.

"Oh... a bit tired now. I was up till three."

He made sure he didn't touch her. He figured she was about done with the vulnerability of all that skin she was showing. But she turned to talk to him better, and her knee touched his leg and stayed there. And while she kept her voice light, her eyes were big and scared, and he cursed himself for letting her out of his sight.

Gradually, with Jon making jokes on one side, what Kane hoped was his reassuring presence on the other, and Darren relegated to the opposite side of the table, her shoulders eased and she settled back into her chair. Kane had turned sideways, and with his arm on the back of his own chair, his hand brushed her shoulder. Ellen leaned in a little.

"I Get a Kick Out of You" had started playing. "Will you dance with me?" he said.

She said, "Yes, please," and he allowed himself the pleasure of taking her hand.

He'd waited so long to get to here, with her hand in his, the scent of her surrounding him, and her body swaying closer to him with every step. Putting his hand on her waist was like coming home; he could feel the jewels in her dress cut into his palm, and the play of muscles as she danced. Her own hand was on his hip under his jacket, and when she splayed out her fingers and moved them farther around his back, Kane had to close his eyes for a second.

She's at work, he kept reminding himself, but he looked at her face, and her eyes were half-closed. If he moved in, they would literally be cheek to cheek.

Screw it. He moved in. She smelled so good. Now her other hand was on his chest, with his own covering it. She gave a kind of shuddering sigh and dropped her head, so her breath skittered across his neck.

Were they still dancing? He pulled his head back. One of the tendrils of hair framing her face was threatening to go into her mouth; he reached up to move it.

"Why didn't you ask me to dance sooner, you idiot?" she said, her lips curving up.

"I wasn't about to fight your boss for the privilege."

"You could have fought that bloody Darren Laing."

Kane snorted. "He didn't need fighting. He's just a kid."

"He's my age," she said, her voice hardening.

"You know what I mean. Why did you have to step on his feet?"

She pulled away, scowling. "He was getting grabby, and whose side are you on?"

He didn't like the way her face was closing up against him, but he'd known Darren his whole life. "He just didn't know where to put his hands."

"Look," she hissed, her cheeks going pink as she dropped her hands from his waist. "I don't need you to tell me when I should feel that someone is being inappropriate!"

Was that what he had been doing? "I'm not. I just wanted to tell you that Darren isn't a threat. He's just clumsy."

She flushed redder and made a move sideways, as if she would like to stride firmly away from him. But she seemed to remember that she was the object of scrutiny and stayed where she was.

He sighed. He'd been trying to help and all he'd managed to do was set himself back several steps in her estimation. "I'm sorry," he said. "I don't want to argue with you." He reached for her hand and held it loosely. "I've been dying to dance with you all night, and now I'm ballsing it up."

Ellen quickly looked at the crowd around them and apparently decided discretion was the better part of valor. Kane happily took her back into the circle of his arms, and when the band started playing "It Had To Be You," she didn't take the opportunity to stop dancing. In fact, with each slight sway of her feet, she moved closer to him, until he could turn his head and breathe in the sweet flowery scent of her hair, just as he'd wanted to a week ago. He could feel her breath against his neck again, and her hand had reached around just far enough to tuck into the waistband of his pants, which he could feel all the way around his torso.

The song ended. Ellen turned drugged eyes on him. "I was fine before I met you," she said.

"I know you were," he said, which was true and not true. Whatever it was that made her react to men the way she did was not fine at all. He put his arm around her and brought her to the edge of the dance floor, where she left him to do another round of the tables.

Coffee had been served. People were starting to leave. Barton had taken Darren to meet other colleagues; Jon and Deborah had gone home to the babysitter. Bill Cohen sat with Kane and talked mutual acquaintances. The band played their last song; the waiters began to pick up napkins and glasses, and soon Kane and Bill were the only guests left.

"So," said Bill, getting to his feet, "does this mean I have to stop teasing Ellen for her monastic life?"

Kane could just imagine how much Ellen loved it when he did that. "I sure hope so," he said firmly. They shook hands, and Bill left. Kane scowled after him.

Ellen came out of the kitchen and looked around. Her shoulders fell with relief when she locked eyes with him. He got up to meet her in the middle of the room. "You were incredible," he said. "You made it all look so easy."

"Thanks," she said, reaching down to take off her heels. "Oh, thank God," she moaned, rubbing her toes. She instinctively reached out to fix one of the centerpieces but pulled her hand back. She'd finished her last ball; she no longer had to fix anything. "Well," she said, pulling her hand back, "I'm glad I went out with a bang." For a second she looked sad, almost... bereft.

They collected her coat from behind reception. He didn't see Penny. "How did you get here tonight?" he asked. "Can I call you a cab?"

"I drove."

"You keep a car in the city?"

Ellen shrugged and took her keys out of her teeny tiny purse.

Not wanting to say anything stupid again, he meekly followed her to the hotel's parking garage.

Her car was a highly sensible Toyota with a GB sticker on the back. When they reached it, she moved from under his arm and ducked down to look underneath it. Then she looked in the windows. "What are you doing?" he said.

Ellen stood up, seemed to come to herself, and blushed. "Nothing, just habit."

He knew he shouldn't ask, but she was scaring him. "Did something happen to you? In a parking garage?"

"No. Nothing like that. Nothing happened." She unlocked the car. "I'll drive you home if you like."

"Ellen," he said. She was suddenly finding the concrete pillar next to her fascinating. "Can you tell me? Who it was?"

She turned on him. "Just because I don't want to be pawed at doesn't mean I have some problem for you to fix!"

"Of course it doesn't," he said, feeling worse because that was exactly what he'd been thinking. Damn, he was no good at this. Carl was the touchy-feely one. He would have known what to say. "It's just... I've known Darren since we were kids. He wasn't trying anything, I swear. He was terrified of you, couldn't you tell? He was trying not to paw at you."

She stayed rigid for a second, then she looked down and wiped some imaginary dirt from the hood of the car. "Okay, you've made your point. Do you want a ride home or not?"

With an offer like that, it was easy to drop the subject. Before he'd gotten around to the passenger side, she was already leaning over the seat, moving it back to accommodate his legs.

The car was small. Their shoulders kept touching. After she had gotten them out to the street and had the car aimed at the harbor, her shoulders lowered a few inches from the battle mode she'd been in most of the night.

The car was a stick shift. Kane took hold of her right hand in his left and sighed dramatically each time she had to slap him off to change gears. But it made her laugh, so he kept doing it.

"Why a stick?" he said.

"That's what you learn on at home. And it was cheaper." Four years here and she still called England home.

What took twenty minutes to walk took only seven by car. On his instructions, she drove to the underground parking lot. At the gate, Kane leaned over her and said to the guard, "This is Ms. Hunter. I'm going to give her my second keycard, okay?" And the guard said,

"Sure, Mr. Fielding," smiled at Ellen, and wrote down her license plate.

She found the spot he pointed out to her. She put the emergency brake on, then stared at the steering wheel.

"Thank you," he said.

She looked at him. "You really piss me off sometimes."

He grinned. "I'll take that over indifference any day of the week."

Ellen sighed. "I suppose I'd better get used to this," she said, reaching out to muss his hair. In the tight space it brought her closer to him. "And how bloody good you smell," she added, her voice getting lower.

Kane again waited until he was sure she was sure before he moved closer and kissed her. Her lips were so damn soft, and she moved them over his so confidently that he wondered how he'd waited until now.

She put both hands in his hair and pulled him to her, turned her head, and deepened the kiss. When their tongues touched, he backed up just long enough to breathe her name into her mouth. Her hair was tickling his face, her back warm and sleek under his hand, which was now free to roam. She moaned a little and touched the back of his neck, which sent a jolt of heat right down into his gut.

Ellen broke off the kiss. "Bloody handbrake," she said in her normal voice and rearranged herself. Kane needed some rearranging too, but it wasn't going to happen in this little car.

"I'd better get out of here," he said.

"Okay." Her slightly swollen lips and half-fallen hair made him need to rearrange himself even more.

He opened the door. "I'll call you." He started to get out but got back in again. "When I say, I'll call you, you know that I'll probably be bothering you in about..." He ostentatiously looked at his watch. "Eight hours. So sleep well. Hope you're hungry for brunch."

Chapter 12

"I'll take you on a picnic," Kane said.

"It's the middle of November."

"I'll bring handwarmers—"

"I bet you will."

"No! Real handwarmers. And thick blankets and soup. I'll take you up Blue Hill and ply you with hot rum."

So here she was, dressed in her long, thick coat and hood—with long johns and a couple other layers underneath—snuggled up close to Kane, a wool blanket straight out of the Highlands of Scotland wrapped around them both, looking out at the skyline of Boston from a comfortable fifteen miles away, while hikers passed them and, blissfully, completely ignored them.

One brunch, three dinners, a trip to the movies, and this picnic—that was the sum total of their dating life so far. And their photo had been in the papers each time. At first it was a cell phone photo taken at the diner, but by the end of that week Ellen knew that whenever they left a building, someone would be there to take their picture. She tried not to worry about it, but the taglines were always suggestive in a way that made her blush at the idea of her mother seeing them.

Today the rest of the world seemed far away. Kane was breathing easily as no more fires had been reported; the security cameras were going in as fast as they could hire the contractors, and she was getting used to him giving her looks that tried to melt her clothes right off her. Apart from the epic kisses, though, he hadn't tried anything else, which she appreciated. Yes. Appreciated. She did *not* want to get him alone and arch her back so that he could get one of her breasts in his mouth.

"What?" he said.

"Umm." Her cheeks were flaming again. "Nothing. So, to coin a phrase, do you come here often?"

"Used to. It's the kind of hike you can take five whiny kids on, with a real view at the end to look forward to." He got that look, again, that she'd sometimes seen flicker across his face—the boy who'd lost something important, and only occasionally remembered how much it hurt.

"Do you get to see your sisters much?"

"All the time." He grinned. "More than they want, probably. Cat especially."

"I'm sure that's not true."

"Ah, she's always been pissed at me for something or other. Now she invites me to Thanksgiving like it's the biggest hardship to even acknowledge we're related. But, you know, siblings, right?"

She didn't really know. She and Adam had always got on well; in a family that sent the children to boarding school as a matter of course, their time together was precious. Still, everyone was different. And it wouldn't matter, except that Kane looked so bewildered by Cat's antagonism.

"There must be some reason why she's mad at you."

"Hell if I know what it is," he said, looking out at the view with his hands wrapped around his thermos. "Even when we were kids... Dad and I would be talking about the business and she'd always interrupt." He took a drink of the spiked apple cider. "But she's got a lot to deal with too. She nursed Mom through her cancer. Basically raised Sam, Thea, and Megan after Mom died and I was so busy. She and Antonio had just gotten married; it can't have been easy for her."

She loved hearing him talk about his family. It brought out all the warmth in him that his playboy image worked so hard to erase. She pulled back her hood, leaned in, and kissed him. "Can't have been easy for you either," she said.

He held her eyes. "Well, you know me. Arrogant bastard that I am. I figured it out."

Ellen let it go, but she hoped he knew that she knew he was barely covering up the pain.

♦

In the end, it was Carl who called Kane. "The hell, man? Where have you been?" was the first thing he said.

Kane adjusted his carry-on and held the phone closer to his ear. "Right. Sorry." He had called Carl the first weekend after the fires, as he'd planned, and Carl had left several messages for him after that, but he'd been too busy or too distracted or too involved with Ellen to call him back.

"That's okay," said Carl. "You were starting to scare me."

They often went over a month without catching up, so three weeks shouldn't have bothered Carl. But there'd been another fire. Kane's own fear was flaring up like the pictures on the local TV stations. And Carl, being Carl, would know this and would want to help.

"I scare myself," Kane replied. "You should see the faces on the building supervisors when I show up."

An announcement over the loudspeaker cut through the air. "Where are you?" said Carl.

"San Diego airport."

"I figured. You're in the *Journal* today," Carl said. Kane had this sudden, irrational image of one of the photos of him and Ellen appearing in the staid, boring pages of the *Wall Street Journal*. But no. Of course it was the fires. This latest had happened the day after their idyllic picnic in the hills, in one of Fielding's recycling facilities in California.

Another random, destructive, pointless act. All it did was put people out of work and give the insurance companies—and Kane—heart attacks.

Carl said, "You should have called me."

Kane put down his bag and pushed his hand through his hair. "It sucks too much to talk about."

"I know. That's why you should talk about it, you idiot."

Kane snorted. "I knew you'd say something like that."

"Yeah, well. I know this is eating you up."

Kane didn't say anything. Carl had been his best friend since before Robert had died. Without him, Kane didn't think he could have finished college. But there were times when he didn't want Carl's sympathy. He needed to take control of the mess the fires were making of his business. He needed to show everyone that they were going to be fine. If he shared his fears with anyone, even his best friend, it made them more real. Like that first press conference after his father's death, when each question from the press had beaten into him the reality that Robert had really gone, that Kane was on his own.

"So anyway," Carl said, apparently deciding not to push it. "My turn to get up there for a weekend, isn't it?"

Kane shrugged his shoulders to try and remove the weight on them. "Yeah. That'd be great. Can you come for Thanksgiving?"

"Not this time. Sal's rented a house on the Island; she's somehow found about a dozen people with no family over the holiday and invited them all."

Sal was Carl's mother, a judge who liked Kane just fine but was always just a little intimidating. She and Carl had been alone his whole life. He reckoned one of the reasons Carl liked him was because of his big, noisy family and the house in Newton that had held three generations of them. Kane didn't know anything about Carl's father, and since Carl had never volunteered the information, Kane had known not to ask.

"So maybe after that?" Carl went on.

"Sure. Maybe things won't be so crazy by then." He hoped to God.

"So." Carl paused. "Okay, obviously you're gonna make me drag it out of you. Who is she?"

Kane groaned. "Dammit. Don't tell me the pictures have made it to New York."

"No. But I'm not above Googling someone when they go AWOL on me. What? Why don't you want me to know?"

"It's not that." The truth was that if he spelled out their

relationship to Carl, he would have to acknowledge how much he was coming to rely on her.

"Holy cow," said Carl when Kane's silence went on too long. "She's really important to you."

Kane winced. "Maybe." It was hard to admit even that much. "Anyway," he said, hoping he sounded less intense. "She's leaving in a few months. So it's just for—" Damn, he couldn't even say that. How could it be fun, when all he wanted when he woke each day was to talk to her?

He'd told himself not to think about her visa. He was seeing her tonight, if this damn airplane would just come to the gate already. She'd finally trusted him enough to invite him to dinner at her apartment, and that was as far into the future as he let himself imagine. "Oh, they've called the gate," he lied to Carl.

"No, they haven't," said Carl on a laugh. "Okay, I'm definitely coming over after Thanksgiving. Try not to mess it up with her before then, 'kay?"

"Okay, jackass. Later."

Chapter 13

When she first opened the door, all Ellen could see were sunflowers. There must have been five dozen of them tucked into the crook of Kane's arm. "Oh, *wonderful*," she said, took them from him, and backed up to let him in.

She only got two steps before he had a hold of her. He threw the flowers on the table just behind her, then got both arms around her waist and crushed her against him as if she was the only thing holding him upright.

Ellen happily melted into him. She hadn't seen him for five days, and she was just as desperate to get close as he was. She brought her hands up to his hair, pulled him to her, and kissed him hard and deeply, making him groan. He tightened his arms around her back. Even though he tasted like too many cigarettes, he still smelled amazing to her, and when he said against her lips, "Oh God, Ellen, I'd forgotten how delicious you are," she could absolutely agree.

"I'd forgotten..." she got out between kisses, "how badly you... need a haircut." Which made him laugh, but not let go. He ducked his head and shook his hair in her face, then brought up his own hand to run it over *her* hair before he buried his face in it.

"You smell *so* good. I've smelled nothing but smoke and sweat and men for five days."

She hid her face in his neck. In their few hours together she'd gotten used to how easy it was to fit herself to him, how she hardly had to drop her head to tuck into his shoulder, to kiss his collarbone if it was available.

Eventually he said, "I have to sit down before I fall down." And he did literally pivot and fall backward into her couch. He made the couch, and her whole flat, look laughably small; with his feet stretched out, he almost reached the TV. Ellen gathered up the flowers and went over to the kitchen. She had maybe two vases to her name; the rest of the sunflowers were going to have to sit in the sink for now.

"How was the flight?" she asked from there.

"Fine." He sounded completely spent. "No cabs though. Had to take the shuttle. This keeps up, I'm going to have to get a driver. I left my bag outside, by the way. Didn't want you thinking I was making any presumptions." He opened one eye to squint at her over the back of the couch.

"No, we wouldn't want that," she tried to joke. *Mouth... breast...*

The water overflowed the vase.

Penny might have made fun of Ellen for obsessing over Kane *before* she met him, but it was nothing compared to her thoughts these days. She supposed it had started when she saw him in that tux at the Queen's Ball. The simple shawl collar jacket had fit him so precisely it emphasized that the breadth of his shoulders was all-natural, and he always looked especially edible in black. When he'd given her that special smile just for her, that crinkling of his eyes showing he was remembering their last kiss good night, Ellen had trouble recalling that she was at work.

And yes, okay, maybe he'd had a point about Darren Laing. But since he himself had unsettled her so much, she held him partly to blame if she'd overreacted. Kane was not safe, and yet she found herself wanting to be nowhere but in his arms.

While he'd driven her to the picnic a week ago, she'd found herself staring at his hands whenever he changed gear. She hadn't realized until then how sexy it was to watch a man drive a manual transmission. Maybe it was something to do with the flexing of his thigh muscles. Anyway, she'd been light-headed the entire trip.

The next day, Kane had gotten the call about the fire in California just as he was about to go over to her place for dinner. Asking him into her sanctuary was a huge step for her, but in the end, she hadn't been tested and had almost welcomed the delay, even though she hated the reason for it. She still didn't have her head on right about him.

He'd called her from the West Coast every night as he checked on his buildings, got craven assurances from managers, and read reports in the newspapers about the panic setting in. He told her that the company's West Coast deliveries had finally been affected by the fires. The insurance adjusters weren't being helpful anymore. The FBI agents were frustrated with hearing the same story from every mill: the security systems had been working, but had been bypassed, or the electricity shut down. There hadn't been time to get cameras on every site, and the arsonists seemed to know this. Kane took it personally.

Ellen wanted to tell him to let someone else hear all the details. He didn't have to talk about insurance or sprinkler systems; he didn't have to tire himself out by personally inspecting every warehouse in the state. But if she delicately tried to suggest it, he would send a black silence down the phone line, so she had to let it go.

Tonight, she promised herself, was just about helping him relax. She didn't have to decide on anything else, didn't have to worry. Didn't have to be stupidly nervous, changing clothes three times and straightening pictures, trying to make the spider plant and its offspring look less untidy. Didn't have to have this constant running commentary in her head that said not to give in to all the signals her nerve endings were sending her. She could trust him. She was sure she could.

She put the two vases of flowers on the dining and coffee tables, changed the music from classical to Van Morrison, and got Kane a drink.

He had his head back on the couch, and his eyes were closed. When the tumbler of scotch touched his hand, he jumped. "Damn. I dozed off. Thanks." Ellen tucked her legs under her and sat close enough to him that her knees touched his thigh.

He didn't look well. His eyes were black from the shadows around them, and new lines had appeared on either side of his mouth. He was looking at her as if she'd disappear if he closed his eyes again. "Chin-chin," she said, clinking glasses, trying to lighten the mood.

He smiled. "So many weird phrases, so little time."

Eventually Leo Palmer, Kane's PR man, had had to put out a brief statement saying that she and Kane were dating, after the calls to both their offices began to number in the dozens. Ellen understood why; better to be providing the information than have it ferreted out. But she hated the way the newscasters said, "Seen here with his current girlfriend," as if it would be mere seconds before he moved on to a new one. They also usually began a sentence with, "Fielding, who was last seen with Holly Oladele at the premier of *Wanting More...*" as if that was his rightful place and being back in Boston dating a nobody was just an aberration.

If she'd sent out that press release, she would have begged the media for a little privacy, for a little room to grow into her new bravery, to learn how to trust her feelings for him and believe in his feelings for her. But it apparently hadn't occurred to Leo or Kane, so she'd kept silent and prayed that her parents didn't have any other contacts in America.

She said, "Dinner's whenever you want it."

"What I want," he said with his head back and eyes closed again, "is just this. Right here." She leaned sideways so her head was near his. "Then I'll probably spend the rest of the night trying to get under your shirt."

She gasped, and he opened one eye and gave her that sideways grin. "Just kidding," he said. "Mostly." And Ellen got so caught up imagining his hands on her breasts that she missed his next sentence.

"Sorry, what?" she said.

"Why are you blushing? I said, before I forget, when are you leaving for Thanksgiving?"

"Oh..." She pulled her mind away from the vision of his big hand on her white skin. The truth was, she hadn't booked the plane tickets. First, it was because of the ball. Then she'd told herself she kept forgetting. It would be awkward that her parents would expect her to know her next job posting when she saw them, and she kept putting off the meeting with HR. But the real reason she hadn't ordered them yet was sitting with his legs taking up most of the floor space in her studio. "Well, I didn't get around to booking my flight just yet."

"Just yet?" he exclaimed. "Thanksgiving's next week!"

She took a drink of her whisky. "Mm."

"Is this because of your mom? Did you have a fight or something?"

"Lord, no," she said at once. "One doesn't 'fight' in my family. And one doesn't stop talking to people just because one has a disagreement." One does, however, hedge every time one's mother asks what time the plane's coming in, and chicken out every time one is about to tell her that one doesn't plan on coming home.

She pointed to the pictures of her family on the bookshelves, and Kane got up to look at them. "That's Adam and Jen." Her brother looked exactly like her: thin and blond with blue eyes. Jen was his exact opposite, with dark-brown skin and eyes, her hair cut close to her head, showing off incredible bone structure. The photo next to them showed that Ellen's nephews had inherited it.

Next in line was the posed photograph her parents had had taken on their thirty-fifth anniversary. Her mother was sitting, her father behind her with his hand on her shoulder in the standard pose. Her smile would have made the Queen proud—small, polite, hardly moving her cheeks. Ellen's father, on the other hand, had a big goofy grin on his face. He wasn't even looking at the camera; he was looking down at his wife. Ellen had chosen that one out of the rejects; it was exactly their two personalities. "You have your dad's smile," Kane said.

"No, I don't." She stood up to look at it as well. "I have my mother's."

"No. *This* is how you smile when you've got that stick up your butt"—she punched his arm, which he seemed not to notice—"but *this* is really you." He looked at her face. "You act like your mom, but you're really like your dad."

"I'm glad you think so. Dad seems to have a lot more fun in life than Mum; she spends her whole time worrying that her face'll crack if she lets out an emotion." Ellen took in a hard breath; she rarely acknowledged even to herself how cut off from her mother she felt.

"Maybe," Kane said. "Maybe you could ask her about it."

"You're very funny. Have you met me?" She pointed to herself. "You know, English? Stiff upper lip? Children seen and not heard, old fruit? No emotions that can't be pushed down with a bracing round of cricket and a cup of tea?"

"Okay, okay." He held his hands up in surrender. "Anyway, I'm not sorry you haven't decided if you're going back yet. I wanted to ask if you'd come to my sister's house for Thanksgiving."

She was almost speechless. She knew the significance of inviting girlfriends to Thanksgiving. "Are you sure?" she blurted out.

"Yes. Please, will you come to my snotty sister's house for Thanksgiving and help me deal with her? It's a great offer, I know." He said it flippantly, but he was looking very hard at the books.

"I'd love to come."

"You sure?" he said, now turning back to her. "They'll all be there, except Sam, of course."

She didn't know why that was of course, but still, even three sisters and a husband sounded pretty intimidating, especially with the way he talked about Cat. She guessed that having asked her to come, he was giving her a chance to back out.

"I'm sure. Thank you for asking me."

He grinned and kissed her. "Thank you for letting yourself in for my family."

"Maybe I'll take *you* to *my* family for Christmas." Why had she said that? That was a terrible idea! She was leaving the country two months after that!

His grin was instant. "Does your mom make mince pies?"

Okay, she shouldn't have said it, but now the pride of the Hunters was at stake. "Better than anything you'll get here. With custard."

"What the hell *is* custard?"

"It's like gravy for mince pies... uh... sweet gravy, oh, never mind. I'll make it for you."

"You're obsessed with gravy," he said, snaking an arm around her.

"I'm not!" she said against his lips.

"Nothing but food, food, food," he murmured. "One of the things I find most attractive about you." He bit her lip gently.

Ellen couldn't help but moan a little. Kane turned with her so her back was against the bookshelves and her front was pressed all the way along his. She breathed in jerky gasps at the feel of his hand at the base of her spine and pressed herself even harder into him. They kissed each other like they'd only just learned how to do it, which for Ellen was almost true. Kane made her want to crawl out of her skin and get into his, and it was scaring her and exciting her in just about equal proportions. *You can trust him*, she thought, and, *oh help.*

When her hand went to the back of his collar, he grabbed her wrist and lifted her arm above their heads, holding it against the shelf. "Not again. You know how bad that turns me on?" Ellen shuddered again, and her chest was curved into his now. Kane began to drop kisses down her neck and into the V of her oversized sweater, and she put her other hand in his hair, either to pull him off or keep him there, she wasn't sure which, but she didn't move it, and half of her prayed that the V would pull down a little farther, and half of her began to panic.

She could feel how much he wanted her, could feel the strength of his hand holding hers above her head; she could feel the speed of her heart rate and the flush on her skin and the scratch of his stubble against her chest, and she could smell the whisky on his breath and hers, and that and her own drugged excitement sent her spiraling into full-blown terror.

Now she'd done it; she hadn't said no soon enough, and he wasn't going to want to stop. This was how things had started with Edward too; he'd been drinking and wanted more, and when she didn't because he was drunk, he turned into someone else and hadn't listened and had held her still and she had to get away and the only way to do it was to—

Bringing her knee up into Kane's groin was easy, but it made his knees buckle, and he fell against her even more heavily, so she had to hit him several times in the side of the head before he finally moved to the side, away from her. In a blind haze of fear, she ran to the door and opened it.

Chapter 14

Kane was on his knees, cupping the part of himself which until a few seconds ago had been so happy. She was shouting something from the door, but his ears were roaring from her very professional punches to his head. He put out the hand that was holding the bookshelves to keep him from collapsing to the floor and tried to say her name.

"*Get out, get out, get out!*" she was yelling. Farcically, as his hearing came back, he noticed that Van Morrison was singing "Sweet Thing."

Ellen was at the door, holding it open. His overnight bag was still outside. Was he ever going to be able to lift that thing again? Was he ever going to be able to *walk* again? He put his hands on his knees.

"Wait a second—"

"I might have *known!*" she raged.

"Known *what?*" he gasped. "Argh, shit, I think you—"

"This is hopeless. Just get out. You only ever did want—"

"No, listen, wait—"

"No, just get out, get the fuck out!"

"Ellen, would you just—"

"No! This is what you wanted all along. You never would have taken me out if it wasn't for—"

Finally, he was mad. "All right, that's *enough!*" Even though it hurt to do it, he could shout a whole lot louder than she could, and his voice echoed out of the doorway and down the hall. He made a Herculean effort to stand, even though he wanted to curl into a little ball and weep for a few hours, and hobbled toward her. She flinched, which would have broken his heart if he hadn't been in so much pain. He slammed the door, at that moment not caring if someone stole the entire contents of his overnight bag.

"It's time you gave me a little fucking credit, Ellen," he snapped. He towered over her, leaning heavily against the door. Her face was as red as it had been in his office, her hair crackling around it. "You know damn well I've let you in where no other woman has gone. I've told you things about my family the press would pay you thousands to find out. I haven't taken *one step* toward you without being sure that was what you wanted. You know, or you should by now, that I would *never* hurt you or do something you didn't want, no matter how carried away I got. Don't cringe, dammit. You only had to tell me to stop. Now, go sit down."

"Don't order me around—"

"*Don't* freak out on me and then try and shut me out!" She looked a little more sorry and went to sit on the couch. "And quit looking like a wounded bird just because you're getting yelled at. I'm the one mortally injured here." He limped over to join her, the blood beginning to re-enter his legs. "Now," he said. "You are going to tell me who he was."

She looked up at him, and he could see the terror in her eyes before they slid away from his. "Who who was?"

"Look, I'm tired. I'm in more pain than you can imagine, and I don't want to take this bullshit from you anymore. I let you in, Ellen. Now you are going to tell me who did this to you and what he did. I've been avoiding it to save you the memory, but I refuse to fight a man I don't know anything about and get beat up for something he did."

Ellen looked at him, at his face, his hair, which was falling over his eyes, before dropping her gaze to her hands in her lap. She didn't say anything for a long minute. Then she said, very quietly, "He's nothing like you."

She took a very deep breath. "He's blond, slick, the perfect son-in-law material."

Somewhere in the back of his mind, a voice said, *and I'm not?*

"The right parents," she went on. "The right circles, you know. We were together for two years. He's a real estate agent, flat in Holland Park, the whole package." She gestured at the pictures, at the life she'd had. "I was going to marry him. At least, I thought I was. My parents loved him—still do. His mother and mine are very good friends. They lunch a lot."

Kane nodded. That could explain part of her problem with her mother.

"He was really very nice to me, most of the time. I thought he was... everything I wanted—clean-cut, well-bred, the right schools, the upper-class thing my mother adored. Dad liked him too; they played golf." She closed her eyes. "He found my brother and sister-in-law their first house, got them a really good deal, especially for London. I loved him for that. It was like he did it to impress me, you know? And I thought that was what we'd do... get married, announcement in the *Times*, have a few blond babies and fight to get them in the right preschool, you know the kind of thing. Adam didn't like him, though. I thought he was being overprotective, but... I guess he saw it before I did." She rubbed her forehead. "Or perhaps he saw... that I..."

She was making lines in her jeans with her fingernail now. "What did I know? I thought the whole thing was kind of messy and a bit pointless. I hardly knew anything about it before Edward; I just figured that was what it was like... for me."

"Are you talking about sex?" Messy and pointless? Holy God.

The flush was coming back to her cheeks. She didn't meet his eye. "Mm-hmm. We'd been dating a required number of weeks or whatever it was; it was time. But I didn't... I mean, we'd read our Jilly Coopers and Jackie Collinses in school, but I didn't think any of that could be real life. Besides, my mother made the whole thing sound so... icky..." She turned her face completely away from him. "I didn't know until meeting you."

Kane held his breath. The admission wasn't the victory he'd expected it to be. It was just sad that she'd had all this passion and nothing to do with it, for so many years.

"So what changed?" he prompted when she was quiet for a while.

"He'd gone to a stag night... a bachelor party. I wasn't expecting him to come over afterward; it must have been three in the morning. I only let him in because he couldn't keep his voice down. He said... he'd seen some serious action that night, and he was going to show me how it was done." The lines from her nails must have been going into her skin by now. "He said... that I was just a... dead fish..."

"God, Ellen."

"...and it was time I had some lessons... to make some decent use of that body." She said it as if her body no longer belonged to her. "He said I was a big disappointment, and I tried to tell him I wasn't interested that night, but he said that I was just a tease, and he... got me pinned on the sofa and he... was so different. He talked about... others, that he'd had to go to because I... wasn't any good... and he *ripped* my pajamas!" she finished with mild surprise, as if she'd learned he didn't like strawberries.

Ellen's voice was getting quieter. "I mean, I don't think I'd ever seen him angry. He was always so poised before. And I tried to stop him, I really did, but I suppose I didn't try hard enough because I never really believed he would—

"But I was trapped, and he was so heavy and strong and before I could stop him, he... pushed in—inside me—" Kane abruptly stood up. "But just once!" she hurried on, as if that made it better. "I got so mad, then, you've never... Well, maybe you have a bit... but I've never been so angry in my life. I suppose the pain... I punched him a lot harder than I did you. Got my nails in there too. When I got him off me, I used a pair of heels I had on the floor to get him in the crotch. He said he couldn't sleep for a week for all the pain I caused him."

"*You* caused *him*?" Kane half turned to her, then turned back. A fire burned in his chest; if he looked at her face now, he'd throw something. "He had the—he dared to talk to you again after that?"

"Oh, yes," she said, as if it was normal. "I told you, his mother and mine were best friends. I think it was his way of paying me back. He didn't want me anymore either, but he wasn't going to make it easy for me to leave."

"But what about the police?"

"What would I tell them? He was the one with all the injuries—"

"Not all of them, Ellen, for fuck's *sake.*" He folded back down onto the couch and took her into his arms.

She held herself stiffly at first but didn't pull away, and after a few moments, she let out a long breath. He felt her tears on his neck. He held her as close as he could, moving her legs so they crossed his, and rocked her a little. When she started crying harder, he kept on rocking.

He'd figured it had to be something like this that had held her frozen for so long, but having it confirmed like this—in such a matter-of-fact voice—brought tears to his own eyes.

All the years that this had been in her, like a cancer, spreading into every aspect of her life and infecting every interaction she had. Every friendly compliment, every eye contact that went on too long, every genuine attempt to get to know her better, every chance for her to let out some of that passion, strangled at its base.

When she'd calmed a little, and with his face hidden in her hair, he said, "So no one knew? What happened when you said you were leaving?"

"I just told everyone we'd broken up, that I was going to be transferred." She gave a shaky laugh of derision. "My mother and Edward's were extremely vociferous in their disappointment." The grim memory of that time was clearly fresh. "But I didn't care what Edward told his mother. I just knew I had to get away from him. I knew they'd never stop inviting him to our house unless I told them... and there was no way I could talk to my parents about it. Or Adam, he has a vile temper when he's pushed too far. I really think he might have killed Edward if he knew."

Kane agreed completely. The thought of any one of his sisters going through this...

"I asked for the transfer, and here I am."

"But you brought him with you."

"Guess so." She gave another shuddering breath, this time of release.

They sat silently, arms wrapped around each other, for a long while. Then he said, "I don't really have the words for this. Carl's the one with the background in helping trauma victims. And I know you're downplaying it because that's what you would do, to try not to make a fuss. But..." He pulled away to make sure she was looking at him. "Don't ever excuse him, Ellen. Ever again. He deserved prison. And an ass-kicking. If I name what he did to you, I'm going to punch a hole in your wall, but don't ever downplay it to yourself. If I ever get in the same room as him, he'll be going out a window, and I don't care whose mother is watching."

She was crying and laughing at the same time.

They sat quietly until she was calm again. Finally, she lifted her head, her hands at her mouth. "I kneed you in the groin," she said through them, in an awed whisper.

"Yep." He smiled. *Yeah, sure you can smile about it now.* "Right in the plums."

"And you're still here." Her eyes were wide above her fingers.

He shrugged, trying to make light of it. He was very afraid he knew exactly why he was still here. "Someone promised me a meal."

"Oh!" She jumped off his lap and walked over to the kitchen.

"I was joking," he said feebly, but now that he thought about it, he was starving. He hadn't eaten since lunch, and it had to be around ten o'clock.

She gave him a bowl of beef and beer stew she'd had ready in a crockpot. Kane took the bowl but held her hand so she was stuck leaning awkwardly over him. "You know what I need more than this?" he asked.

Ellen looked wary again. "What?"

"An ice pack."

"Oh! Oh, jeez, Kane, I *am* sorry."

She hurried over to the freezer, and Kane thought, *She said jeez.*

The ice pack was a huge improvement to his evening. After the stew, they ate ice cream and watched the news. As the fires were now a five-day-old story, Kane was thankfully not on it. Then they watched *The Daily Show*, which made them laugh so hard they had to rewind it a couple of times to hear everything.

Before Ellen could switch to Colbert, Kane muted the TV. "Ellen," he said to the top of her head, which was leaning against his chest.

"What? We're missing it."

"They yell 'Stephen' for five minutes anyway. Listen." He pushed her away from him so he could watch her. "Let me stay the night."

She went very still, her eyes sliding away from his.

"Not like that, obviously. Look, I'm harmless. I'm out of action here. And you need to remember what it's like to fall asleep—I mean it, don't look at me like that—fall asleep in a man's arms." He moved his head so he was in her line of sight. "You need to trust me."

She sighed, looking unconvinced. "Fall asleep."

"Scout's honor."

"With you."

"For lack of another eligible male in the room."

She looked over to the screen that separated her bed from the living room. "There's not much room."

"I don't take up much space. Just give me six square feet, and I'll be fine."

"You'll be sleeping standing up, then."

She got up, went to the door, and brought his bag inside.

"I'm not saying I trust you," she said. "But I don't... not."

Kane beamed at her, but suddenly the travel and the jet lag, and the physical and emotional trauma of the past few hours caught up with him, and he fell back against the cushions with a groan of relief.

She was adorable. He watched her fidget, cleaning the bedroom area that didn't need cleaning, straightening her bedside table as if he gave a damn what angle everything was at, apologizing for not having something similar on his side of the bed, asking him if he needed a lamp or towels or water or anything else. She ran into the bathroom with her pajamas when she could have just told him to stay on the other side of the screen.

Kane stripped down to his boxers and got into bed, loving the scent of her on the cream-colored sheets, and the pure masculine pleasure of immersing himself in a woman's world.

Ellen came out of the bathroom and froze at the sight of him. "Oh, crap," she said, her eyes dark. "Could you *please* not be all... chesty and bicepy and... hairy without warning me first?"

He laughed and flipped her sheets down. She lay down next to him on her back, just her head turned toward him. Kane kissed her gently and took a hold of the hand that was closest to him. Right away his eyes drooped for real, which was a shame because he wanted to enjoy the feel of her for longer.

They stayed like that for a few seconds, or Kane may have slept a little, but then she moved forward and kissed him. "I missed you so much when you were away," she whispered, and Kane fell in love with her so hard he couldn't breathe for the ache.

Chapter 15

Gabriel, Thea's husband, had so little imagination that when Kane found the bar he was in, he didn't even run. He was dressed like Kane, as was most everyone else in the bar, in jeans, boots, an old Sox Henley, and padded vest. Kane wore his baseball cap low, but he didn't think anyone would recognize him in this crowd. These weren't the kind of guys that bought the newest cell phone so they could snap pictures of unexpected visitors to their local bar. The music was Irish folk, but it was quiet. This was a place to drink and commiserate and drink more, not dance.

Although Kane was itching to seize the kid by the front of his shirt and yank him off his barstool and into the nearest wall, he managed to control himself enough to walk up and just tower over him. Gabe had gone pale, his eyes wide, his normal get-away-with-anything smile replaced with horror. "Did she—has she..." he stammered.

"Yes," Kane ground out. He still had his car keys in his hand. He didn't plan on staying.

"D'you hear that, fellas?" Gabe tried to say to the other men at the bar—this was not a bar for women. "I'm a da again!"

Kane was pleased to see that no one congratulated him. Every one of them looked away, embarrassed. They obviously had Gabe's number.

He couldn't resist any longer; he took a hold of the back of Gabe's neck and pulled him off the stool. "You piss on the idea of a father," he said. Gabe reached for his glass, but Kane pushed it out of his hands, far down the bar where it threatened to slide off the end. Kane kind of wished it had. "Thea's still soft enough to want you to come see him. And that's the only reason I'm not punching some teeth out of your useless head."

Gabe didn't put up any more resistance, and no one came to his rescue, but before Kane could get out the door, the bartender, in a hopeful tone, said, "He's got a tab, chief."

Kane let go of the younger man long enough to pull a bill out of his wallet, crush it into a ball and throw it at the bar. "Stop serving him then, moron," he said, and made sure that Gabe hit the doorframe on the way out.

He kept hold of Gabe all the way to his car, and if the kid's head hit the frame, too, as he roughly pushed him in, well, the guy had been screwing with Thea's life for ten years. He deserved every bruise.

In the car Gabe was quiet for a long time. At one point when Kane was looking at the traffic to his right, he could see that Gabe had tears running down his cheeks. "Oh, for God's sake," Kane said.

"You gotta know," Gabe said in a choked voice. "I love 'em both, so I do."

"Yeah, that's one way to put the way you treat them. And there are three of them now." They pulled up to a light. When Kane turned to look at him, Gabe flinched. "The stupid thing is that I believe you. So this is the way it's going to go. Thea's finally done with you. After you go to the hospital, where you will *not* try and convince her to take you back, because you know how much better they'll be without waiting for you to take off again, we're going back to the apartment and packing up your shit." Gabe had his face turned away from Kane's now, wiping tears away as he looked out the window. "Then you're going to sign papers agreeing to provide child support, and *then* maybe she'll let you be a part of those boys' lives. The moment—the *millisecond*—I hear you missed a payment, you lose all visitation rights."

"Ah, Chrissake, Kane," Gabe said, still not looking at him. "It was just—I lost that last job. I couldn't face her."

"And yet, when you're a grown-up, you face the tough times. It's called being a man. When I think about what you've done to Jacob, the role model you've been for him..." The light changed, and as Kane went to change gear, his hand "accidentally" swept up and backslapped Gabe right on the nose. "Oops."

"Jaysus!" Gabe shouted, holding his nose, checking for blood.

Jaysus was right. Gabe did deserve a fair amount of abuse, but he wasn't going to learn how to be a good father from Kane slapping him about. And it wasn't just Gabe's behavior that Kane was taking out on him.

Kane had been furious for two days, ever since Ellen had told him about her... He still couldn't say the word. He thumped the steering wheel, and Gabe yelped, "What now?" but it was Edward he wanted to have under his fists now. It was Edward, and the damage he'd done, both physical and psychological, to Ellen, that put Gabe in such immediate danger. And it was three fires and no pattern to how they were done, except cut security feeds and total destruction. Now every building had two security guards patrolling at night. Every building. And Kane still wanted—needed—to go look at them all himself.

And yes, he admitted it, he was horny as hell. Waking up next to the warm, soft, pliant body of the woman he was now permanently and irrevocably in love with had been painful. Very painful. He'd had to get out of there before he gave himself a blood clot or something. It didn't matter how many times he reminded himself that he had no intention of even bringing up the subject and that he was a good man for being so understanding. He'd spent all last night dreaming about her, and his body was telling him in no uncertain terms that his hands-off policy was fucking stupid.

Kane dropped Gabe off at the front entrance, and while he parked the car, he tried to calm down. He had to deal with his older sister now as well, which wasn't going to help his temper any, but he was going to ask her if he could bring Ellen to Thanksgiving, so he needed her in a good mood. Not that he'd seen Cat in a good mood for about ten years, but still, hope sprang eternal. And handling his sisters was the one thing guaranteed to shut his libido down. He slammed the car door hard, making the window rattle. *Yeah, right. You're a freaking oasis of calm.* Letting the keys bite into his fist, he walked into the hospital.

♦

Three days later, Ellen was the one fighting to improve her mood. Penny called and said, "Bryson got a head for someone else's figure."

"Well then, he's out of his tiny number-crunching mind." *Oh good,* she tried not to think. *We can talk about Penny's problems tonight, and I can stop obsessing over mine.* "I'll tell you what. Come with me to the gym tonight. I've been dying to get you in there. You can make big eyes at the new boxing instructor."

"Ugh. Really? That's your answer to my trauma? Boxing?"

"Come on," Ellen said bracingly. "I'll pick you up at seven thirty."

Penny, in tight black capri pants and a shocking pink T-shirt that made her look straight out of *Grease,* was morose and weepy when Ellen picked her up, not at all her usual bubbly self. She wiped away tears on the drive to the gym as she talked.

"The worst of it is"—she sniffed—"that it was the languages he couldn't get past. He didn't understand why we bother learning them, when 'everyone speaks English now.' If it wasn't about numbers, he didn't want to know."

Ellen considered it part of the fabric of their friendship that every few months, she would have to take Penny out and listen to the tale of her latest breakup. Bryson hadn't lasted long, and Ellen reminded her that this was good; Penny hadn't yet invested too much in him.

Penny looked like a beautiful, kicked puppy. "You never say 'I told you so,'" she said.

"I never did. Not this time, anyway. He seemed just fine." Truthfully, Ellen hadn't spared a thought for Penny or her boyfriends since meeting Kane. The guilty twinge she felt made her decide to spare Penny the boxing lesson tonight. "Okay, honey, now what did I tell you to call this kind of man?"

Penny gave a reluctant half smile. "A wanker."

"That's right. He's a total effing wanker." Ellen pulled another tissue from the center console and gave it to Penny. "Don't give him another thought. That floozy he chose over you probably says *irregardless.*"

Penny laughed, hiccupped, and blew her nose. By the time they got into the gym she had repaired the damage to her makeup and was ready to beam at the male receptionist.

"Okay," she said after they'd signed in, "what are you going to teach me today? The thumb-in-the-eyes trick? The old faithful knee to the groin?"

Ellen winced. "No, why don't we just get on the ellipticals today, since I was here yesterday for my sparring class, and you're feeling delicate?"

"Oh, thank God for that." Penny put her machine at a pace that looked like slow, graceful swimming.

They talked about work for a few minutes, but now that Penny had had her pep talk, Ellen was beginning to settle back into a melancholy of her own.

Finally, Penny said, "Okay, who left the sugar out of your coffee?"

"What?"

"You've been frowning for the last five minutes. And I've been very funny, despite my heartache. So, come on, what's going on?"

Ellen tried to marshal her thoughts, to tell Penny just one of the army of worries she had. She went for the safest one first. "Well, it's the fires, of course."

"Did he call you today?" This morning's papers had the fire in New Hampshire on the front page.

Ellen shook her head. "I wouldn't expect to hear from him until late. He beats himself up so much, he has to go over every inch of every Fielding building within reach. He only came back from New Jersey on Saturday because his sister had gone into labor."

"Did you get to see the baby? I'll bet it's gorgeous. Probably already has chiseled cheekbones."

Ellen smiled briefly but said, "I told you, I haven't seen him or anyone else since Friday. He's either been at work or with his family."

"Okay, well, that's understandable. So you miss him."

Ellen snorted. "How could I miss him?" she said tartly. "All I have to do is turn to the pages of the *Herald*. Or go on Boston.com. Oh, and who's that next to him? Yes, there she is, 'current flame, Ellen

Hunter,' aka deer-in-headlights girl." She grabbed at her water bottle and fumbled it, sending it flying down between the other machines.

"You do not look like a deer in headlights," Penny said, happy to stop her lazy pulls on the handles and get it. She gave the bottle back to Ellen and leaned on her machine. "You look rocking, thanks to me."

Penny had let out a squee of joy when Ellen had asked her to take her to buy "a couple of new suits." One Saturday afternoon, two thousand dollars that made Ellen's credit card groan, and a very happy Nordstrom assistant later, Ellen had a waist and legs again.

"That's not the point. Well, all right, it is, but how would you like being looked at every minute you're out in public?"

Stupid question. Penny dressed to be noticed. Her fearlessness was one of the things that had drawn Ellen to her.

She took a slightly more controlled sip of her water. "I don't know how much longer I can do this."

"What, date the hottest man in the state? Uh, I think you could hold on a little."

"It's not funny, Pen. The media are obsessed with him, and I told him before that I couldn't handle it." She sped up her pace. "And I can't *not* handle it because the fires are *tearing him up*."

"They're obsessing *because* of the fires. When they catch whoever it is, they'll stop."

"Will they? They've got my cell phone number, did you know? And are you gonna get back on that thing or not?"

With an exaggerated grimace, Penny climbed back on and half-heartedly pulled on the handles. "Sweetie, I think all this is a moot point. You and Kane *are* together; you *do* care about him; you're *not* about to leave him, no matter how many pictures there are of the two of you—and, I'd like to point out, there have only been three—"

"Because I've hardly bloody seen him!"

"Yes, okay, and not for lack of trying on the photographers' part, I'm sure. So look," Penny went on, slowing down again so she could lean a little closer, "the media aren't the threat to your relationship, and you know it. Your visa status is."

"Oh *God*." Ellen stopped moving. "Do we have to talk about this?"

"We'd better. When does yours expire?"

"March."

"So. Tell them you want to stay."

Ellen scrubbed at her face with her hand. "I *don't* want to—"

"Ellen."

"It's career suicide."

"Do you really want to leave? Tell me true, now," Penny insisted, her face uncharacteristically serious.

Ellen looked at Penny, who was so important to her. She'd made a few other friends at work, also ex-pats, but Penny was the only one who was Boston born and bred. Even Francesca was due to be transferred around the same time as Ellen. Penny was part of the reason that Boston had begun to feel like home.

She felt tears starting at the back of her eyes. "It's not that simple. I want to make good money. I want to be management. I want to follow Jon up the ladder if I can, but I have to go away for at least four more years before I can do it." Her throat tightened. "So, you see," she continued when she could speak, "there's not much point in helping Kane through the fires when I have to leave soon anyway."

"Well," said Penny, patting herself with her towel even though there wasn't a drop of perspiration on her, "I think you'll find your priorities have changed. I'm pooped. Let's get a smoothie, and I'll tell you what I see."

Ellen didn't have the mental energy to protest. At the smoothie bar, Penny continued. "I see the 'career' Ellen. She lived in her own little cocooned world, where she went from work to home to work to home, never did anything fun, never so much as looked at a man, let alone let him flirt with her or even say something nice, and where the most exciting thing that happened was getting a new instructor at the gym."

Ellen's mouth fell open. "Shit, Penny."

"And then, there's the Ellen I see before me, the one I knew was hiding under there all along. Who smiles more at silly old farts like Bill Cohen, who's doing a better job at work because she doesn't bark orders so often—yeah, you did—and who's stopped dressing as though the Puritans are still in charge."

It was impossible not to be insulted. "Bloody hell, Pen. I didn't know I was so hard to be around."

"You're not, you idiot. That's what I'm saying. He's brought out the best in you. Don't even think of going back."

Ellen didn't know what to say. She sucked on her smoothie, a delicious concoction of mango and passion fruit that hid the taste of the protein powder.

"Besides," said Penny, with the air of pulling a rabbit out of a hat, "you can't go back. Your accent's changed."

"Okay, now I shall have to summon a policeman."

"Nice try, Ms. Poppins. You called me 'honey' before. When has that word every been part of your vocabulary? You just said, 'How ahh ya?' to our server here. Don't try and kid a linguist. Those R's aren't going away 'cause you're English; it's because you're falling for a chowdahead."

"I'll tell him you said that." But she could feel her cheeks heating up and knew that Penny was right. She was digging herself further and further into this life, this city, and Kane, even as she should be breaking away.

"So now," said Penny, taking the lid off her smoothie and drinking it as if it were a frozen margarita, "the only thing left to complete your transformation is some mind-blowing sex."

Some of Ellen's smoothie went up her nose. "Shh!" she gasped, looking around her. The gym was full, and the smoothie bar was right next to reception.

Penny wasn't concerned. "How the hell you let him walk out of your apartment on Friday morning without jumping his bones is beyond me."

"I told you," Ellen hissed. "He was tired."

"You really don't know anything about men, do you? No man has ever been that tired."

"Well, he was." All Penny knew was that Kane had fallen asleep at Ellen's apartment after his long flight. Ellen had never told her about

Edward, just that she'd had bad luck with men back in England, and that was why she had steered clear until now.

Before telling Kane, Ellen had almost convinced herself that Edward and that last horrific hour of their relationship hadn't happened, so it had been easy to keep the story from Penny. But in the quiet hours she'd had while Kane helped his family, she'd gone back over what she'd told Kane and his reaction. What it meant, and what she'd been hiding from herself. By allowing herself to pretend that Edward hadn't "really" raped her, she'd absolved him of much of his culpability for the assault and put that blame on herself.

"Call it what it was," she'd said to herself in the mirror the night after Kane left. "It was... rape." She squinted at her reflection, finding the word as hard to say as it had been to think. "Edward raped you. It wasn't your fault you couldn't fight him off at first."

And she'd cried some more and made herself a cup of tea and more beans on toast, and felt a little better. Relieving herself of all of the guilt would take more time, but she was closer.

She was also closer to telling Penny what had happened because it explained so much that had puzzled Penny.

"And he didn't make *any* moves in the morning?" Penny insisted.

"No." Actually, when she'd woken up, he'd already been in the kitchen, making oatmeal. And he'd gotten out of there within fifteen minutes. Ellen had had to admit to a little disappointment.

"Is he sick?"

"No!" She lowered her voice even more. "Look, the truth is..."

Okay, she couldn't go *there* in this crowded gym, but this part was true too.

"I told you that I had a... bad experience in England." Penny nodded. "Well, my..." She didn't even want to dignify Edward with the word *boyfriend*. "The man I was seeing told me... that I... wasn't any good at it," she finished in a whisper. Now her cheeks were flaming.

"You've got to be kidding me."

"So... with all the experience Kane has... I don't want to—"

"Oh my God. Don't even go there. Who was this jerkoff?" Penny's voice had risen; she brought it back down to a whisper. "I'm sure you couldn't disappoint a guy if you tried."

Ellen put her hands to her hot cheeks. "Well, I didn't know... much. He was only the second man I..."

"How long were you together?"

"Two years. According to him"—she began folding her straw paper into a tiny square—"two very boring years."

Penny made a sound of disgust in her throat. "Well, I have to say that that was his fault because I know you, Ellen, and under all that stiff-upper-lip crap, you are the most passionate woman I know."

"Ach." Ellen waved her hand in front of her heated face. "You're full of it."

"Don't even try and deny it. I've seen you sing along to Adam Lambert. And I snuck in and watched you and Kane dance at the Queen's Ball, and if that wasn't foreplay, you can call me Susan."

"Keep your voice down!" But as outraged as Ellen tried to be, she couldn't stop a slow smile from taking over.

"Uh-huh." Penny folded her arms. Just then, someone passed so close behind her that he bumped her into the counter. "Ow!" She turned to glare at the man.

He wasn't dressed for the gym, but he seemed at home there. "Oh, hey, I'm sorry," he said with an insolent grin. "Mind if I join you?"

"Yes," both women said at once.

"Okay, okay." He put his hands up. "I'll just set myself down over here." He indicated the seat two down from Penny. "That work for you?"

"If you must," said Penny, in such an icy tone Ellen rather thought she'd learned it from her. Penny purposely turned her back on him. "So," she went on as if the interruption hadn't happened, "how do you expect to spend Thanksgiving weekend, if it isn't..." she lowered her voice, "horizontal?"

"If I survive his family, you mean? I don't know. I think he might have to work. He said he might not even be allowed to rebuild one of the factories right away. Even if he does, of course it's going to be months before anyone can work in it. And he's got a whole lot of security guards at every other site now."

"That's a lot of security guards."

"Hundreds of thousands of dollars' worth. And the unions are on his back to tell them when they'll be working again. He's trying to help out by running extra shifts at the plants that are still open, but that means he has to cut hours, and he's still paying the men the same amount. It *has* to be crippling him." She used her straw to stir the remains of the smoothie, but she'd lost her appetite for it. "He sees all the people relying on his factories—hundreds, now, without a place to work—and it's killing him, Pen. He told me last night about meeting everyone at the Bristol place yesterday. That plant was the biggest employer in town. They were all looking at him to give them something to do, and he's standing in front of them with the words of the insurance companies ringing in his ears."

"Oh, sweetie." Penny patted her hand. "You only have to—" A cell phone rang, loudly. The man behind Penny again. She spun on her seat to glare at him.

"So sorry!" he said, equally loudly, and put the phone to his ear.

Penny's pretty face screwed up in annoyance. "You done? Let's go."

The air outside was full of sharp needles of sleet; they paused at the door to put their hoods up. Someone stepped in front of them and said, "Ellen?"

She instinctively looked up. A camera flashed barely five feet from her. The car it was in disappeared around the corner, tires squealing a little on the slick road. The man who'd been at the counter came out behind them and grinned at her, before setting off up the street at an easy jog.

"You fricking creep!" Penny yelled after him, but Ellen held her back when she took a step toward him.

"Forget it," she said heavily. "That's what they want. Interaction."

Penny was shaking. "Okay, okay. God, I get it now. That sucked."

Ellen put her arm through her friend's, and they walked to her car. Sassy, bubbly, busty Penny, bright and shiny like her name. She'd been defending and praising Ellen since their first meeting.

"Have I ever told you...?" Ellen began. But the words got stuck in her throat. She stopped walking and looked at Penny. "I mean," she tried again. *Just tell her she's important to you! Can't you do even that? Haven't you lived here long enough?*

"Aw, hon," Penny smiled, patting her arm. "I love you too."

♦

Ellen purposely avoided the papers the next day. She hated, loathed having her photograph in the paper. Every time another newspaper or unfamiliar cell phone number appeared on her caller ID, it was like undoing the three locks on her front door and inviting the world in. Her pepper spray couldn't save her from the lewd stares of men as she walked down the street. She didn't get much work done, even counting the early closing they got for the holiday. When Jon told her to get the hell out of the office, she went down and helped the front desk with the clog of guests coming in for the weekend, rather than go home and think.

She'd texted Kane when she'd gotten home from the gym, and he'd texted a quick good night back, but she hadn't tried to contact him today; she knew he'd be in meetings or, hopefully, coming home. She hadn't told him about the camera; it would just be one more thing for him to worry about.

She was in her pajamas, switching off her music and closing up her book to go to bed, when the door buzzed. Her first instinct was fear; it was eleven thirty. She didn't know anyone who'd be up this late on a Wednesday. Then she reasoned that it had to be Kane, and besides, that was what the intercom was for, so she pressed the button. "Hello?"

"It's me."

It didn't sound like him, so she kept her door locked until she saw him through the peephole. He looked terrible. As she opened the door, she took in his two-days' growth of beard, unkempt hair, and the smell of cigarettes and wet ashes that filled the air around him. "Oh, Kane," she began, reaching out a hand, but he stepped away from her.

"Who have you been talking to?"

Her sympathy at his croaking voice was quickly overtaken by confusion. He was looking at her as if he didn't know her. His eyes were so narrowed she could hardly see them beneath his eyebrows. The two faint lines on either side of his mouth were now sharp creases. One hand held a lit cigarette. "What?" she said.

He held up a newspaper, folded to the picture of her and Penny.

"Well, of course I didn't talk to that man," she said reasonably, not understanding his anger. "You can see he surprised us outside the gym."

"Look closer, *sweetheart*." He pushed the paper into her chest and stalked into her living room, taking a drag on his cigarette. When she could pull her eyes away from the way he filled her apartment, she looked down at the paper.

"*Has Superman Met His Kryptonite? Ellen Hunter spills: Kane Fielding may finally have met his match in this arsonist. According to her, the great Fielding empire is on the point of crumbling. The company will not be rebuilding the factory in Bristol, NH, for lack of funds.*"

Chapter 16

"God," she said, letting the paper fall. The man behind Penny, of course, listening in. Probably calling a friend outside to wait for them. She sank to the armchair.

"Don't look so sorry for yourself!" he shouted, striding over to her. "Do you know what shit I've had to wade through today, to convince those people I'm not going to close the mill? How much did they give you to buy that prize-winner?"

"Nothing, for heaven's sake, Kane!" she exclaimed, leaning back as he towered over her.

"Oh, great, you blew up my life for free. Great."

He waved the cigarette at her; the ash was threatening to fall.

"I didn't say anything to them!" she tried to say, but he was already interrupting her.

"If this was a public company, you would have just sunk the entire stock! What the hell—"

"I *didn't talk to the press!*" she shouted over him. "Do you hear me? I—didn't—talk—to the press!" She stopped leaning back in the seat, sat up straight so her head was about at the level of his waist, and glared up the long length of him. "Could you move, please? You need an ashtray."

He did back up but snarled, "I'm not staying."

"Well," she said over her shoulder, swallowing the hurt his words evoked, looking in the kitchen for a saucer that she didn't care about too much, "that would be a shame because I was looking forward to you coming back. I didn't realize you left your brains in New Hampshire." She gave him the saucer; he snatched it, and then went over to the window and opened it to smoke, which at least showed some small consideration.

Ellen, trying to ignore all the smoke in the air, picked up the newspaper. "Come on, Kane," she said a bit more calmly. "I'd never do that to you. Come on."

He stubbed the cigarette out on the brick outside the window—she appreciated this saving of her saucer—and came over to the sofa, sitting down so heavily he pushed it back a couple of inches. He scraped both hands through his hair, then covered his face with them and let out a long, low roar that she was sure could be heard on the street outside. Still with his face covered, he said, "Then how did they know?"

"I was at the gym with Penny." She sat next to him. "I was worried about you, and I was telling her some of why I was. This man came and sat behind Penny; we didn't realize he was listening in."

Abruptly he stood again and began pacing the few steps around the sofa. "Don't you see?" he said, not looking at her as he paced. "You can't just go anywhere you like and talk about the company like that! People make decisions based on this shit. We're talking about a hundred jobs, Ellen."

She stayed where she was. With him on his feet, she hardly had any room to stand anyway. "I'm really sorry, Kane. But I wasn't 'talking in public;' I was talking to my best friend. Quietly, at a counter where we were barely a foot apart. I didn't think they'd go to those lengths to hear us."

He'd gotten another cigarette out and caught it between his teeth. She must have made a face, because he growled, "I'm not going to light it," and started pacing again. When he got over to the kitchen table, she thought it might be safe to go to him.

She could see he was fighting to keep his anger. "Then why the hell didn't you call me today?" he said.

"I knew you'd be busy. I didn't look at the papers. I knew the picture would be there, and I didn't want to see it."

He silently paced a few more times. "Did you tell her about Thea?" he ground out, and she knew that this scared him more than any of the rest of it.

"Well, yes—"

"Goddammit!" he shouted, throwing his hands up. "Now that'll be *tomorrow's* headline!"

"Kane, you spent all day at a hospital. I'm surprised no one took your picture then. I told her about Thea over the weekend, not yesterday."

Kane was breathing hard, his throat sounding overused and scratched. The cigarette had disappeared. His legs stretched out in front of him where he leaned against the kitchen table. Ellen put her hand on his arm, dared to get closer to him.

He looked at her, finally seeming to *see* her, and the intensity of his black gaze made her own breath catch.

"I'm warning you now," he said. "I'm going to kiss you. Real hard."

And he did. And Ellen met him with just as much ferocity. Mouths open, tongues tangling, they set a torch to the sparks that had flown around them, and Ellen couldn't get enough. She turned his head so she could kiss him more deeply, but Kane pulled her hair back so he could lift her chin and kiss his way down her neck. She heard herself making sounds that were almost like sobbing because she couldn't do without his mouth on hers for a second, unless it was when he was running his tongue over her collarbone.

For the first time in her life there was no thought process. She was acting on pure instinct, and her instinct was to get Kane as close to her as humanly possible, as quickly as possible.

With his lips on her neck, she had to content herself with pulling his shirt out of his jeans and getting her hands on the burning hot skin of his stomach and back. Still making his way past her collarbone, he shrugged out of the coat he had never taken off, and Ellen let her hands move higher, into the thick pelt of hair on his chest. She found a nipple and flicked at it, and he groaned and spanned her waist with his hands. When his fingers went under the waistband of her pants at the base of her spine, she shivered and pressed closer, unconsciously asking him to move lower. But he moved back around to the front, feeling the curve of her stomach, his fingers reaching under her pajama top to just below her breasts.

Kane broke away long enough to murmur, "Thank God, no bra."

Ellen grabbed his head again and pulled it down to where the buttons began on her top, then she made a noise of complaint and let go of him long enough to direct his hand up her rib cage. Kane obeyed while he took her mouth again in a broiling kiss. Ellen arched into his hand that now cupped her small breast completely while his thumb ran over the nipple. She was making little gasping noises into his mouth, and somehow her leg had found its way up beside his hip on the table, so she was almost sitting on him. The proximity nearly blew the top of her head off.

She wanted his hands on every part of her, and when he moved, she wanted him back where he'd been. He had both nipples now, and she yelped and pulled his shirt all the way up so she could find his. When she lowered her head because she absolutely had to touch that nipple with her tongue, he lost contact, and she had to slip down his leg a little, but she couldn't help it. If she didn't kiss his skin, she was going to weep. She felt the moan in his chest before he let it out and she smiled up at him. His hands couldn't reach her anymore, just her shoulders and her back through her top, and she rejoiced at the frustration on his face.

Suddenly he got his hands under her arms and lifted her up and back onto his lap, moving so he could cup her buttocks and hold her against him. Ellen arched again, amazed at the hot pulsing that was building deep inside her, that made her grind down on him as hard as she could. Kane's neck was slick with sweat now, and she could feel the same heat on her skin. She brought her knees up, so he was holding her completely, and kissed him again, scratching the back of his neck with her nails.

Kane gasped and suddenly broke off the kiss. "No." He kept holding her to him, his head lowering to her shoulder. He was shaking; they both were. The rest of his body wasn't saying no. "No," he said into her neck and very slowly relaxed his hold so she slid off him.

Putting her feet back on the floor was heartbreaking. Her whole body was humming; her face tingled from his stubble. "What do you mean, no?" she whispered. Had she been doing it wrong? The whole thing had been a blur, an animal response she'd never had before. Was that not right? A wave of cold swept over her.

His head was still down. He moved his hands to her shoulders and held her away from him. "I'm sick," he said. "My throat is sore, and my chest hurts, and when I make love to you, I am *not* going to do it when I'm too tired to see straight."

"You didn't feel tired," she said diffidently.

His mouth quirked up in that half smile finally. "I'd have to be dead not to react to you." He smiled wider. "Oh gods, look at you. You're so beautiful, you're passionate beyond anything, and you're standing there like you did something wrong."

The flush came back to her face. Now he laughed properly and leaned forward to kiss her again, this time gently and slowly.

"Okay," she said against his lips, "but you're going to have to stop doing that."

He kissed her for a bit longer anyway, and Ellen helplessly let him. When he stopped, and she looked at him, he said, "God, Ellen, don't look at me like that. I'm going home."

"Do you at least want something to eat?"

"Yes!" he shouted, and laughingly wrapped his arms back around her. "But like I said, not until I'm better." Now her cheeks were so hot she put her hands to them, making him laugh even more.

"I'll pick you up tomorrow about eleven, okay?" he said, grabbing his coat.

Oh, right, Thanksgiving. "I don't know, Kane. Do you still think your sisters will want to meet me?"

He ran his thumb over the redness on her chin from his stubble. "Come on, Ellen. You came to a whole new country full of uncivilized Yanks; surely a few Fielding women won't scare you?"

Yes, they would, actually, but she would follow him anywhere. "What about you getting sick?"

"It's Thanksgiving," he said simply. "You don't miss Thanksgiving. So, eleven o'clock, okay?" He crushed her to him one last time.

She went to bed but tossed and turned before succumbing and

doing something for herself she hadn't done since the last time she'd watched Tom Hardy in *Mad Max*.

Chapter 17

Cat's house was an imposing Victorian right in the old center of town, with a wide wraparound porch, an enormous corner tower, and a wooden front door that looked original. Three bikes that were strewn across the front steps had knocked over a couple of pots of chrysanthemums. The house was painted a faded green, and the white trim could use a touch-up.

It was where Kane and his sisters had grown up, where their father and grandfather had been born. It frowned down upon Ellen from the moment she pulled up in Kane's car. "Park near the street," Kane said beside her. "We'll need the driveway for basketball." He grabbed an armful of flowers and her bag of groceries from the back seat.

Ellen balanced the pie she'd brought with a bottle of wine and followed Kane's long stride. He ignored the front porch, instead following the driveway around to the rear of the house. Here was more evidence of children: a basketball hoop, balls scattered around the yard, a jungle gym.

Kane took the steps up to the deck two at a time, as he had obviously been doing all his life, and flung open the back door. She followed a little more slowly, telling herself just to keep breathing.

"*Mi famiglia!*" he called and was greeted by "*Fratello mio!*" from someone inside the room. Ellen stepped in behind him and was immediately wrapped in the delicious smells of a kitchen in full Thanksgiving-meal-preparation mode and by the sight of five heads turning to her as one. Kane was being hugged by a man almost as tall as him, but more heavyset, with short, curly black hair and a gigantic smile. Over Kane's shoulder the man's blue eyes twinkled at her. At the stove was a tall woman, her dark hair pulled back into a charming loose knot on top of her head. Three boys sat at the counter, potato peelers in their hands and a bag of mini marshmallows spilling in front of them. One had a pair of headphones on that was playing so loudly she could hear it from the door; he was the only one not looking at her.

Another woman, smaller and thinner than the one at the stove, had hands covered in flour, but rushed up to Kane anyway, who held out the bag and flowers in his hands to block her. "Wait, wait!" He laughed, but Megan—it had to be Megan—got a fine handprint right on his sleeve, craning around the flowers to kiss his cheek.

"Which ones are mine?" she demanded and took her bunch and the grocery bag from him so she could hug him properly.

"Where are mine?" the man said, still smiling. His Italian accent was noticeable but softened after fifteen years of marriage.

"In the bag," Kane answered, and Antonio found a six-pack of Peroni, which he clutched in ecstasy. "And a case in the car," Kane added. "Hi, sis." He went over to Cat, who had hardly taken her eyes off Ellen, and she offered her cheek for him to kiss.

"Little late," she muttered. "Still." She took her flowers, but didn't say thank you.

"Dinner's at three, Cat. I think we're fine. House still needs a coat of paint, I see. Come meet Ellen." Then he was back at her side, his arm slipping around her waist, and Ellen was drawn into the group.

Cat nodded at her as if it hurt to do so. Antonio danced over to her and kissed her on both cheeks. "*Piacere.*"

"*Piacere,*" Ellen replied, instinctively reverting to receptionist mode. Antonio beamed; Cat scowled.

"Just plain old English for me, please," said Megan, enveloping Ellen in a hug. "How youse doin'?"

She was easy to smile back at. "I'm wicked ahsome," she said. "How ahh ya?" Megan whooped, and the two boys at the table that could hear them burst out laughing.

"Please," said Antonio, gesturing to them, "come and meet my boys. Paolo, *e* Matteo. And this is Jacob." He put his hand on the shoulder of the boy in headphones and used his other hand to pull one side off Jacob's ears. "Jake, there is a beautiful lady in the room. Say hello."

Jake didn't smile, and his eyes barely flickered toward her before going back to the potatoes he was supposed to be peeling. "H'lo," he managed. Ellen glanced at Cat, but she had her back to the room again, stirring something on the stove as if it were concrete she had to soften.

"You'll meet Thea in a minute," Megan said. "She's nursing. Is that pie?"

Ellen gave it to her; she took it by unceremoniously dumping Kane's flowers on the nearest surface.

"Mom?" said one of the boys; Ellen had forgotten which was which already. "Now that Uncle Kane's here, can we go play football?"

"Did you finish the sweet potatoes?" Cat said without turning her head. The boys groaned and rolled their eyes and gazed imploringly at their father, whose eyes they had inherited. But Antonio just pointed to the counter and drew Ellen away from Kane's arm.

"Come through, Elena, and get a drink. Where did you learn Italian?" Leaving Kane's side brought on a little panic, but she was curious to see the rest of the house and to meet the famous Thea, for whom Kane had gone to so much trouble.

The front hall was wood-paneled, with old-fashioned wallpaper above, and led to a gorgeous curved staircase, though the stair treads and trim around the doorways were scuffed and dented. Antonio brought her into a library which, she was happy to see, had books in it that looked like someone read them, and then through to a family room, also wood-paneled, with a big old fireplace along one wall and a giant TV set above it, already showing a football game.

She accepted one of the Peronis Kane had brought and chatted with Antonio in Italian until Kane came in. It was very pleasant to feel her reaction to Kane, to know that he was there in this big, noisy family, that he was hers to take home whenever she wanted. Well, not quite, but the principle was the thing.

He flopped down onto the couch between them. "You okay, buddy?" Antonio said. "You don't look so good."

"Nah." Kane scrubbed his hand over his face, which just made him look more rumpled. "I caught a cold somewhere in New Hampshire.

Or maybe it was the looks your wife's been giving me. You gonna drink all those Peronis, honey?" he said to Ellen.

"Maybe I should make you a hot toddy instead," she said, but Antonio had already, reluctantly, handed over the beer.

"Hot toddy!" Antonio said. "Sounds like I should leave, huh?"

"That's totty, Antonio," she reassured him. Kane looked bewildered. "Toddy is a drink, whisky and lemon and honey, for when you're ill. Totty is... Well, it's your old girlfriends," she finished with a big smile at Kane. Antonio laughed aloud and then stood up, saying something about Cat probably needing help.

"Cheap shot," Kane said when he'd gone. He moved her legs so they were over his the way he liked best, then leaned back so he could see the TV. He was really a lot sicker than he'd seemed coming into the house. When he'd picked her up, he'd felt so rough he asked her to drive. She'd had to wake him when they turned off the Pike so he could direct her to the house, and he'd had a pretty serious coughing fit just before they arrived. She kind of hoped no one would come in for a while, so he could rest some more.

But of course, that was impossible. Megan was next. "Hey," she bounced in. "Got any more of those?" And she too took a Peroni. Poor Antonio was going to be out of them within the hour. She took in Kane's prone figure. "Whassa matter, poor baby? You sick?" she said in a mock-concerned voice. "Or," she reverted to her normal voice, "was it a late night last night?" And the wicked grin she gave Ellen made her blush scarlet.

"Take it easy," Kane said, his head still back, eyes now closed.

"Sorry!" Megan said, obviously not even a little bit. "It's so nice to meet you, Ellen. Usually he's too ashamed of us to bring anyone home."

"True," Kane interjected.

Megan ignored him. "How did you meet?"

Ellen gave her a heavily edited story, then asked her about college.

The room was warm and cozy, with some antique furniture and this massive, squishy, frankly hideous sofa they were curled up on.

Their beers were slowly drunk, the game went on, and Ellen began to relax.

Pictures of the family covered the wall; Ellen eventually got up to look at them. They were a striking group, all dark hair and eyes and big white American grins. *Five times braces.* Megan was much younger than the rest of them and had the biggest smile of all. Kane had started smoldering at the camera somewhere around fourteen. It was a little disturbing, so she turned away and saw Cat at the door.

The topknot in her hair had slipped an inch or so, and she looked as though she'd caught Ellen and Kane at it on the couch. "Kane," she said, then again, impatiently, though he'd barely had time to open his eyes, "*Kane.* Can you go get some wood and start the fire in the dining room?"

"Sure," Kane said and immediately got up. Moving made him cough, hard.

"You *still* smoking, bruh?" Megan teased, but Cat answered for him. "Like a fricking teenager behind the bleachers, like everything else you do."

Kane rolled his eyes, gave Ellen a small, sad smile, and followed Cat out.

"Come and meet the baby," Megan said.

"Oh, I can wait. I'm sure Thea wants her privacy."

"Nah, she's dying to meet you," insisted Megan, and went upstairs two at a time, as Kane had done outside, to another equally wide and well-proportioned hallway, where she knocked on a door. "Thea? You decent?" They heard a murmur from inside, and Megan went in.

The bedroom was in the tower. Thea was sitting in an old wooden rocking chair in the curved window, with a bundle wrapped in a yellow blanket in her arms, the cool light of the day outside illuminating her.

Thea looked old; Ellen thought it before she could stop herself. She looked exhausted and drained and scared all at the same time, and it made her look older than Cat, though she was eight years younger. She turned big brown eyes, ringed with gray, to the two of them. "This is Ellen, hon," said Megan, not as loud and bouncy now. She knelt down in front of the chair.

"Hello," said Thea in a small voice. "I'm sorry. I'm not much for company today."

So Megan had lied. Ellen felt herself begin to blush at her intrusion. Megan said, "Don't be silly."

Ellen said, "I don't want to disturb you."

"Oh, just let her see Benji, please, T?" begged Megan. Thea obligingly removed some of the blanket so that Ellen could just see a shock of dark hair above closed eyes, a tiny nose and mouth, and a strawberry mark going down past the baby's ear. Ellen crouched next to Megan.

"He's so beautiful," she said. "He's all Fielding."

"Thank you." Thea turned her head to the window. "That's nice of you to say." One hand came up, and she pressed her fingers to her mouth. Fat tears began falling down her cheek.

"We *mean* it, Thea," Megan said, taking hold of her knee and shaking it a little. "With or without the birthmark, he's the most beautiful baby since Jacob. Don't tell Cat I said that."

Thea almost smiled, but then a sharp voice came from the door. "You shouldn't have this many people around the baby."

It was Cat. She swept in, and Ellen and Megan scrambled back as though Thea were radioactive.

"It's all right," Thea said in a thick voice, but Cat had already glared at Ellen and Megan and whispered, "For God's sake, *now*?" so the two women left. But at the open door, Ellen heard Thea begin to cry properly, and Cat saying, "It's gonna be okay, hon," in a voice filled with love and compassion; a completely different voice than she'd used with anyone else. Ellen froze in the hallway.

"I'm so *scared*," Thea sobbed.

"I know," said Cat. "And I'm so proud of you. That was the hard part; now you can start again."

"They need their father."

"They'll have him. But on your terms. You can make sure he pays child support this way, and really spends time with them when he sees them. You'll see; it'll work out."

Thea blew her nose. "Jake's so angry."

"Yeah, well. He'll get over it. And he knows he's got Antonio if he ever needs anything. And Kane, I guess." This made Thea laugh; a small laugh, but it was there.

Ellen realized she was eavesdropping and turned guiltily away. Megan, who'd gone a few steps farther before noticing that Ellen wasn't with her, grinned the Fielding grin. "Sorry," Ellen said, coming down the hallway. "I didn't mean to do that."

"Don't worry. I'm the youngest. If I didn't eavesdrop around here now and then, I'd never find out a thing."

Downstairs, the boys were done; Kane had forced Jake out of his headphones, and they'd all gone outside to play touch football with Antonio. They needed a sixth player. Megan was happy to leave the malevolent atmosphere around her eldest sister.

Ellen watched them for a few minutes. Kane had found a new burst of energy; he teased the boys, kept Jake near him, gave him noogies if he looked too morose, and shouted insults to Antonio and Megan as if he were perfectly healthy. The boys loved him. They had no problem tackling him even though Antonio kept yelling, "Touch, boys, *touch* is what we are playing!" Kane would just wrestle them to the ground, with his own running commentary.

Ellen was fascinated to see this side of him. She supposed if she'd met him when he wasn't in the middle of the worst threat to his company in a decade, he might have shown her a more playful side before.

In the end her heart was so full, she had to go back inside. Cat was cutting the potatoes the boys had peeled. "Can I do that?" she asked tentatively.

"If you insist." Cat put the knife down, Ellen was rather relieved to see. "Do you need an apron?" Cat said stiffly, her gaze passing over Ellen's thick sweater as though it were made of kitten fur.

"No, I'm fine." She asked how big Cat wanted them, then kept her head down while she chopped, but she was aware of every move the older woman made. Cat had gone back to the stove to stir something, but now she was just standing there with her back to Ellen. The fan over the stove was running, and Jake's music was still blaring out of his headphones, which were next to Ellen on the counter, along with his iPod. Despite this, the silence in the room was torture. Ellen remembered how Cat had been with Thea and tried not to get too defensive.

"So," Cat finally said, turning around, "what's Kane helping *you* sell?"

Chapter 18

"I'm sorry?"

Ellen just held herself back from gaping at the woman. She, and everyone she knew, had been brought up to avoid confrontation at all costs, especially with strangers. She wasn't used to this kind of direct assault.

"All his girlfriends have used him for one thing or another," Cat said with bite. "What's your angle?"

It was so unfair, to both her and Kane, that Ellen began to get angry, and when she got angry, she found she was just fine with confrontation, no matter how much she'd wanted Cat to like her.

She drew herself up to her full height and glared at Cat just as hard as the older woman was glaring at her. "Why are you so angry with him?" she shot back. "You know he's killing himself to keep that company going for you all, don't you?"

Cat snorted, but her eyes slid away from Ellen's. "Don't pretend you care about the company, after what you did the other day."

Ellen had the knife in a death grip. "Don't you think," she started, then realized she was on the verge of pointing it at Cat, and put it down, "that Kane asked me about that?" *Shouted my walls down, more like.*

"Kane has blinders on around women. I'm sure you 'persuaded' him the papers were making it up," Cat sneered.

Shinedown was screaming through the headphones. Ellen grabbed the cord and ripped it out of the iPod. Her hands were shaking. The worst part was that she herself had believed the same thing of Kane when she'd met him. "You don't give him enough credit," she said, squirming inside. "Or me, come to that."

Cat shrugged. "I call 'em as I see 'em," she said, which was a phrase Ellen hated.

"I don't think you've 'seen' Kane for quite some time," she retorted. "And don't presume you know *anything* about me."

The back door opened and everyone piled in, hearing the last of Ellen's words, seeing the two women at battle positions on either side of the center island. "Oops," said Megan, and Kane went to Ellen and put an arm protectively around her.

"Welcoming my girl to your home in your usual warm manner, Cat?" he said, and despite Ellen's anger, a feminine pleasure ran through her at being so described.

Cat didn't seem to want to continue the conversation in front of witnesses. "Megan, did you set the table yet?" she said.

Kane began to draw Ellen out of the kitchen. "I didn't finish the—" she began, but perhaps retreat was best.

Kane and Ellen helped Megan with the table. They took apart Kane's bouquets—leaving Thea's intact—and Megan made pretty little centerpieces with them. She sent Ellen to the butler's pantry to find candles, and when she stood up from rummaging in a low cupboard, Kane was right next to her, ready to pull her into his arms. She hugged him back as best she could with her hands full of candles.

"Just ignore Cat," he said into her ear. "You won't win."

"I don't want to 'win,'" she said impatiently. "Why does she treat you like this? It's totally irrational."

"I'm used to it," he said, giving her that heartbreakingly sad smile. "She's had a lot to deal with since Mom died. Taking on the others, and the house... and now Thea's going to be staying with her until she closes on her new place."

"You've taken care of them too," she insisted. "Why does she still treat you like you're a teenager?"

He shrugged. "I dunno. It makes her feel better. I'd rather she take it out on me than Megan or her kids."

She dropped the candles back onto the counter and put her hand up to run it through the hair at his temple. "Everyone's punching bag, huh?"

He turned his head and kissed her palm. "As long as I'm not yours."

Even the small feeling of his lips on her hand made her tingle. "Well," he said, his voice lowering, "at least not anymore."

They were in a very small space. Kane leaned back against the counter, and Ellen pressed against him, the memory of last night still fresh in every nerve, keeping him immobile so she could kiss him. Funny how one kiss from him could erase any worries she had, how all she could think about was his hands on the base of her spine and his thighs against hers.

"Don't mind me." Megan's voice came from somewhere very far away. "I'll just take these, shall I?" She reached behind Kane to get the candles. "Carry on." She grinned and disappeared.

Ellen dropped her head onto his shoulder, blushing hard. His chest rumbled in a laugh that turned into a cough.

Ellen frowned at him. "Go back in the family room. I'll make you a drink."

"Don't worry about it," he replied, grabbing her before she could leave. "Let her have space for a little longer. I'm going to give Thea her flowers."

Ellen let him go and went into the family room herself, feeling a little at loose ends. But within a few minutes, Kane returned, leading Thea in and setting her up with pillows behind her back and on her lap, to support Benji. He stayed well away from the baby. He started to talk about the game, and Thea began to come out of herself; she obviously knew her football. Ellen let their words wash over her. Sitting on this giant couch with Kane and his family surrounding her, even with Cat radiating hate through walls, she could stay here forever.

One of the boys came hurtling into the room. "Aunt Sam is on Zoom!" he announced. Kane jumped up like he'd had five hundred volts set off under him. Thea said to Ellen, who had almost been thrown off the couch when Kane moved, "Hold him, will ya?" She thrust the baby unceremoniously into her arms and disappeared after Kane.

Ellen looked down at Benji, who solemnly looked back. "Hi, Benji," she whispered, her throat suddenly tight. "Not that I'm thinking about the future or anything, but you sure do look like your uncle." Benji smacked his lips. "Yeah," she said. "Hungry, huh?" And she went to see if Benji's dinner was ready.

The family was gathered around the kitchen island, potato peelings surrounding the laptop Cat had put there. Kane and Thea were in front; Sam was saying, "...not saying anything to anyone until I see me that baby!" So Ellen brought him forward and gave him to Thea. "Wait, who's *that*?" Sam burst out. "You got a wet nurse, T?"

"That," said Megan with satisfaction as Kane opened his mouth, "is Kane's *girlfriend*. Ellen, this is our sister Samantha."

"Sam!" yelled Sam. "Samantha's a witch! Hi, Ellen."

Sam's hair was a lot lighter than the rest of the family's, a reddish brown liberally streaked with natural highlights. Her face was nut-brown and white lines fanned from her eyes from squinting in the sun. Her teeth stood out white against the tan. Ellen could tell she was being examined as well and hoped that Sam saw more in her than Cat had. Behind Sam was a wall with various pieces of paper taped to it, a crooked calendar showing the Pyramids, and part of a window framing a white-hot sky outside.

Ellen responded somehow, but it was the baby Sam wanted to see, so she was happy to stand off to the side, away from the camera, while Thea, with a little more pride this time, unwrapped Benji from his blankets. "Oooh, that birthmark's awesome!" Sam breathed. "On the right side, that's totally good luck." Ellen couldn't see Thea's face, but her shoulders visibly relaxed a couple of inches.

"So you finally threw the bum out," Sam said matter-of-factly.

"Yes," Thea said uncertainly, looking around to see if Jake was there. He wasn't.

"Say it loud and proud, T," Sam said firmly. "Stick to it, okay? You're worth a lot more than that." Thea nodded, her hand going to her mouth again. "And so are the boys, so don't make me come over there and whup your ass."

"Kane's done all the ass-whupping we need, thanks," Cat said in a stiff tone.

"I hardly touched him," Kane protested. "This time."

"Good for you, bruh," Sam said, ignoring Cat's tut of disapproval. "Next time, can you get one in for me? And what's this about the family fortune going up in smoke?"

Apparently, Sam was the blunt one of the family. "Oh, nicely put, Sam," Megan said. Although Kane scraped his hand through his hair, he laughed.

"Maybe," he said ruefully.

"Nah." Sam pulled a face. "They'll catch 'em. This many fires? They have to be making mistakes." And she launched into a story about thieves at a dig she'd been on two years ago.

The boys drifted off, and Jake drifted in. "Jacob!" Sam interrupted herself. He reluctantly came into view, standing next to Ellen, shoulders hunched, head down. The back of his neck was scrawny and looked terribly vulnerable. Ellen wanted to put her arm around him. "Take off the 'phones and say hi, Jake!" Sam yelled. Jake did. "Did you find out about Machu Picchu like I told you?"

His head came up. "Yeah." He leaned forward. "I Googled everything I could about it. I even took out some books at the library." These were the longest sentences Ellen had heard him utter. "But it sucks ("Jake! Language!" snapped Cat); there's so much they don't know!"

"I know, fun, in't it?" Sam grinned. "Maybe one day I'll take you there, and you'll dig around and see what you can find out."

"Sounds cool," Jake said, and he sounded like he meant it. Thea turned around and got her free arm around her son, who instantly backed off and dropped his head again.

"Okay, bud, it's a deal. Be good, okay? Be nice to your mother. And your brother." Jake shrugged. Sam seemed to accept this was all the enthusiasm she was going to get on that subject. "Okay, peeps, I'd better go. Save me some turkey, 'kay? Love you!" They all chorused their love back. Ellen blushed a little at the simple, open affection. "Bye, Erin, wherever you went!" At least three people corrected her with great shouts of laughter. "Oh, Ellen, sorry. Nice to meet you! Don't tick off my brother! I guess if he's inviting you home to Mother

Cat, you must be doing something right. Ha ha, Kane, you should see your face. Bye, baby Benji! I love you! Bye!" And she disconnected.

They all seemed a little deflated after the call, but Cat looked like she was in a better mood. "Let's eat," she said. "Antonio, I'll take a jumbo glass of the Barbera, please."

Ellen could appreciate the antique silverware with the letter F engraved on it; her mother had a similar set and took great pride in keeping it polished. It was often Ellen's job to do it before holidays. The candelabra were equally old and sparkling; someone had been working hard all week. But the family dinnerware also carried the F; Ellen smiled at what her mother would have called the overt American desire to "stamp their name on everything." Cutlery was one thing, her mother would have said, but dishes as well? Rather outré.

The turkey was definitely outré; it was about the size of a baby hippo. "I hope there's enough turkey," Cat sniffed. "There wasn't time to order a bigger one." Kane gave Ellen an amused smile from across the table. Megan was next to her, Jake on her other side, headphones firmly clamped back in place. The other boys seemed to accept this and didn't include him in their fights over the mashed potatoes.

"So, Ellen," said Megan. "What can I get you? What's your favorite?"

Ellen looked around at the ten or so dishes that covered every inch of the table. "Well... I don't really know. I've never had a Thanksgiving dinner before."

Everyone stopped dead and stared at her. "Never?" asked Paolo-or-Matteo, frozen in the act of getting all the marshmallows from the sweet potato casserole onto his plate.

"Umm, no. I've always gone back ho−back to England at Thanksgiving."

"So..." Megan said, "You've never had green bean casserole?"

"Nope."

"Sweet potato casserole?"

"No."

"Sweet potato pie?" "Candied yams?" They all started shouting dishes at her, until she laughed and shook her head. Then one of the boys said, "Stuffing?"

"Yes!" Ellen smiled at him.

"That's just so sad," said Megan, and she grabbed the green beans. "Right, well, here you go, an introduction to the classic American tradition of eating too much"—she ladled a massive spoonful of green beans and fried onions onto Ellen's plate—"and glaring at each other across the table." She cast a dark eye over to Cat, who pretended she hadn't been looking.

"Dark or white meat, Catriona?" Antonio asked, and the focus shifted away from Ellen. Megan only stopped putting things on her plate when there was no plate left to see.

Kane caught her eye. "Gravy?" he said innocently, but his eyes were molten. She had to look away from him before she started panting.

Obediently working her way through the pile of food, the conversation ebbed and flowed around her. Antonio taught at Boston College, and Cat was a third-grade teacher, so they always had stories to tell. Cat was a good storyteller when she forgot to send Ellen the stink-eye. She kept Thea next to her and after a few minutes took the baby from her so Thea could eat. Ellen wondered why they didn't put him down in a crib somewhere, but she supposed he was a kind of security blanket for Thea. She took him back from Cat as soon as she could.

About halfway through the mountain of food in front of her, Ellen began to flag. Or maybe it was the tone of Cat's voice when she demanded, "What are the police doing about the fires? Seems like the arsonists are just going from one town to the next to the next without any hope of stopping them."

"They've been going through the employee lists, all the way back to Dad's time," Kane said, and a hush fell over the table, as though their father wasn't invoked often. "They think they've narrowed it down to a group that's disappeared. Ex-employees. Some recent, some we had to fire back then."

Now he frowned. Ellen knew what was bothering him: he still felt guilty for not being able to hire everyone back all those years ago. "They're trying to find them," he went on. "They say Thanksgiving's a good time; people tend to go home then." He fixed the boys with a dark stare. "No blabbing about this at school, okay, boys?" They nodded.

"I mean it," Cat added. "This is family stuff. You hear?" They nodded feverishly again, even Jake, who had turned off his music at last. "Family stuff" was apparently the magic word.

When Cat stood up to clear, Ellen joined her and made sure she was the first at the sink. She treated each heirloom plate with so much care even Cat couldn't complain. Between them, she and Kane had everything put away before his sister could think of something snotty to say.

Megan had put out the dessert things by then, and Ellen made one last attempt to be nice. "Cat, is it all right if I use the stove? I wanted to make some custard to go with the pie."

"You. Are. Shitting me," Kane said.

"What?" asked Megan, ever sensitive to changes in mood. "What's wrong with custard?"

"Excuse me," said Kane and abruptly went out the back door. She could see him lean against the deck railing, his back to the house. Megan said, "You're making custard? Like, ice cream?"

Ellen tried, and again failed, to describe it. She got out the milk and the powder she had brought with her, and started heating the milk, with Megan looking on. "Oh," Megan said. "It's like hot pudding."

"Ewwwww!" squealed the boys, who had come in hoping for some cookies to sneak.

"Well, if you put it like that," Ellen admitted. "But... well, I like it."

"What's Kane's problem, then?" Megan asked, frowning at the back door.

"Nothing." Ellen allowed herself a small smile. "I'm sure he'll like it too."

When Kane came back in a couple of minutes later—not before

Cat had stuck her head out the door and said, "You better not be smoking out there!"—he pulled Ellen back when she was about to take the pie into the dining room. "This pie's hot," she complained.

"*You're* hot," he growled. "Next time you're going to say 'custard' in front of me, give me a little warning." She laughed so hard she nearly dropped the plate.

Ellen couldn't convert everyone to the custard, but they loved her apple pie, made without spices so the sweet tartness of the apples came through. Antonio got out some port and whisky, and even Cat stopped sucking on a lemon. She'd moved from the head of the table so she could lean against Antonio. Thea had gone off to nurse again, but Cat had insisted she have a little Guinness—Antonio's mother had sworn by it for nursing mothers—so even she'd been looking a bit more cheerful.

The boys had run outside again to burn off their sugar highs. Dean Martin was singing a Christmas song. Kane had his arm around Ellen and was playing with her hand. The room smelled of the fire in the grate, a smell she always associated with him now, and of syrup and melting ice cream.

"So, Helen," Cat said on a slightly drunken sigh, "what exactly are your assspirations with my brother?"

"That's none of our business, *cara*," Antonio said gently.

"Yes 'tis," Cat objected. "My only brother, isn't he? Baby brother..." She closed her eyes.

"I've been bigger than you since third grade," Kane said.

"Don't matter," Cat breathed, leaning farther into Antonio. "Those actresses... used you, din' they? Poor innocent Kane." Kane coughed out a laugh. "Dropping trou for any chick that bats an eyelash..."

"Aw, Cat," Kane said. "You were doing so well..." But Cat had fallen asleep. Antonio smiled apologetically at them.

"Is that really what she thinks?" Ellen asked. "That you're desperate for affection?"

"*In vino veritas*." Kane smiled. "Ah, who knows? I gave up trying to figure her out years ago."

"She is protective of you all," Antonio said quietly.

"Well, she doesn't have to protect *me*, for f... crying out loud," Kane said, his face immediately changing from indulgence to annoyance. "She still thinks I can't run the business, doesn't she? She still thinks I'm twenty-two."

"She does not say so," said Antonio. "But you also, you do not think she takes care of this house?"

"That's just a coat of paint," Kane said. "And you're always complaining about the heat on the third floor. Why you don't just buy a new furnace..."

"We do not have your income, *fratello*." And when Kane took an angry breath, he held up his hand. "The trust fund is for the boys, you know that."

"There's more than enough for college *and* the repairs," Kane said roughly. "God, I'll give it to you myself. I don't want this place to fall apart because she's too stubborn to take her own money."

"But it *is* her money." There was ever so slightly more edge to Antonio's voice now. "And we bought the house from the estate."

"So you're just going to let it fall apart? What is it with my bloody sisters?" He stood up abruptly, depositing Ellen back in her own seat. "Sorry, hon," he said, and he banged out of the back door.

Antonio and Ellen smiled apologetically at each other. "Welcome to Thanksgiving," he offered.

Ellen didn't answer. She had a feeling swelling in her chest she didn't know how to define. This was the first time she'd really spent time with an American family. She'd been here for four years, and all she'd done was hang out with co-workers, half of whom were from other countries. As soon as family holidays happened, she ran back to her own, putting up with a few days of the painful ache she got when she looked at her mother or heard her talk about what Edward was doing now because it was easier than noticing how empty her life was here.

Today her sphere of acquaintances had grown by nine, ten if you counted Benji. And she'd been thrown into the middle of whatever the family found important as if she'd been part of it for years—adding to Cat's aggravation against Kane, used as his sounding board, teased by Megan, drawn into Thea's problems. The frightening feeling she got as she looked across the table was that she didn't ever want to leave.

Chapter 19

Kane went up the driveway to the front porch, away from the boys, and lit a cigarette. How his family could make him love them so much, and yet piss him off so badly, always astonished him. Having a cigarette was one more small, admittedly stupid, fuck you to his sister.

Cat always got mad when they talked about the business or about their father. It was one of the reasons they didn't bring Robert up much. When their parents had been alive, Robert had talked about the company all the time. "Ten generations," he'd say. "We can't let it fall on our watch. You see that, don't you, son?" Kane, idealizing his loud, charismatic father as they all did and wanting nothing more than to follow in his footsteps, had fervently agreed.

Then Cat would say something like, "But don't we need to focus more on our supply chain at the moment? And what about the recycling plant? Can't we do more with that?" And if he even let her finish her sentences, Robert would pat her shoulder indulgently and say, "Don't worry about it, sweetheart. You've got your own career to think of."

And the next day Cat would yell at Kane for hogging the TV too long or not taking out the garbage or taking their parents' car when she wanted to use it, or any number of violations he couldn't possibly anticipate.

Actually, she'd been right. Robert talked about the family legacy so often because he was in serious danger of failing it, as Kane discovered when he took over. And converting to recycling was the direction he'd chosen to take. But he and Cat had never discussed it.

He leaned on the railing and looked out at the deserted road in front of the house, at his old Audi that Ellen had driven here so expertly. The fact that she drove a stick was enough by itself to make him love her. She had no fear of Boston drivers—"Hello. I learned to drive in London"—no fear of his sister, no fear of living thousands of miles away from home. He didn't know how she did it. No matter what his history with Cat was, if he couldn't stand on this particular, slightly crooked porch, feel this splinter-laden railing under his hand, argue with her, fix stuff for Thea, and get teased by Megan on a regular basis, he'd feel like the ground was gone from beneath him.

But Ellen had fit right in. She'd taken Cat in stride, charmed Antonio within seconds, and had Megan treating her like just another sister. He'd taken a risk, bringing her here, because she was now part of this fabric. If she decided to leave the country, she'd leave a huge hole, and he didn't know how he'd bring the pieces back together.

The front door opened. Thea, without the baby for once, hissed, "Quick, put it out, she's woken up!" but Cat was already there, apparently completely sober after her nap, scowling so hard he was surprised she could still see. Kane turned around lazily to face her and, stretching his arm in a wide arc behind him so she couldn't miss it, deliberately flicked the ash off his cigarette.

"You're such a *fucking* child," Cat spat out. "Go ahead and get lung cancer, the hell do I care?" and she pulled Thea in with her and made to slam the door. But Ellen had come up behind her and caught it. She slowly padded over to Kane—at some point she'd taken off her boots, and even her feet in thick woolen socks turned him on—and matter-of-factly took the cigarette from him.

Of course, in front of her the whole thing did seem childish. Cat tutted loudly, said, "Oh, *sure*," and went inside. Ellen walked down the steps, stubbed the cigarette out on the grass, came back, and put her arms around Kane. He settled back against the railing and buried his face in her hair, his arms holding her fast. *This'll work out,* he thought. *This'll just have to work out.*

"I'll apologize to Antonio," he said against her hair.

"Sounds like a plan," she said, holding him a little tighter.

After a while the music started playing "La Vie en Rose." Kane swayed with her. Then he began singing along to the song. In French.

Ellen pulled away in surprise.

"Yeah, you see?" he teased. "You're not the only one with the fancy-pants languages." He put her head back on his shoulder and gave her another verse. "Okay," he admitted. "That's all I got. I learned it to impress this exchange–"

"Surprise, surprise," she interrupted.

"Uncle Kane!" came a yell from the side of the house. "B-ball! It's getting dark! You promised!"

"Come on," he said. "Go find your shoes. You're playing this time."

♦

The boys looked doubtful when Ellen came out the back door, but they were soon wishing she was on their side. "Netball," she explained, laughing, when she'd scored her fifth basket. Her only problem was her tendency to stand still, not dribble, which meant Kane could catch her too easily, and he would pick her up and squeeze her until she dropped the ball.

"I don't think LeBron would like it if you did this to him!" she'd gasp, and he'd just grin and get a perfect layup.

The hoop had a new net, but the rest of it looked as old as the house. A window above it, on the second floor of the garage, was covered with plywood except for one pane, and that had a baseball-sized hole in it. "Did you do that?" Ellen asked Kane, pointing up in an attempt to distract him.

"No!" yelled Matteo–she'd finally figured them out–"I did!" And he barreled into Kane to try and knock the ball out of his hands.

This sent Kane into a coughing fit that stopped the game. When Ellen put her hand to his forehead, he was burning up. She apologized to everyone around them, which would have made Kane smile if he hadn't been trying to catch his breath, and said that she was going to have to take him home.

When they got inside to say goodbye, Cat also touched his

forehead, and her lips tightened. "You stupid ass," she said, and Kane said, through a shiver, "I love you, too. Be nice to T and Megan."

♦

The dilemma of what to do over the holiday weekend was solved for her. Ellen spent it taking care of Kane, who ran a fever for two days and couldn't get out of bed.

She made a trip to her apartment to pick up some things early on Friday and was photographed driving away from his building. For a little while she'd thought the press had nothing on Cat for unsettling her, but the picture coming up on the internet, with the usual lewd suggestions underneath, still made her insides clench. She didn't tell Kane.

♦

Constant application of hot toddies and painkillers meant that in the middle of Saturday night Kane woke up, sweating like a linebacker and feeling much better. He stepped out to look for a fresh set of sheets and noticed that the door to his guest room was ajar. His living room was tidied, a bottle of single malt sat on the kitchen countertop, and the apartment didn't smell of cigarettes anymore; Ellen's flowery scent had taken over. He changed the sheets, took a shower, then went to the door of the guest room.

Her clothes were neatly folded on the chair; a comb and mirror stood on the chest of drawers, and she had put an old-fashioned alarm clock on the bedside table. She was lying on her stomach in the bed, one arm thrown above her head, presumably from moving the pillow, her head to the side, her blond hair half covering her face.

He stood there for a moment, enjoying the squeeze of his heart as he looked at her. Whatever happened after this weekend, she was his for now.

He padded over and gently took the covers off her. When he rolled her over and picked her up, she opened one eye a crack. "Better?" she asked sleepily.

"Mm-hmm," he said, and carried her back to his room. She was asleep again before he put her down.

♦

Sitting at opposite ends of his enormous couch the next day, her feet against Kane's thigh, newspapers strewn all around them, a wintry rain outside the floor-to-ceiling windows, Ellen was giddy with how desperately she liked this.

The papers were full of pictures of two people the cops had arrested "in connection with" the fires. They'd each been happily tucking into turkey and stuffing at their parents' houses on Thanksgiving. The man and woman weren't saying much, but they had bus tickets from New Hampshire, and the cops had found a van with every kind of device needed to make explosives, mechanical or chemical, as well as two laptops, in the airport parking lot. The man had clocked in as one of the security camera installers at the plant in California. His ID had been faultless.

"If the FBI holds a press conference," Kane said from behind his newspaper—the building's concierge had delivered it that day—"I'll probably have to be at it."

Ellen said, "Uh-huh," but a molten dread went through her. What if the journalists asked him about her? What would he say? Would he laugh her off, dismiss her to show them that nothing had changed, that there was nothing to worry about? Or would he try and rein the press back in by giving them a tidbit about his personal life, that was now *her* personal life, that she didn't think she could stand him sharing?

Kane put down the paper and let his head fall back, pinching the bridge of his nose. "Not too soon, I hope."

"You're a lot better today than yesterday."

"Yeah. Well enough to be pissed off that I'm sick." He rolled his eyes over to her. "Prettiest nursemaid ever." Ellen had to smile back.

Kane looked back up at the ceiling. "Why did they do it?" he said, going back to the two suspects. "I mean, one of them was just some kid that did IT for us for a summer. What did we do to him? And that girl. She's from Nebraska, for Christ's sake. There aren't even any trees in Nebraska. Kidding."

And then, as if he couldn't help asking even though he didn't want to know the answer, he said, "Do you think Tennant will keep going?"

Henry Tennant was one of the last names on the list of ex-employees the Feds hadn't been able to trace.

The FBI had told them that Tennant had been in the building on that day thirteen years ago when the boiler had exploded. That he'd been two rooms away from Robert Fielding. That he'd been crushed by a wall, suffered fourth-degree burns on twenty percent of his body, and third-degree on most of the rest. That two years ago he had stopped going to the doctor, stopped picking up his worker's comp checks, stopped paying rent, and disappeared from his apartment. That a sweep of library computers in his last known location had turned up searches for arson, chemical fires, and warehouse layouts.

"He can't do much without his IT guy," she said. "And whatever it was the girl did. And his picture's all over the place now. He won't be able to get anywhere near your buildings."

Kane nodded but still looked bleak. She stretched herself out next to him at his end of the couch and wrapped her arms around his wheezy chest.

He dropped his head to hide his face in her hair. One hand was crushing the newspaper at his side. Very quietly, as if he didn't want to say the words aloud, he said, "There were people in the mill in Bristol."

"Who all got out," she reminded him.

"Yeah, but..." He didn't finish the sentence. Ellen heard the thump of his heart through his chest and kept on holding tight.

Kane had spent years cultivating an image of a fearless businessman, optimistic to the point of arrogance, laughing and carefree in the face of the glaring problems the company had had when he'd taken over. He'd made it look easy to change Fielding Paper to recycled products, to explore new materials like hemp, to save hundreds of thousands of acres of forest. And he'd done it all virtually alone. From what she'd seen, the only sister that could have supported him chose to treat him like an annoying child, and his best friend was hundreds of miles away. And Ellen might be stereotyping, but she would bet he'd never discussed business with any of his previous girlfriends.

She couldn't imagine the weight of responsibility he carried every day. And now he took every man hour that had been lost, every stick of every destroyed building, every firefighter that put themselves in danger to fight them, on himself.

He didn't have to tell her this; she'd read between the lines of his phone conversations from California and New Hampshire. To add the idea that his employees might actually get injured, or worse, because he—as if it had been his responsibility to keep tabs on Tennant—had let someone slip between the cracks, must be unbearable to him.

How could Ellen help him when she didn't know where she'd be in three months? When he'd spent what little time they had together worrying about media attention or her own emotional demons? When her upbringing just about forbade the kind of questions Americans seemed to find so easy to ask? She knew she was the only person within light years who could help Kane with the strain he was under, but she didn't know how to go about it.

Casting about for something cheerful to say, she went with, "Tell me more about Carl. How long have you known him?"

"We took some business classes together. He's literally a genius. Very handy guy to have around when you've got a paper due." Kane gave a semblance of his old smile, but it soon faded. "I don't know how I would have gotten through those last couple of months of college without him."

Ellen held her breath. This was the first time he'd voluntarily brought up that period in his life.

"After the funeral, and that press conference," he went on, "he sat with me in my dorm room for two weeks, watching movies and drinking whatever made me drunk the quickest." He scrubbed his hand through his hair. "Better than years of therapy. The hangover was, too."

Ellen lifted her head from his chest. He was smiling again, his dark eyes softened. "I'm glad you had him," she said.

Kane let go of the newspaper to run a finger along her jawline. "I'm glad I have you."

Ellen blushed but didn't duck her head as she would have done a few weeks ago. "Anytime," she said, or tried to say, lightly. Forever, was what she wanted to say, but there was still the issue of her visa and of just how serious Kane could ever want to be with her, when he had so many other commitments in his life.

The press were rabid now. Leo gave a statement, but it didn't stop them calling or setting up shop outside Kane's building, and seeing Ellen leave it early on Friday morning sent them into ecstasies. Megan counted three of them when she came to check on Kane that Saturday. Kane's apartment was twenty stories up and faced the harbor, but just in case, Ellen had pulled the sheer drapes across his huge windows.

Kane's friend Paul had called with supposed sympathy but actual plans on how to monetize the situation. "You know, if you guys had come to me first, we could have avoided all those awkward photos," he enthused. "A few well-staged ops, that's what you were missing."

"Thanks, Paul," Kane said, "but we don't plan on staging anything. Staying out of spotlights, that's us from now on."

"You sure? I'll bet *New England Home* would pay good money for a lifestyle piece."

Kane snorted and said, "Lifestyles of the boring and congested. No, thanks. See you later, Paul," and firmly hung up.

"Anyway," Kane said now, "you'll meet Carl yourself soon. He's coming to visit in a couple of weeks."

And then he had a sneezing fit. Ellen went to put the kettle on while he blew through a few dozen tissues. She decided to heat up some of the gallon of turkey noodle soup Megan had brought over yesterday along with more groceries, for which Ellen had been grateful, because it stopped her having to run the gauntlet of reporters again.

Looking back at Kane, who was now sitting with his head on the back of the couch, holding the bridge of his nose again and swearing, Ellen faced another problem. Even congested and disgusting as Kane was, now that his fever was down and her nursemaid instincts weren't needed, her female instincts were getting louder and louder. Kane sounded like he was talking through a tube, and he smelled like eucalyptus, but the sight of him in plaid pajama pants, his bare feet propped on the coffee table, sent warm flickers through her belly, and she'd had to concentrate not to knead her feet into his thighs like a cat. She was glad to have her baggiest sweatshirt with her because her nipples had been at attention all weekend.

But what could she do if he made a move? She'd told Penny the truth: the sheer number of his ex-girlfriends was disconcerting at the very least, terrifying at most. Just as she was hoping that she was becoming important to him, she didn't want to fail at this most basic test of their compatibility.

So she stayed on her side of the kitchen counter and stirred the soup and told her body for the twentieth time that day to calm the hell down.

Chapter 20

"Ellen, it's your mother," said the voicemail message when she got home on Sunday night. As had the three other messages she'd left that day, while Ellen was at Kane's. "Goodness, where could you be all day? Did you know your mobile voicemail is full? Do call as soon as you can, dear."

Hearing Charlotte's voice was jarring, after the days Ellen had spent enmeshed in Kane's world, the clipped English tones unfamiliar after all the broad Boston vowels. Ellen should have called her. She always called on Sunday. But she'd allowed herself to forget because for the first time, she really had something happening in her life, and it was not something she wanted to share with her mother. Each of the last three Sundays had been studies in avoiding the subject.

She was glad to have the excuse that it was two o'clock in the morning in England not to have to call back right away, but she was up early on Monday morning. She couldn't avoid her mother any longer.

"Hold on," said Charlotte. "I'll call your father."

Andrew was at work. "Let's just you and me talk." She winced at the bad grammar, knowing Charlotte would pick up on it. "I have to get ready for work soon anyway."

"All right. Well." Charlotte seemed to be gathering herself. "Well, Eleanor, I'm afraid your father and I have heard some ridiculous rumors, and I just wanted to make sure everything was all right over there."

Ellen closed her eyes and leaned her forehead against the kitchen cabinet. "Rumors?" she stalled.

"Yes, well, you remember my friend Barbara Welsh, from church? Her daughter Saskia emigrated about the same time you went away"–they never said that Ellen had emigrated, just that she'd "gone away," as if she was in a mental institution or prison or something—"and she told me that... well, it's ridiculous of course, but that you've been photographed in..." Charlotte's voice lowered. "In a *compromising situation*."

Ellen laughed silently, but it turned into a sigh. Only her mother would use the phrase "compromising situation," as if Ellen were a politician caught with a prostitute. *Oh, Mum, if you only knew what kind of positions I've been dreaming about being in with Kane...*

"All right, here it is," Ellen said with a deep breath. "Actually, can you get Daddy on the phone too? I'd rather tell both of you at once."

Charlotte put her on hold so fast Ellen almost couldn't finish her sentence. "He'll be here directly," she said after a short pause.

You're not a receptionist, Mum, Ellen thought dismally. She sat down at the kitchen table, extra-large cup of tea at the ready.

Her father's voice came on. "Darling!"

"Hi, Dad," she said, finding it easier to smile. Her dad would back her up on this one. Not that she had to defend herself for anything. But she was beginning to feel a pinch between her shoulder blades.

"So all it is," she began, "is that I've starting dating"—a word her mother wouldn't approve of; Americanisms seemed to be popping out of her mouth unchecked these days—"a man who's a minor... celebrity around here. So the press have been taking pictures of us when we go out. That's it."

"*Dating?*" her mother said, predictably, scorn dripping from the word. "He's American, then, I assume."

Her father said over Charlotte, "Wasn't there something about you being in a fire?"

"No, no, Dad. His company makes paper, and some of their mills and warehouses have been set on fire."

"Oh, well, thank goodness for that," said Andrew, which made Ellen smile a little.

"Yes, yes, I saw that," Charlotte said impatiently, which meant she'd deigned to go online and look Kane up. "But who *is* he? Why didn't you tell us about him?"

"He's..." How could she sum up Kane, who had become so much to her in so few weeks? She struggled to find terms her mother would accept. "His family has been here for generations. Old Boston stock." As for the other question, Ellen decided to pretend she hadn't heard.

"And he... makes paper," said Charlotte. Why did she make it sound like he cleaned toilets?

"You want to see his balance sheet?" Ellen said impatiently. "He makes millions of tons of paper. Recycled, most of it." Not that that would impress Charlotte. Recycled smacked of hippies to her.

"Of course I don't want to see his balance sheet," Charlotte scoffed, but again her father's louder voice talked over her. "Nice people, darling?" and Ellen was able to fervently reply, "Very nice people, Daddy."

"Treat you well, does he?"

"Very well." She allowed herself to drift for a moment, remembering their kiss goodbye the night before.

"Thanks for taking such good care of me," Kane had said.

"You're welcome," she'd said—Americanism, again—and kissed him delicately. "But you'd better look a lot better next time we meet, or I don't know if I'll be able to be seen with you."

"Yeah, jeez." He'd put his fingers to the bridge of his nose. "I was such a superstud before you came along. Never a hair out of place. Well, you know what I mean."

She'd messed his hair up even worse than it already was. "Sucks to be human, huh? Well, you'd better shape up, as the song says, or I'll have to look elsewhere for my superheroes."

"Funny," he'd said and pulled her into his body in a crushing hug. She'd put her arms around his neck and buried her face in his shoulder, breathing in whatever strength she could—and a little Vicks—before facing the staring eyes of the cameras out front.

"That's all well and good," interrupted Charlotte now. Ellen sighed again and took a sip of her tea. "But why are *you* in the papers? Why are they interested in *you*?"

This was the tricky part. "They're not, really. They like him. His company's a bit of a fixture around here. And the fires at his mills have made him even more interesting." She didn't mention the other, more famous girlfriends, but if her mother had been online...

"But, dear," her mother insisted, "you know, it's really not the done thing to get yourself all over the papers. I thought you'd value your privacy more."

"I haven't 'got myself all over the papers,' Mum," Ellen said hotly. "We didn't choose this. Well, Kane did, before now, but now he'd much rather be left alone."

"So why on earth are you going out with him? He doesn't look like your sort at all." Meaning he looked nothing like Edward. "I just don't understand, dear."

"No." Ellen blew out a long breath. "I didn't think you would."

"Is this why you didn't come home at Thanksgiving?"

"No, Mum. I told you. I tried to book it too late, and all the flights were full." It was a lie, but the best she could come up with at the time. "I'll be home for Christmas instead, and for longer." She cleared her throat. "Actually, I was hoping I could bring Kane with me."

She heard her mother give a little snort and say under her breath, "*Kane.*" Out loud, she said, "I thought you didn't get much holiday time over there." That was another excuse she'd handed them, to explain her infrequent visits. Ellen didn't say anything. "And can *he* take that much time off?" Charlotte added.

"He owns the company, Mum. I think that means he can take as much time as he needs."

"One of these jetsetters, is he? Too much money and nothing to do but spend it?"

Ellen fought to control her voice. "No," she explained, proud of how calm she sounded. "He hardly spends money at all, if you must know. He drives an old car and his apartment is..." She thought about it. Okay, bad example. "Well, it's not the penthouse. Though I'm sure he could afford it."

"Yes, well... there are more important things than money."

Ellen's mouth fell open; her calm evaporated. "You just said...! And anyway, that's not what you said when you were telling me how much money Edward's family had!"

"I did nothing of the kind, Eleanor. I don't talk about that kind of thing. I merely mentioned that their family was a good, established one. You thought so too, at one time."

"Well, Kane's family has been here since about 1773, so I'd say that makes him pretty established too, wouldn't you?" She'd made up the date, just needed to snap something out.

"There's no need to get snippy, Eleanor," Charlotte said quellingly.

"Are you all right, darling?" Andrew said, again breaking over his wife's voice, as if he couldn't stand them arguing. "You sound a bit out of sorts."

That tends to happen when your mother questions every single decision you've ever made and treats the man you love as if he works on the docks. But to her father, she said, "I'm all right." She took a couple of breaths. "Look, I don't like those pictures any more than you do, but..." She faced it even as she said it. "I like him more than I don't like the photos."

There was a pause at the other end. "It's serious, then?" Andrew said, more quietly now.

Ellen's heart was hammering a jazz beat in her chest. "Yes," she almost whispered. "For me, anyway. Yes."

"Ah," said Andrew. "Right."

Silence fell again.

"But what about your work, darling?" said Andrew. "We thought you might be getting moved again soon. Isn't that what you told me they'd be doing with you next year?"

Ellen gripped her cooling mug. She'd told them that months ago, long before her life had changed beyond all recognition. "Yes, I know. Usually, it is."

"Usually?" Charlotte came back. "What do you mean?"

"I don't really know what I mean. I... haven't figured that out yet."

"'*Figured that out?*' I think you've been in America quite long enough!" said Charlotte. Then she gave a horrified squeak. "Oh, Lord, you're going to marry him so you can stay in the country, aren't you?"

"No!" Ellen shouted. "No. Absolutely not."

It had crossed her mind; of course it had. She knew it had crossed Penny's mind as well. But she was damned if she was going to force him into any kind of a commitment he didn't want, no matter how badly she wanted to stay, no matter if the alternative was leaving him.

"No," she said again, just in case they hadn't understood. "I might... be able to ask for a permanent position, then I could apply for a green card." If Jon would still have her.

It was the first time she'd admitted as much, even to herself, and she realized as she said that she had changed her plans without conscious thought. That the idea of leaving made a fist tighten in her throat. That she was going to throw herself on Jon's mercy and whatever professional reputation she had and beg to stay.

"Green card?" said Andrew. "Permanent?"

"Maybe."

"Oh. Well, dear," he continued, "we were sort of hoping that you... well, that you might be thinking of coming *home*... permanently."

Ellen looked at the clock; she should really be getting in the shower. "But... you knew about the transfers..."

"Yes, but you didn't take the last one. We thought perhaps you'd decided not to move around so much, that you'd—"

"We thought," Charlotte said, her voice impatient, "that you'd stopped being angry with us for whatever it was we've done and would come back to your real life!"

Ellen felt as though she'd swallowed ice. These last four years of her life were just a temper tantrum to her mother—she knew Andrew wouldn't have seen it that way—just a snit Ellen had to work through, and then she'd fall back into line.

She wanted to put the phone down, but that wasn't how her family worked. "I think you trained me well enough, *Mother*," she said coldly, "to know that temper tantrums are not in our vocabulary."

Yet she *had* run away, had acted on pure emotion, after Edward's attack. She'd gone straight to human resources, asked them about international transfers. She'd jumped through every administrative hoop in a kind of frenzy, and before the season had changed, she was on a plane. She'd allowed her emotions to direct her life for the first time, and she'd been determined never to acknowledge that. So much for the logical career move.

Whenever she'd been homesick and wondered if she'd made the wrong decision, she only had to think of Edward, and the impossibility of returning to England would soothe her. But despite this, she'd never really considered her situation as permanent. The fact that she *could* go home had always been there. Now... now she thought about leaving. Not just leaving Kane, though that was enough of a punch to the heart, but leaving Penny and Boston, the city she'd learned to love more than anything she'd left behind. Leaving that house full of women who also loved Kane, who embodied his sense of home, who were the reason he worked and worried so hard.

The morning radio was on quietly. Ridiculously, the accents of the hosts brought tears to her eyes. She'd emigrated, she realized, without even noticing.

"I'm sorry, Mum," she said hoarsely. "But I'm not coming back."

Andrew gave a soft "oh" of disappointment, but Charlotte said, "Because of *him*?" And now she sounded angrier than Ellen had heard her in years. "Because I've seen all the other pictures, Ellen, with the other women. Are you sure he feels the same way about you as you say you do about him?"

There it was, the question Ellen had been pushing away all weekend. How did she know that Kane didn't consider the blissful day they'd had yesterday just another hangout with just another girlfriend? And Ellen had to be a lot higher maintenance than those others.

"You might be right," she said. "But even if..." She could hardly say the words. "Even if he and I don't... work out... my life is here now."

"And what about *us*?" Charlotte burst out.

Typical. "I'm sure your friends will forgive you for having a daughter who went over to the dark side. Look, I have to get ready for work. Say hello to Adam and Jen for me, will you?"

"But, darling," her father began, but Ellen couldn't take any more.

"Bye, Daddy," she said and carefully and non-temper-tantrumy pressed the off button. Then she covered her eyes with her hands and let the tears fall. She didn't even know what she was crying about. If this was what letting out her emotions meant, then it stunk.

Chapter 21

At work, still feeling a little delicate but determined to get back to whatever normal was now, Ellen made her usual bumper mug of tea and tried to read her emails. But she found she couldn't settle down enough to read until she'd Googled her name and Kane's. Okay, sure, the only place that cared enough to post a picture of her car driving out of his parking garage was some gossipy website with so many ads no one probably bothered to load it. But the arrests, and the aftermath of the fire in New Hampshire, were still news.

Kane's picture, taken after that fire, made him look as drawn and ill as he'd eventually become after Thanksgiving; the lines on either side of his mouth had deepened, his eyes more shadowed and haunted than ever. The business pages speculated wildly about what was making him look so worried, and despite his assurances last week, everyone was figuring that some mills were going to have to close.

Her blood began to boil again. Didn't they see that they put *more* pressure on him when they made these ridiculous guesses? What was the point of Leo Palmer's office putting out press releases when they ignored them? But even with the photographic evidence that Kane was taking the fires hard, his silence over the weekend, coupled with the fact that she'd stayed in his apartment, led the media to suggest that he was fiddling while Rome literally burned.

Work, she reminded herself. *Get back to work.* If she was going to ask Jon for a permanent position, she was going to have to be perfect at her job over the next few days. Maybe it would be better to wait a couple of weeks before she asked him. Maybe after Christmas would be best. Her fingers shook a little as she replied to an email. Maybe in the new year.

At about eleven o'clock, she went back into the kitchen for her second cup of tea. A couple of colleagues met her in the hallway, and they both greeted her with a lot more interest than they'd ever shown before. One of them had asked her out a couple of years ago, and he seemed unable to stop staring at her, even, she sensed, when she was walking down the corridor away from him. Her cheeks flushed, and she cursed such an obvious sign that she was upset. *This is not professional. The papers can say what they like. Just keep doing your job.*

But it was hard to focus when everyone who came in contact with her gave her that same curious look. By lunchtime her nerves were shot, and she thought she might stay in her office and have a Snickers bar for lunch, rather than go outside and get stared at some more.

Then she jerked up out of her seat. Dammit, no. She was *not* going to change her habits for these assholes. Head high, she went and bought a sandwich as usual.

Coming back through the lobby, Francesca saw her and waved her over. Sighing, Ellen went to her, hoping that the conversation would be short. She didn't want to blow off her friend, but she really didn't want to discuss Kane or the newspapers.

"*Hola, chica.*" Francesca smiled. "How are you today?"

"Brilliant," Ellen said grimly.

"*Si,* I thought so much." Francesca squeezed her hand. "Your cell phone's mailbox is full, did you know?"

"Oh, right." She'd turned off her phone over the weekend for the same reason Kane had. "I'll clear it. Did you need something?"

"No, cara. Just wanted to check on you." Then her heart-shaped face went from concerned to mischievous. "So nothing new for reporting?"

"Oh, for God's sake, Francesca, don't you start." Ellen pulled her hand away. "You try living in this goldfish bowl for a few minutes."

"You're right. I sorry."

"And you can tell that to Penny as well. If she wants to find out the juicy details, she can come here and get yelled at herself."

"*Si,* I get it, okay, Elena. Wow." Francesca gave her that same appraising look she'd been getting all day. "I have never seen you like this."

Her cheeks were hot again, and she was ready to throw her strawberry lemonade at someone. "I'm sorry," she said, and tried to mean it. "I'm just… not much company right now. I'll see you later." She started to walk away but came back. "He had the flu, all right? All weekend. Tell Penny that."

"Okay, I will tell her." Francesca wasn't smiling anymore. "We are happy for you, you know. Or we were. Should we not be?"

"Buggered if I know," Ellen said, and went back to her office.

By five o'clock she knew she'd done about the worst day's work of her life. She hadn't called any clients this afternoon, had put a few more off via email, had lost an entire day not setting up a conference that was starting right after the new year because she didn't want to call the suppliers, and had even contemplated pretending she'd caught Kane's flu and just going home. She hated people who did that. Officially her day was over, but she almost always stayed later; it had become what Jon expected of her. But today she didn't have it in her. She was too mad to talk to anyone, and there were only so many emails in the world. She shut down her computer, grabbed her bag, and stepped out into the hallway.

Jon, damn him, was right there. "Hi," he said in surprise. "You going home?"

"Um, yes." She drew herself to her full height, which was a good few inches taller than him, and tried not to feel as though she was playing hooky. *Don't explain yourself. It's past five.* "Feeling like I, uh, might be coming down with a cold." *Dammit.*

"Okay," Jon said. He looked concerned, but that didn't explain how hard he was looking at her. "You do look a little flushed. You getting a fever?"

Of course she blushed even harder under his scrutiny. "Maybe," she squeaked. "Better go before I contaminate you." *Ellen, you're a big fat liar and a slacker, and he's never going to let you stay.*

"Sure." But he didn't walk away. He looked as if he was screwing himself up to say something, and she did. Not. Want. To hear it. "You okay?" he finally said. "Everything okay?"

What possible answer was there when your boss asked that question? "Yes," she said firmly. "I'm fine. Everything's good."

"Okay, good," he said, but he still looked uncertain. He looked up and down the corridor to make sure no one was near them. "Listen," he went on. *Oh, Lord, here it comes.* "I shouldn't tell you this, but HR called me." He looked mortified.

HR meant Claire Holland. "Bloody hell," she said between clenched teeth. He didn't have to say anything else. This was exactly what she'd been worried about when she'd first refused to go out with Kane. Rosette employees did not have their picture taken with the city's biggest playboy. And they did not have their sex lives hinted at in the local newspapers. Far from proving that she was an asset to the company, Ellen was fast becoming a liability.

"So, look," said Jon, looking just as uncomfortable as she felt. "Just... whatever you can do to stay under the radar."

She had to snort at that. "I didn't do anything to get *above* the radar," she snapped.

"I know." But she could see he thought that getting involved with Kane was a bad decision. "Look, I hope you'll... see that I'm speaking as your friend, not your boss. I told Claire that your private life is none of the company's business."

"Well, thanks for trying." They both knew it was an empty gesture; Ellen didn't have a private life anymore. And as soon as her name was linked with the Rosette in the papers, it had become their business.

She sagged back against the wall for a moment. "It's not fair, Jon," she said quietly, running her hand through her hair like Kane did. If she was doing half the things with Kane everyone thought she was, maybe the gossip would have been warranted. She'd be having a hell of a lot more fun, anyway.

"No," Jon said. He patted her arm a little awkwardly. "I'm on your side, though, okay? For what it's worth."

She appreciated it but could only smile rather weakly at him and let him walk away, before putting her weight back on her own two feet and going to the stairwell—the employee stairwell, this time. She had no intention of facing the stares of anyone in the lobby.

She no longer feared every dark corner and isolated stair. She didn't check under her car, and only one key stuck out from her knuckles. Kane had made her feel safe. The memory of the way she'd been, and how far he'd brought her, made tears prickle behind her eyes.

As she got into her car and began to drive home, she thought of Jon's face, and Francesca's, and the man she'd turned down two years ago, and the woman who was with him. And the smirk on the face of the guy at the gym. And her parents' assumptions, her mother's instant rejection of Kane based on some gossiping woman thousands of miles away.

By the time she stopped at the first traffic light, she was steaming. If they only knew just how boring her relationship with Kane was—they couldn't go anywhere, they couldn't do anything, and he'd been sick for days so even if she'd gotten over her fear of not being any good in bed, they hadn't been able to do anything about that either.

She pulled away at the light with a squeal that turned the head of a policewoman at the street corner. Her jaw set, Ellen made sure to keep her foot off the gas as she turned toward home. But she just got angrier and angrier. Her full mailbox. The cameras outside. Cat and her sneers. Two strangers who were fucking up Kane's life and some nutcase who seemed determined to destroy him.

Suddenly, what Ellen could do to make Kane feel better, and herself at the same time, became abundantly, gloriously clear.

Instead of turning right, she turned left, drove up to his parking garage, flipping the photographer who was still there the bird as she did so, parked in a visitor's spot, and stalked to the elevator.

Kane had stayed home that day on her and Anna's orders. They hadn't planned to meet up that night, but he was grinning when he opened the door. "Hey," he said. "This is a nice—"

Ellen pushed him inside the door and slammed it behind her. She kept pushing him until he came up against the wall of his entryway, and then she pulled his head down to her and kissed him.

How the hell had she stayed away from him for so long? His height was intoxicating all by itself, and the woodsy smell, unsullied by cigarettes after his days with her, surrounded her as he happily put his arms around her and lifted her so he could reach her better. She felt as though her body had been a useless appendage until just this moment.

He was still in pajama pants and a T-shirt, and Ellen, her anger not abated, almost ripped the T-shirt right off him in her hurry to feel his skin against her palms. She kissed him hard, opening her mouth, taking great open kisses from him, her hands gripping his hair.

He yelped a little when she bit his lip, and he pulled away. "Whoa," he said, smiling but puzzled.

"Whoa, indeed," she said, grabbing his hand and pulling him through the living room toward his bedroom.

When he saw where they were headed, though, he slowed her down. "Honey, wait a second..."

"No," she said, pulling on his hand. "Now." She walked backward, looking at him so that he could see exactly how serious she was. "Now, Kane. I don't give two shits how sick you are. Now."

They got a few more steps toward the bedroom. "Why?" he said. "I know I don't care, but... why now?"

Ellen got him the rest of the way into the room and slammed that door, too, shoving him up against it and grabbing at the bottom of his T-shirt. He obediently lifted his arms so she could pull it off, but she kept the material tangled around his hands and held them above his head with one hand, pressing her chest against his and kissing him again, light-headed with the power she had over him. "Because," she said, using her other hand to run her nails down the middle of his chest, making him gasp. "Because fuck 'em, that's why." She moved her hand to the waistband of his pants and slipped around to the back, scratching the base of his spine. "And me," she added hoarsely. "Do that to me."

Kane shuddered, and Ellen pressed her entire body against him, using her hand behind him to cup his buttocks and push into him further, feeling exactly how ready he was.

"Are you—ah!—sure?" he said one more time, and she loved him even more for thinking of her first, when she was obviously offering herself up to him on a plate. She'd never been so sure of anything in her life.

In answer, she pulled his hands, still wrapped in his T-shirt, down and led him by them to the bed. She got him flat on his back, straddled his legs, and leaned forward and kissed him, long and slow. "We're going to do what I've wanted to do since the second I met you," she went on, flattening her hands over his chest, enjoying watching him grit his teeth when she grazed his nipples. "Since before then."

She crawled down his legs and pulled his pants off with one movement. Kane had shaken the T-shirt off and started to reach for her, but she pushed his hands away. "Not yet," she said. She ran her hand up his leg, grasped his thigh, and followed her hand with her mouth. "Your damn thighs," she said, kissing and biting her way up them. "They've been driving me crazy since that first day in your office."

Kane groaned. He was biting his lip, unable to touch her, his hands gripping the sheets in fists. She stopped kissing his thighs before she got all the way up and sat down on them so she could take off her suit jacket. She was exploring his chest and shoulders again, flicking her thumbs over his nipples, digging her nails into his biceps. Kane had closed his eyes. "Ellen, please—let me—" But she pushed away his hands again, unbuttoned her pants, and stood up to remove them.

He managed to get his hand around her leg before she could back up, and he pulled her close. She put her hand on his chest, so he couldn't pull her onto the bed, but he took the opportunity to explore her thighs as she'd explored his. Each sweep of his fingers against her skin, the brief touch against her buttocks, made her shiver and arch her neck.

"Ellen," he said, and she realized she'd nearly given up control. She got away, went back to sitting on his legs.

"No," she said. "You have to stay there. You're sick, remember?" She leaned over him again. "You have to let me do everything."

The feel of his crotch against hers, with only one piece of fabric between them, sent heat writhing up her torso. She sat down harder, and Kane snarled, "Dammit, Ellen!" and she kissed him and laughed, and he groaned, and she felt like a queen, able to control him with one shift of her hips.

She took his hands and put them under her blouse. In seconds, he'd found his way inside her bra and was stroking her nipples, and it was Ellen's turn to gasp. She leaned back and took off the blouse, feeling as if she had the greatest rack in the world because of the way he was looking at her.

Kane pulled down the straps of her bra. He took hold of her upper arms and pulled hard, so she fell forward and he could take one breast in his mouth.

Ellen lost the plot completely for a while. She didn't know when she'd started sweating, when the feel of his equally slick skin had gotten so erotic, when sweeping her hair over his chest had started turning her on so much, when the skin of his hip had become so intimate, so utterly hers.

"What now?" he prompted, grinning, his hands on her hips. He gripped one strap of her underwear and pulled, hard. She cried out at the ripping sound, but then decided he had the right idea, and ripped the other side. The little bit of cotton disappeared.

Naked and feeling glorious and beautiful and powerful under his gaze, she said, "This," and leaned sideways to open his bedside drawer to find the condoms she'd seen there. In her whole life she'd never been confident enough even to think about doing this herself, but now she slapped his hands away when he automatically reached for the packet, and put it on him, before shifting her hips and sitting down on him so accurately they both yelled.

She fell forward again and let him move her hips for her, lifting her up and down while Kane angled his head so he could kiss her more deeply. They caught each other's moans, and Ellen felt herself melting and put her hands on his shoulders to brace herself while she rose and fell even more precisely. Kane lifted his hips just once and held there, and Ellen screamed and shuddered and laughed, and he tightened his grip on her hips and climaxed inside her, and she sat down as hard as she could and he laughed and gasped and relaxed.

Ellen fell on top of him and he rolled her to her side while their heartbeats slowed. "Don't go anywhere," he said, as if she could have moved, and he was gone and back in seconds, gathering her back into his arms.

"So this is what knackered really means," she murmured against his chest and, at peace for the first time in years, she slept.

Chapter 22

Kane was sitting on his bed, still unable to believe what he was looking at. Ellen was leaning against his headboard, naked, a plate of Thai food in her lap, her skin luminous against his charcoal-gray sheets. Her blond hair was loose and fell to, but didn't cover, her breasts. He felt, as he'd felt for three days, as if he couldn't blink or she'd disappear.

She was—there was no other word for it—magnificent. The buttoned-down Ellen he'd met had been beautiful and smart and intriguing and queenly. This Ellen was an empress—demanding, imperious, and more passionate than even he had imagined. Kane had grown up feeling that he was pretty much the equal of anyone he met. Ellen left him in awe.

She had gone home early on Tuesday morning and come right back on Tuesday night, and again last night and tonight. The only concession she'd made to outward appearances was to leave her car at work and take a cab to his building, to throw off the cameras. They had caught her through her driver's window flipping them the bird, which endeared her to him even more, but which he guessed probably hadn't gone down too well at work. But Ellen seemed determined not to do anything anyone told her to, and that included Kane.

Perhaps more precious to him, though, than Ellen's awakened passion, were the hours they spent talking, when her hand rested on his arm as they lay next to each other and squeezed him every now and again while he talked about his father. And he found himself sharing things with her he hadn't even admitted to himself—his fear of losing the company that sent cold sweat down his spine each time he saw a burnt-out building and the mantra that still plagued him, the *next time, next time,* that made him dread a ringing telephone. Ellen listened and nodded and didn't run screaming from the room.

And then she'd crawl away from him to the other side of the bed, her butt in the air, and he'd forget whatever it was he'd been worrying about.

"Let me ask you a question," she said, pinching up some noodles with her fingers and dropping them into her mouth. Kane was instantly turned on so badly he had to shift positions. He had loved watching her eat from their first dinner together. "This apartment. Did you make any decisions about the décor at all?"

He looked around him. He'd lived here for five years. Except for that one night when he'd questioned his choice of couch, he hadn't once thought about his surroundings. "Why?" he asked. "What's wrong with it?"

"Nothing!" she said, flipping over the sheet in her lap. "All this gray and purple. Very…"

"Masculine?"

"I was going to say, funereal."

"I see," he teased, getting closer to her and putting his bowl of curry on the bedside table. "Three days in my bed and you're changing out the drapes already, huh?" He picked up one of her noodles and began to spiral it around her breast. Ellen drew in her breath so hard she almost dislodged it, but she stayed very still while he did the same with the other breast.

"Not just in your bed," she pointed out in a strangled voice, and then "Ah!" when he began to take the noodles off with his mouth.

"Mmm," he said. "My new favorite way to eat pad Thai." And he reached for another noodle.

But, as he'd expected she might, Ellen moved, pushing him off her. She picked up a noodle of her own and said, "Now what shall I wrap this around?"

Was he aware that Ellen had to be in absolute control every time they made love? Of course he was. Did it hurt that even at this stage, she still didn't trust him enough to let him take over? Yes, a little. Could he make himself care a whole lot at this exact point in time? *Hell* no.

◆

"You get the paper," Kane said several mornings later, kissing the tip of her nose. "I'll make eggs."

Ellen groaned and sat up in bed. The bedroom faced west, and at this time of year, the sun was barely up when Kane's alarm went off. She squinted up at him so she could enjoy the sight of his bare bum before he put his pajama pants on, then roused herself and threw on his bathrobe.

Listening at the front door to make sure no one on his floor was opening theirs, she got the paper and tucked it under her arm. Then, as had become her habit, she scooted Kane over a little at the stove so she could reach the kettle, fill it, and set it to boil. The teabags she'd brought over especially were close to hand. While she waited for the kettle, she sat at the counter and opened the paper. From here she could wake up slowly and watch Kane cook, her body languorous, her heart peaceful.

Until she saw page five, anyway.

She shot out of her seat. "Oh, fuck."

Kane spun round at the tone of her voice, but she was already running for the bedroom.

"What?" he said, following her.

"Shit. Fuck. Shit," she heard herself saying while she fought with her bra and knickers. She'd begun to leave some things at Kane's so she wouldn't have to get up so early. Useful today. She threw on her clothes without even showering.

"What is it?"

Ellen waved an impatient hand back at the kitchen, at the newspaper she'd flung to the floor.

Kane went out. *Oh God oh God oh God oh God*, she thought as she dressed.

He came back in with the paper in his hand. "Honey..."

Ellen dashed into the bathroom, with some vague idea that she had to brush her teeth. *Nope. Takes too long.* She ran back.

"Ellen." Kane's voice was getting firmer. "This doesn't mean you."

She took a precious second to glare at him. "Why else do you think they're doing it now?"

The paper had done some "investigation" into the Rosette's habit of employing people from outside the country, and suggested, very cleverly, without making any overt accusations, that some of those employees were here illegally.

"Okay, but hold on," he said while she panic-brushed her hair into static-induced knots. "Let's just… take a minute here."

"No time," she snapped. "I have to get to Jon. Like right now."

"But what are you going to say to him? What do you have to prove? The visa's right there, in your passport, with its extension." But Ellen hardly heard him. "Ellen," Kane tried again, "talk to me." He reached out to catch her hand, but she dodged him and ran into his showroom of a living room to find her shoes.

"There's no point," she said, and then remembered saying that to him when he'd asked her out. The memory made her pause again in her headlong rush.

From the look on his face and the way he pulled back his hand, he remembered it, too. "Really?" he said.

But Ellen was too full of fear and remorse to respond to the hurt in his eyes. "Look, I'll tell you what happens later," she said.

"Let me at least drive you to work."

"No," she said at once. "That'll just…" She waved a hand toward the window, and the cameras outside. "I'll take the T." Which was another sign of how far Kane had changed her. She'd always had a vague, amorphous anxiety around the T and the people on it. He'd helped her move away from all those fears.

She felt tears start then, but she told herself she didn't have time to indulge them. Instead, she kissed Kane quickly, promised she'd call him later, and hit the elevator call button several times in quick, fear-induced jabs.

She barreled into Jon's office, not even bothering to go to hers first.

But Claire Holland was already there. She sat in one of Jon's guest chairs and looked up at Ellen as she burst in. Claire somehow managed to look like Ellen's old headmistress, if her headmistress had had a helmet of bright-red hair surrounding her pinched little face. Claire had reminded her of a snotty teacher since the first day they'd met.

No matter; all the pride and anger that had sustained Ellen over the past week and a half had left her. "Listen," she gasped. "I didn't say *anything* to *anyone* about my visa, or anyone else's—"

Jon had instinctively stood when she entered, and now said, "Go ahead and sit, Ellen," but she was shaking too much, now that she was at this dreaded meeting, to move more than her first few steps from the door. Jon closed it behind her.

Claire was holding the newspaper. "I have a meeting after this with the USCIS," she said. It was typical of Claire's pedantic nature that she would use the full acronym for what everyone else still called the INS. "They want to see the records of every L-1 employee we've *ever*"—she paused as if to let that sink in—"brought over here."

"But all the visas are legal, aren't they?" Ellen said, aware that she was pleading. "They won't find anything."

"It's our reputation that's been damaged," said Claire. "You know how this works, Ellen. According to the newspapers, we're guilty until proven innocent."

She closed her eyes briefly. Yes, she knew that. She'd known from the second she'd opened the paper that morning.

"Because your situation was... different," Claire continued, and she cut her eyes over to Jon. Ellen had a pang of guilt that he'd been drawn into this terrible spotlight as well, just for keeping her on over the usual time period. "They've chosen to *suggest* that not only are you here illegally, but that it's a practice we use regularly."

"Yes. I read it."

This was all because she flipped them the bird that day. They'd stopped painting her as the slightly exotic foreigner and decided to go for the jugular. And they'd succeeded. She felt as if she were bleeding out.

"It's all very well written," said Claire. "Our lawyers probably won't be able to pin anything definite on them for libel. They'll print a small retraction in a few days. But the damage is done."

Ellen nodded weakly. She waited and worked on breathing past the great mass on her chest.

"In any case, this has brought up another problem," Claire continued. "Am I correct in understanding that Kane Fielding is a client of ours?"

"No," said Jon, but Claire was looking at Ellen, and the expression on her face gave the woman the answer she wanted.

"I can't believe," she said with obvious relish, "that I would need to remind *you*, Ellen, of the line you've crossed."

"He's not a client," Ellen said feebly.

Jon echoed her, more strength in his voice. "Fielding Paper didn't hire us because Ellen was leaving. They were never clients." This was not strictly true. Ellen had never followed up with Lucía. They usually met every week at the gym, but Ellen had been so wrapped up in Kane she hadn't worked out since she'd taken Penny there almost three weeks ago, and when she had seen Lucía before that, she'd always put her off.

"Potential clients, then." Claire shook her head. Ellen felt like Alice in Wonderland after drinking the shrinking potion. Claire was only saying what she herself had said to Kane six weeks ago.

"Under the circumstances," Claire went on, apparently getting to her grand finale, "we think it would be a good idea to bring up your transfer date. Since you've applied for time off over Christmas, it would seem appropriate for you to start your new job right after New Year's."

She'd expected this, but the speed... "That barely gives me three weeks to pack," she protested.

"The relocation company can forward whatever you still have in your apartment when you leave," Claire said, not a trace of sympathy on her face. "We have openings in Rio, Singapore, and Delhi." She stood up and handed Ellen three sheets of job descriptions. "Think about it, and let me know by the end of the week."

Ellen automatically took the sheets, unable to speak. Claire nodded to Jon and swept out of the room with the air of a person who believed she'd performed her job admirably.

Jon looked miserably at Ellen. "I tried, Ellen, believe me."

"I do," she said through white lips. "I'm sorry about this. All of it." Tears came to her eyes so suddenly she was caught by surprise. She dashed back to her office and shut the door, just managing to close the blinds in the window facing the hallway before falling, sobbing, into her chair.

What was she going to say to Kane? That this hopeless dream they'd been sharing was now going to last barely two months, instead of four? That she'd been right from the beginning? That she loved him? What good would that do?

When the first shock of tears had subsided, she tried to reassemble her dignity with tissues and a makeup mirror, then turned to her inbox. She stuffed the job descriptions in her purse without looking at them. She already had voicemails and emails from clients to return. "No, of course the newspaper is wrong," she said about twenty times that day. "The Rosette has no need to try and get around the INS. And neither do I."

"So you're staying?" a few of them asked.

"For as long as they'll have me," she hedged.

One of the first voicemails was from Lucía. Ellen waited as long as she could before she called her back.

"What the hell's going on over there?" said Lucía without saying hello. "I don't see you for weeks; I haven't had any follow-up on the proposal, and now you're getting thrown out of the country?"

"I'm not getting thrown out of anything." At least, not for the reasons Lucía thought. "My visa is fine. It still runs out soon. And... I didn't follow up about the contract because... well, once I started going out with Kane it wouldn't have looked very good, would it, for you to hire my hotel?"

"I'll tell you what, Ellen," said Lucía, sounding more pissed than Ellen had ever heard her. "The fact that you're leaving is more of a reason for me not to use the Rosette than whatever's going on in your private life, and I would have thought you'd have enough faith in me to know that."

Ellen dropped her forehead into her hand. "Well, thank you. And it's not a question of faith, Lu, it's ethics."

"Like not dating a guy you were trying to do business with?"

Ellen winced. "Exactly. Look how great that's turning out."

"I can't look, can I, because I haven't seen you for weeks."

"The papers are happy to—"

"Oh, sure, now she thinks I'm going to listen to gossip about her. Jeez, Ellen. I thought we were better friends than this." And she hung up.

Ellen tugged on her hair with both hands. Her friends had been everything to her, hadn't they? That and her career. Six weeks with Kane and it was all going to hell. Maybe she should just get out before she hurt anyone else. Or herself.

At lunchtime she got a text from Kane. **What did they say?**

She couldn't call him. Her throat closed up at the very thought. At least he wasn't expecting her that night, as Carl was coming in from New York. She had planned a nice evening curled up in her own space, enjoying her own bed while dreaming about the blissful ten days she'd just spent in Kane's.

Hi. It wasn't that bad, she texted back. **I'm okay.**

What kind of okay? he texted right back.

Fine. Don't worry. Going to work late tonight though. Have fun with Carl.

After a pause during which she could almost feel him glaring at her, he replied, **I can help, if they fire you.**

No, you can't. **They haven't fired me. It's all good. Got to get back; talk to you later.**

Although how she was going to do that, she had no earthly idea.

Chapter 23

She did work late that night, until past ten o'clock. The regular lot she used near her apartment was full at this time of night, but she sometimes used a ground level lot a few blocks away. As she walked toward her apartment, she went over the day, over the options Claire had given her, and tried to think logically about what she wanted to do now. She could quit, of course, but that would mean going back to England. She could look for another job here, but there was no time. Once her sponsorship from the Rosette was over, she would have to leave.

And then there was... whatever Kane might do. He was enough of a gentleman to offer marriage just to help her out. She winced; she meant what she'd said to her mother. Whatever her future held, it sure the hell didn't include a pity wedding.

She was so preoccupied, she didn't notice the two men coming up from behind until they spoke to her.

"Ellen," one said.

She spun around, thinking they were journalists, but one glance showed her they weren't. One was larger and stockier than the other, in a tight, hooded tracksuit with dirt patches on the knees and down the front. The smaller man had a broken nose and tiny blue eyes. Both men were filthy dirty, their white skin dark with it. They came very close to her. Ellen instinctively backed up, but hit the wall of the office building behind her.

This could not be what it was. She had worried and planned and trained for this moment for four years, but she had let down her guard over the past few weeks. One key was sticking out between her knuckles, but her pepper spray was in her purse. And now her mind was a complete blank. She couldn't run or scream or even feel her hands in her pockets.

"Henry Tennant says hello," said the big man. His cheeks were pouchy and pushed the corners of his mouth closer, like a line between two parentheses. *Great, Ellen, that's a really handy observation.* She should be focusing on the fact that these men had been sent by the man who wanted to ruin Kane.

"What do you want?" she said. Her voice was cold and clipped, the voice she'd used around men for years before Kane came.

"We'll take the purse," the small man said and smiled at her. He had perfect white teeth, a little too large for his face, but still weirdly perfect. "Figure you're not short of money now you're around Kane Fielding."

He had to move closer to her before Ellen could stop thinking about his teeth and react. If she could remember only one thing from her self-defense classes, it was that a bag of money wasn't worth fighting over. She let the purse fall off her shoulder to the ground, taking her hand out of her pocket to do so. Her hand was still hidden in the folds of her coat, but now she could feel the chill of the key against her knuckles and got some kind of strength from it.

When she went to step away from the bag, the larger man told her not to move and came right up to her, grinning as he swept down her body to crouch and pick up the bag. Her coat was open and the night was cold, but not as cold as the swirl of fear that started in her stomach when she looked down at him. He was at eye level with her knees and the curves of her ankles and calves. His hand shot out suddenly and clasped one leg, getting a good feel before she jumped away.

Meanwhile, the other man had been watching her. "You were in the paper today."

"So?" she managed. She was beginning to shiver now, with the cold and the fear. They were supposed to go away when she gave them her purse, not stand on each side of her, blocking the way to her apartment and her car.

He looked over at his friend. "Scamming the system. Got no visa or something." His eyes went back to her. "Fucking foreigners. Even the ones who speak English are taking our jobs."

Ellen closed her mouth tight, her breath coming fast and labored through her nose. *Make them go away*, she prayed.

"Fielding's lost it," the small man continued, flashing those beautiful teeth at her. "No business left to run, I heard."

She might throw up if he put his face any closer. "I also heard," he said, his voice lowering, "that you've been putting out for him like a frickin' whore. Got any left over for a coupla regular guys?"

Somewhere behind her terror, Ellen noted that he said, "Haa" for "whore." Her linguistics professor would have lunged for a tape recorder.

The large man was to one side of her; she couldn't keep him in her view without turning her head, and if she did that, she would touch the other. "Henry just told us to–" the large man said.

"And we did what Henry asked," the small one reminded him. "This is just between us." His smile turned hungry. "Isn't it, bitch?"

Some spittle from the word hit her, and she flinched.

"'Sides," the small one continued, "Tennant wants to get back at Fielding, don't he? I don't reckon he'll be too bothered how we did it.
"

"Okay, then me next," the large man said. He was closer to her than she'd thought. She didn't have room to swing her hand, and the realization of this almost buckled her knees. It was only her determination not to touch the small man that kept her rigid.

He wasn't tall enough to be a threat, but the other man was, and his words and the sinister way he gave that perfect smile had her shaking. Suddenly he jerked his face so close to her his nose touched her cheek. She gasped and tried to step back again but couldn't; the rough cement wall behind her caught her hair and her coat.

Both men could now turn in front of her. The smaller one pushed against her, planting his mouth on hers. Ellen made a noise in her throat and twisted her face away as violently as she could, but the other man's face was right next to her. She screamed in his face, making his ears ring, so at least he backed off a little, but the small man's body was still jammed against hers, his hands going under her coat.

The tried and true method finally came back to her. When he went to nudge her legs open, whispering obscenities at her while he tugged her shirt out of her skirt, she brought her knee up so fast his eyes almost fell out of his head. She felt the kick pleat in the back of her skirt rip. He fell back, coughing and swearing. Ellen tried to run past him, but a huge hand came from beside her and punched her on the side of her head, sending her flying to the ground.

She hit the ground and skidded a short distance on her side, her coat useless as it bunched up around her. Her right leg and forearm were exposed to the sidewalk, which had recently been gritted for the winter weather. Her skin felt as if it had caught on fire.

For a second she lay there, pain darting around behind her eyes, her knuckles scratched and bleeding from the keys still in her hand. When she opened her eyes, it was to see the larger man kneeling next to her, working on his belt. "Get away from me," she whispered through the darts.

"I'm gonna fucking *kill* her!" the small man was shouting from his prostrate position a few feet away. "I'm gonna fucking do to her what she did to me!"

The large man was grinning again. "See," he said, "you gotta not play so hard to get, then you won't get hurt." She screamed again and tried to roll away, but he easily stopped her by hitting her again, and straddled her.

She was so terrified, her breath wasn't doing enough to keep her conscious. But just as the fat man was finding his way up her leg, not looking at her face, she got a surge of angry energy. Not *again*, she thought, brought up her hand, and slashed at his face with the key.

The key dragged slightly as it tore his cheek. Then he was yelling, falling half on top of her, blood spraying onto her clothes and bare stomach. As she frantically pushed him off her, she saw the other man trying to reach her, and her whimpers of fear became grunts of desperate exertion. She left one shoe behind under the large man and ran back toward her car, jumping over the crash barrier that surrounded the lot.

Her keys were still clutched in her hand; blood was running down her arm and leg and from her mouth. When she pressed the key fob to the lock, leaving blood on the metal, she also hit the panic button and the siren went off, threatening to pierce her eardrums. But she just got in the car, trapping her coat in the door, and used both hands to control her shaking fingers long enough to get the key in the ignition. She reversed with a shriek of the brakes, hitting the car behind her, then spun the wheel and nicked the corner of a minivan as she flew out of the lot, splintering the entrance gate, her siren still wailing.

She stopped what traffic there was at that time of night for blocks and pulled up haphazardly to Kane's building, bumping up over the curb and narrowly missing a fire hydrant. As she staggered out of the car, the concierge came out and blocked her way. "M−Ma'am," he stammered, "you can't leave your car−" Then he saw her face in the light from the door, the blood trickling down the side of her mouth, and froze.

"Could you please..." she croaked out. "Call Kane Fielding?"

The concierge made the connection. He stood there for a second with his mouth working like a marionette. Then he led the way to the revolving doors and hesitated before he let her go in front of him. As soon as she'd made it inside, she leaned against the windows that flanked the door, listening to the siren that wouldn't quit on her car.

"Mr. Fielding?" she heard him say into the phone. "There's... I mean it's... I mean I think Miss Hunter is here." He eyed Ellen. She had begun to shake uncontrollably, now that she had reached the relative safety of one door between her and the outside. "Well, she... she don't look too good, sir. I don't think I can ask her to go up." He hung up the phone, as Kane had obviously done on him, and stood there eyeing Ellen uncertainly, while her heart roared in her ears, and her head left a bloody smear on the window.

She heard the elevator moving, the clicks as it went down the floors. *I just have to stay standing for twenty more clicks... ten more clicks... five more...*

Kane came out of the elevator at a run but stopped dead when he saw her. "Holy shit Christ," he growled. "Ellen."

She slid down the wall as he ran to her, until she was sitting on the floor, her knees up by her chin, shaking so hard her hair, which had been in a French braid, fell around her face. He crouched by her and picked her up, and with the movement the blood left her head altogether.

Chapter 24

If Kane hadn't had his hands full, he might have socked the concierge. "Call the cops," he barked at the man. "And an ambulance." The concierge seemed to come out of a trance and reached for the phone. Kane set his jaw against the horror of all the blood on Ellen and took her upstairs.

Carl was waiting at his front door; he looked pleasantly curious until he saw her. "God," he exclaimed. "What happened?"

"The fuck would I know?" Kane snapped. "Can't you see she's fainted?" Carl stepped inside, and Kane laid her on the couch, holding her as gently as he could while he removed her coat. The blood was spattered across half her face and chest. Her perfect cheek was hidden under a welt whose bruise got worse as he watched. Her lip was swelling under the cut, her hair dirty and lank on her face. He sat back on his heels and looked at her, tears coming into his eyes.

Carl picked up a throw blanket from another chair, put it over her, moved to Kane's room, and brought out his comforter to add to it. Then he got out his cell phone and called the police.

Kane didn't stop him, was only dimly aware of all this, though he was grateful that the thick layers of warmth seemed to be stopping some of Ellen's shivering. She was still gripping a bloody set of keys in one hand. There didn't seem to be a single part of her he could touch without hurting her, so instead he scraped his hand through his hair and kept it there, his head down, while Carl moved around, doing something practical, no doubt.

Ellen stirred, and her eyelids fluttered. The light made her wince. Kane gestured to Carl, and he turned everything off but one lamp across the room. Kane could see the glitter of Ellen's eyes as she focused on him. "I'm okay," she whispered.

"No, you're not," he stated, not caring that he had tears on his face. "This is not okay."

Into his line of sight came a glass of brandy, followed by Carl, who crouched down next to him. "Hi, Ellen," Carl said.

"Hi, Carl," she said, and unbelievably, smiled a little. "Nice to meet you."

Kane could feel his heart rate slowing just from having Carl there. All Kane could think about was how deep the injuries went, and why Ellen in particular had been targeted.

"Kane," Carl said. The brandy hovered in front of his face. "Drink this. Drink it," he insisted when Kane pushed it away because it was between him and Ellen. Kane obeyed, but it just seemed to make his blood burn even more at the sight of her.

"The police'll be here soon," Carl said to Ellen. "We can't get you cleaned up until then, okay?" She nodded. Carl paused, then said delicately, "Are you hurt anywhere else?"

"Just my leg," she said. Kane didn't think he could stand to look at her. That wasn't what Carl was asking, and the potential answer was killing him, but he couldn't take his eyes off her. "Oh," she said, and reached out to Kane. It was the hand with the keys in it, so he still didn't touch her. "No. They just took my bag."

Kane rocked back so he was sitting on the floor and hid his face in his hands. The relief was agony. He heard Carl say, "They?"

"I parked my car farther away," she explained, her voice still low and hoarse. "Because it's late. They took my bag... and then they..." She stopped. After a few seconds he heard, "They thought they'd seize the day."

"You're covered in blood," Carl said.

"Mmm."

Kane managed to look at her. She was examining her forearm and hand. "One of them hit me, and I hit the ground pretty hard." She said it so calmly it made Kane groan. "Don't worry–"

"Don't *worry*?" he broke in, his voice cracking.

"I got him back." She gave that small smile again. "Kicked one in the nuts–you know I'm rather good at that–and got the other one with these." She shook the hand holding the keys. "I think that's why there's so much blood." It was still seeping from her arm and leg onto the couch. Ellen suddenly went to sit up. "Oh, Kane, your sofa!"

It was so absurd he just gaped at her. It was Carl who said, "No one cares about the couch, Ellen. Just relax."

The concierge rang up then, and soon the police were in the room. Ellen sat up, and Kane even saw her make an attempt to smooth her hair, which exasperated him and hurt his heart all at the same time. The detectives called back to have someone go to the street where she'd been attacked, and then spent the next several minutes asking him and Carl exactly where *they'd* been tonight, even with Ellen saying with increasing force, "It wasn't them. Hello. It wasn't them."

Kane had been so pissed today, at himself mostly but also with her. What she'd said would happen had finally happened: a news story so damaging she really could have lost her job. And she'd shut him out. After the week they'd had, the intimacy they'd shared, not just physically but emotionally, in those hours when they'd talked about their lives, when he'd told her about his relationship with his father and she'd talked about the hurt she felt whenever she spoke to her mother, after all that, he thought she'd come to trust him, even to rely on him the way he did her. Even, God help him, to consider a future with him. But today she'd gone right back into the cold, aloof Ellen who shut away all emotion. And he didn't know how to get her back.

And now... this. He'd felt scared and helpless when his mills had been attacked; when he'd closed the plant thirteen years ago and had to let people go; when he'd been told his father had died and knew that if he didn't do something, the company was going to die too. But it was nothing compared to this. She had been attacked because of him, he was sure of it, because he'd dragged her into his crazy life in front of cameras and with journalists ready to believe anything they liked about her sex life, just because she was with him. He couldn't even bear to look at his own hands.

But when the police talked about going to the hospital, it was

Kane she turned to, her eyes pleading. She tucked her head into his neck and held him so tight his breathing was restricted, but he held her even more closely. "I don't want to go," she said into his shoulder.

"I know, hon," he said, his voice still rough. "But let's help them catch these assholes, huh?" He brought up one hand to stroke her hair.

"Don't leave me there," she whispered.

"Not for one second."

"I'm sorry about your sofa."

Her and her constant need to say sorry. He loved her so damn much he had to laugh. "We'll get a new one. This one always was too big anyway." He picked her up because she didn't have any shoes, and felt her laugh against his side.

Carl drove them to the hospital in Kane's car. Ellen had finally been able to let go of her keys, but since they were evidence and had DNA on them, her car was towed out of the way.

"I don't see any cameras," Carl said when they pulled out of the garage. Kane lifted his eyes from Ellen long enough to look around, and he didn't see the bulk of a photographer leaning against the bushes across the street either. It must have been so late they'd gone home. It was an almost insignificantly small mercy.

Ellen was cleaned up and patched up and covered in bits of gauze and given a hospital gown, and she sat in Kane's arms while she gave her statement. She often had to pull on one of Kane's hands to remind him to loosen his grip on her.

When they were done, Ellen had the nurse help her to the bathroom and sent Kane out for a break. He went outside and had two cigarettes, lighting one off the other, which he'd always sworn was the sign of a true addict. Then he got a soda, not that he needed the caffeine, and, taking a deep breath, went back in. Ellen had been watching for him and gripped his hand tightly, making the cuts on her knuckles bleed again. Kane focused on finding another piece of cloth to dab them so he wouldn't scare her with the fury in his expression.

By the time the police had left, it was past three in the morning.

The hospital suggested she stay overnight, but she looked to Kane again, so he said, "Does she have to?"

While they waited for her discharge paperwork to be finished, Ellen sat on the bed, leaning hard against Kane. He wanted to tell her he was going to take her to and from work from now on. He wanted to tell her she had to leave that tiny little Bay Village studio and move in with him and a parking garage and 24-hour security. He wanted to erase the sight of all that blood on her from his mind.

What he said was, "It's my fault."

Ellen sighed. "Yes, you egotistical bastard," she said affectionately. "This is all about you." She waved at the cup of water that was on the bedside table, and he gave it to her.

"You're saying that to make me feel better, I know," he said. "But it's not okay. Not by a long shot." He'd thought losing her job was the worst thing that could happen to her? He'd been as naïve as those arsonists who'd gone home for Thanksgiving when the whole country was looking for them.

Kane took them home, driving as though the car itself had done the mugging. He got Ellen into the apartment, and she sat on the ruined couch, saying she figured any blood the hospital missed couldn't make it any worse. Kane went to run her a bath. It was closer to four o'clock now. The apartment seemed to echo strangely in the early hour.

When he came out of his bathroom, he could hear Carl and Ellen talking. He paused at his bedroom door.

"—Assistant DA in the Sex Crimes Unit," Carl was saying.

Kane wasn't planning to eavesdrop. He just didn't realize his feet had stopped moving.

"That sounds like a lot of laughs," Ellen said.

"Well." Carl paused. "We get by."

"Sorry. I didn't mean to make light of it."

"Kane always says I take myself too seriously. Don't worry about it."

Their heads were bent toward each other. Kane could see them from his corner of the room. "So tonight wasn't new for you," Ellen said.

"No. I don't usually come into the picture until the next day, or whenever the complaint is filed, but... no."

"Not that today was... the same as what you have to deal with."

"No." And his head got closer to hers suddenly, urgently. "But don't minimize it, Ellen." Carl shook her shoulder. "It's a terrible, terrible thing for a man to do, to use his strength over you that way, and you have every right to be traumatized. Thank God you got away. It could have been—"

"I know." She smiled at him. But in the dim light from the lamp across the room, Kane saw her face fall and her shoulders start to shake. Carl crossed the last inches between them and put his arm around her. Ellen stayed where she was, but her head was naturally cushioned in the crook of his shoulder, and she gave several long, low sobs while Carl said, "That's it... It's okay... Go ahead..." And Kane turned away and put his useless hands to work turning off the faucets in the bathroom, though his own sight was blurred and he could hardly see them.

When he came back in, she was sitting up and batting at her face with her hands, sniffing mightily. She said, "No, he feels bad enough already—"

"Your bath's ready," he said loudly. Ellen jumped. She leaped up from the couch with such a guilty look at Carl that Kane's mouth twisted, said, "Okay, thanks," and dashed past, trying to keep her face turned away from him. Kane let her go and walked over to stand just behind the couch.

"So, she's finally been able to let some of it out," Carl said, hooking an arm—the arm that Ellen had been able to show her feelings to, Kane noted sourly—over the back of the couch to look at him better.

"Yeah. I heard."

"Did you? Okay, good." He did a double take at Kane's face. "Hey, don't be looking at me all pissed. She had to let down that stiff upper lip; I was just there."

She was letting it down just fine until this morning, Kane thought gloomily.

"Don't worry," Carl went on. "She's going to be crying on you plenty the next few days. You've got to remember, she'll be reliving the other time, too." Kane had told him about Edward because Kane been looking for reassurance that he'd handled that first night the best way he could. "Even though tonight wasn't"—Carl made finger quotes—"'as bad,' she's going to be going through scenarios in her head for a while."

"How do I help her?" Kane ground out.

Carl stood up and stretched his arms up over his head, making his back pop. "You know, bud, you can't solve every problem for every woman in your life. Just be there; I reckon that's a start. I'm going to bed. I'll take a cup of coffee about eleven o'clock."

"You wish," Kane said automatically and reluctantly headed back to his bedroom.

Ellen was in the bath for more than half an hour, during which Kane sat and stewed. She seemed to have no desire to sleep anywhere but with him, however, and just as it was getting light, she woke up from the first nightmare, moaning and begging and sweating. Kane stroked her hair and talked to her, and she curled up into a ball in his embrace until she stopped shaking.

Chapter 25

Ellen woke midmorning and tensed up at once, until she remembered where she was. She was alone in the bed. The light was washing over the bed from the floor-to-ceiling windows across from her, curtained only in sheer drapes. She was high off the ground, behind well-locked doors and concierges. She was safe.

She didn't feel safe.

She wrapped her arms around her knees and hid her face, unable to stop the waves of fear rolling over her again, intensified by the dreams. She swore she could still smell the small one's breath, feel the weight of the bigger one against her thigh as he pulled off his belt. This was how it had been after Edward, as well. Weeks and months of sudden flashbacks, icy dread filling her at any moment. Seeing men she'd been working with for years and not being able to look them in the eye. Trying to keep her distance from people in the crowded underground trains. It had all come back. She had never gotten away from it, and now she never would.

She took a shower, pulling off the bandages Kane had changed only a few hours ago so she could scrub every inch those men had touched, until she was bleeding again and had to spend another few minutes stemming the blood.

Finally, hunger drew her out into the living room. Kane and Carl were in the kitchen. The apartment smelled of fresh coffee. Kane's hair was about as messy as she'd ever seen it, falling over one eye. He was dressed only in pajama pants, and the sight of all that skin that she had come to know so well made her want to weep. It had been such a nice dream.

Kane had been smiling, but he must have seen a change in her because he stopped and quickly came over to her. "Another nightmare?"

Oh God, he smelled good too. Like coffee and maple syrup. "No, no. I'm fine." If wanting to bury her sore cheek in his chest and at the same time get on a plane counted as fine.

But Kane didn't take her in his arms. He seemed to be keeping a calculated distance from her. "You want some coffee?"

She appreciated that he didn't touch her. She wasn't sure how she'd react to him. "Mm-hmm. Are those pancakes?"

She sat next to Carl at the counter, feeling suddenly shy. Last night she'd wept on him, but she really didn't know who he was. He had short, curly, dark hair, amber-brown skin, and dimples that showed when he smiled his good morning at her. She was grateful that at first he didn't try and talk to her. Kane busied himself at the stove, handing over pancakes as soon as her plate looked empty.

When she'd started on her fourth pancake, Carl said, "You've been on the news."

Ellen stopped mid-chew. "Well," she said, bravely swallowing, "I figured someone would tell someone. Oh, crap!" She suddenly stood up, the scrape of the chair legs echoing in the large room. "I didn't call the office!"

"I did," Kane said, putting out a hand to slow her down. "Jon heard it on the news. He was trying to get a hold of you, but of course, he was calling your cell and your home number. You might want to call him when you're done. Penny too, or she'll remove parts of my body I'm pretty fond of."

She dropped her knife and fork and called Jon right away. She had to reassure him five different ways that she wasn't badly hurt.

"Well," he said, "and not that there's a bright side to this, but Claire Holland's eating crow. She's accepted that you're going to be out for several days and has had to admit that maybe you're not an attention-junkie after all."

"Small mercies," she agreed, but it didn't make much difference. She'd tried doing things this new way, tried letting her emotions out a little more, and look what had happened.

Next, she had to call her parents, which she did from the bedroom, with the door closed and Kane outside it. She couldn't bear to see the guilt on his face if he heard what she knew her mother was going to say. She pretended that Kane didn't have Zoom because she didn't want them to see the huge gauze pad on her cheek.

"Why can't he download it?" demanded Charlotte. "We'll wait five minutes."

"It's a work computer," Ellen lied. "He's not allowed."

"I thought he was the owner—"

"Mum, can I just tell you this now? It's on the news, and I don't want anyone else telling you."

"What is it now? Yet another photograph? What did you do?"

Ellen closed her eyes. How else could she say this? "I got mugged last night."

"Oh! My *God*," said Charlotte, which she hardly ever did.

"I'm fine though!"

Charlotte said, "Hold on, I'm getting your father on conference." There was a pause while she reached Andrew at work.

"You see?" she said when she got back on the line, her voice shaking. Ellen could hear the other phone ringing in the background. "You see? You wouldn't come home and now look what happened!"

"Darling," said her father, and the crack in his voice brought tears to her eyes. "What happened? Frances said Mum said it was an emergency. Are you hurt?"

"No. Well, yes, but only superficially. Grazes. I was just coming home, walking from my car. Not paying attention." Letting down her guard, as she'd sworn she'd never do again. That was the lesson Edward had taught her, that she'd forgotten to follow, that had left her vulnerable.

"That bloody city!" said Charlotte, another word Ellen had never heard her use. "Come home, Ellen. Right now. This weekend."

"I can't, Mum."

"They won't even give you time off for this?"

"It's not that." She let the tears fall. "I'm being transferred. After Christmas. So I have to stay and wind up things here."

"Where?" said Charlotte, as Andrew said, "I thought you were staying in America."

"No." Under the pad, her tears were stinging her cuts. "I changed my mind."

"Can you still come home for Christmas?" Andrew asked carefully. "Please do, darling."

Ellen squeezed her eyes closed again and tried to keep her voice steady. Her parents used words like "darling" all the time, but they could still never tell her they loved her, and neither could she. Still, that kind of reticence seemed soothing to her right now. "I will. I want to."

"And where was your precious *Kane* in all of this?" demanded Charlotte. She still said his name as if it were a bad joke. "Letting you walk around a city at night by yourself!"

"Mum, I was just coming home from work. This is nothing to do with him." If she told her mother why she'd been targeted, she wouldn't need a phone to hear Charlotte's shriek. "It was my mistake. I'm at his apartment now. This is the number here. My cell phone and keys are with the police at the moment. I'll... I'll call you when I get home."

"Do you want me to come and get you?" Andrew asked.

With a sudden rush she realized how badly she wanted her father, a need she hadn't had in years. To hide her face in his shoulder and feel as if the world had receded, to breathe in the sympathy and support of the one person who never questioned her.

But it was Charlotte who said, "Oh, Ellen," in a completely different voice, one Ellen hadn't heard in a long time.

She had to cover the phone with her hand to stifle a sob. "'M okay," she tried to say.

"Ellen, dear," Charlotte said, and Ellen couldn't resist the sympathy, the compassion she heard. "All we've ever wanted is for you to be happy. If you're not happy there, then just come home. Don't wait until Christmas."

"*Mum.*" She couldn't hold back the tears now. For the first time in years, she believed that Charlotte really did care about her feelings. "I want to."

"What's stopping you?"

"Whenever I came home," she said, "you talked about Edward. You told me how much you wished–"

"Oh, Ellen," said Charlotte. "I just meant that the last time I really saw you happy was with him. I was looking for the thing that would make you happy again."

"I thought your Kane was making you happy," her father interrupted.

"He–he did–he..." She wanted to say, *he does*, but she was too used up today. Too in love and too hopeless about it.

Her parents gave her time to finish the sentence, but when she didn't, the silence spoke volumes.

Charlotte broke it first. "So you'll come home? Even to regroup for the holidays? I promise not to... not to ask you any questions."

"Yes." Ellen made the decision and the strength left her limbs. She fell sideways onto the bed, the phone trapped under her ear. "I'll come home."

The word had begun to mean something else to her, someone else. But she'd been dreaming.

"Oh, good," Charlotte answered, not knowing how the capitulation had shattered Ellen. "We have missed you, darling."

"Mum," Ellen whispered, tears having taken her voice. "Don't. I can't take that right now."

"No, of course not." Of course the declaration of actual emotions was undesirable. "Well, call us when you know your flight."

"Okay."

She hung up and hid her face in her hands. Could she go home and start again with her mother? Her father's love was always uncomplicated. It didn't matter how long they spent apart; they picked right up with their banter and jokes. Charlotte had always been more prickly, seeming harder to please. Every emotion on her part had seemed like a duty grudgingly fulfilled.

But now she'd told Ellen that she wanted her home, and not

because she didn't approve of Americans, but because she was worried for Ellen's happiness. She'd missed her for herself, not because she wanted a son-in-law and grandchildren. Perhaps Edward hadn't killed off all of Ellen's life in England. Perhaps she could go home.

Home. She had begun to believe in the possibility that home was wherever Kane was; that she could share her life with him, trust in her own feelings, and admit them to him. She went into the bathroom for another box of tissues. *You should have known.*

She had to call Penny next. Within half an hour, the concierge was sending her friend up.

Penny looked murderous, but when she saw the parts of Ellen's face that weren't covered with the bandage, her face fell. She hugged her tight for a long time. Ellen was surprised at how glad she was to see her.

"Good thing I'm wearing my waterproof mascara," Penny said bracingly as she swiped at her eyes when they pulled apart. "Here's your spare key, before I forget."

She was a vision in Christmas circa 1955 today, with her signature red lipstick and a tight dark-green sweater with a large black flower and leaves appliqued down one side. In honor of the cold weather, she was wearing drainpipe pants and booties with a fur trim.

Somehow, the fact that Penny looked just as she should was soothing to Ellen. She introduced her to Carl first, as Kane was extricating himself from his laptop on the couch. Predictably, Penny's eyes lit up. Carl was dark and solid and had a sweet smile and killer shoulders.

When she got to Kane, she began with, "I thought I'd told you—"

"Oh, *don't*," Ellen interrupted. "He blames himself enough as it is."

Penny hmphed; Kane raised an eyebrow and went to sit on the couch. "What's the press like out there?" Ellen asked.

"I didn't see any. Haven't you been watching the TV?"

"Of course not. More innuendo and assumptions. They're probably saying it was—"

"Whoa, whoa. Okay, you should definitely hear them. Carl, do you know where the remote is?" Carl obediently turned away to get the remote, which gave Penny a chance to fan herself ostentatiously in Ellen's direction.

They all faced the huge TV that was installed over the fireplace. "You know, putting electronics over a fire isn't good for them," Penny said vaguely, but her eyes slid over to the back of Kane's head.

A local lunchtime pseudo-news show was on, and the two women were having a field day. "This is what comes," one of them gushed importantly, "of the media's obsession with celebrities. Even someone barely connected with it can be attacked because of who she is!"

"See?" said Penny. "Everyone's on your side now. Look, they don't even have any photos of you there. Trying to pretend they weren't part of it."

The second bobblehead leaned in. "An insider told us that Ellen got one of them with the heel of her Louboutin. You go, girl!"

"Oh, for Pete's sake," Ellen muttered. "You think I can afford Louboutins?"

"They think Kane buys them for you," Penny said.

"Great. Just great."

The women on the screen went on. "Let's go to our correspondent, Mary Caminiti, live from the scene."

Poor Ms. Caminiti was several dozen feet away from the scene, behind police tape, but she gainfully gave what small details the eavesdroppers to the police radio had. Even at that distance, seeing the wall of the building she'd been pushed up against made Ellen shiver and turn her face away.

Kane noticed first and was next to her in a second. "Turn it off," he barked at Carl.

"No, no." She pushed at Kane's chest. It was the first time she'd touched him since she'd woken. His chest was warm and hard, and it broke her heart. "I'd like to know what I'll have to deal with when I... get back out there."

Kane looked as though he wanted to argue, but the phone rang. He took it into the bedroom. Penny spent the time tucking Ellen into a corner of the couch (which was now covered with a blanket) and finding a Hepburn-Tracy movie to watch.

Katharine Hepburn had just delivered her first zinger when Kane came back. "It was the police," he said. "They got a match on the DNA, and they found your purse in a trash can. They followed the bloodstains, but they reckon the men found some rag or other in the trash to cover the guy's cheek, because the blood stops after that. Both men have a record; that's how they have their DNA. The last they knew they were both homeless, but the police are pretty confident they'll find them."

He was next to Ellen, who'd sunk down on the arm of the couch. More gently, he said, "Will you be able to go and ID them when they get them?"

Ellen drew a deep breath. "Of course," she said, though her heart had begun to speed up at the fleshing out of these two into men with histories, with names, with lives and crimes that stretched out before their encounter with her. What else had they done and to whom?

Kane sat on the arm of the couch and rubbed her shoulder. Ellen leaned in. He really smelled soooo good.

"We can go and get your purse whenever you like," he said.

"Oh." She turned her head into Kane's side.

"Not yet," he soothed, moving his hand to rub her back. "You can stay here as long as you like."

Just stay, a voice in her head said. *Just stay here.*

No, she answered. *This isn't my life.*

The phone rang again, and Carl, who was closest, threw Kane the handset. He kept one arm around Ellen as he pressed the button. He listened for a moment and then said, "What? *Today?* No, I'm glad to hear it, but..." He took his arm away from her to scrape it through his hair. "What time? Okay. Thanks." He hung up, looked around at the three of them. "They caught the third arsonist. They're having a press conference at four."

"Where was he?" asked Carl.

"In Canada. That's all the agent told me."

"Do you have to go all the way up there?" asked Ellen. She was counting the minutes she had left with him as it was.

"No, they said the press conference will be here. I think Leo might have had something to do with that. I'd better call him."

"Kane," said Carl. "Let Leo do the conference. You didn't sleep last night."

Kane stood up fast. "No. It has to be me, as I've been telling you from the beginning." He towered over Ellen, and today, all she wanted to do was grab him around the legs and not let him go. Until she had to, anyway.

Carl didn't seem cowed. "They know about Ellen. They'll understand."

"Yeah, sure. They'll understand that I put my private life before a couple of thousand jobs."

"That's what people do," Carl said mildly.

Kane turned back to Ellen. "I'll just be gone a couple of hours. That's okay, isn't it, hon? You see that I have to be there, don't you?"

She saw that he was once again refusing offers of help, refusing to give himself the comfort of knowing other people had his back. She'd hoped that she'd given him that for a while, but now here she was, running to him as soon as things got tough in her life, just like his sisters, just like everyone else. It was another reason they wouldn't have worked. "Sure, of course," she said.

Chapter 26

"Yeah," Leo Palmer said. "That's it. You look—"

"Chrissake, Leo, can we *not* have a discussion about how I'm supposed to look for once?"

The press were in the media room Leo had insisted they fit out years ago when Kane had started this whole dog and pony show. Kane was at his window in his office, dragging on one last cigarette; Leo was there to give him his talking points. But they always spent a good part of the conversation on Kane's appearance and manner. It had been funny once. Now he felt as if he were being strangled. He knew Leo was itching to pull his tie just a little bit looser, to indicate his serious concern for his employees, rather than loss of profits. He wanted to rip the thing off altogether, but loosened it himself instead. Like the well-trained monkey he was.

Leo sat on the corner of Kane's desk. "Calm down. I'm on your side, remember? You know most of the work is done by how you look." Kane blew smoke hard out of the window. "Think of it as helping you."

"So what am I supposed to look like today? Pissed-off shareholder? Concerned employer? Traumatized son?"

Leo winced. "You know that was never part of the..." He paused.

"Act," Kane finished for him. Shit, how much of the last thirteen years had he spent acting? Did he even know anymore when he was and when he wasn't?

Yeah, he knew. When he was with Ellen.

From the minute he'd met her, he'd wanted to be more to her than just the playboy he showed everyone else. Thinking about how easy it had been to let her in made him feel as vulnerable as that kid from the first press conference: the kid that hadn't been schooled in how much to loosen his tie, whether he should have his hands in his pockets, or which reporters responded best when he looked at them. The kinds of things that had been his native language for years. That press conference and this were overlaying each other in his mind. He was worried that he'd slip today, let out some of his fear and uncertainty. And that if he did, they would come down on him like ravenous wolves.

"All right," said Leo. "Yes, it's been an act, and a damn good one, and you're welcome." He caught Kane's eye, and Kane gave a reluctant, one-sided smile. "Remember," he went on more seriously, "you can shut down any question you don't want to answer."

He meant any question about Ellen. The feeling that he had lost control of his life intensified.

She was pulling away from him; he could see it. Every set of her jaw, every time she said she was "fine." Even when she did hold on to him, he got the sense that she was doing it while she still could.

He'd wanted the comfort of switching to work mode; he'd always been able to make things go his way at the office. But here he was, and he was dreading the press conference, and he wanted to be home with her, letting someone else deal with Fielding Paper for a few hours. For the first time he began to think his time might have been better spent attending to his private life. He hadn't had enough time, he thought, stubbing out his cigarette. Not enough time to become as indispensable to her as she was to him.

Anna came in. "Agent Hernandez and Superintendent Nolan are here."

"Okay," said Leo. "We'll be right there." Kane stood up and straightened his shoulders, trying to put on the mantle he had created for himself, that now felt like a noose.

♦

The FBI agent and the superintendent said their piece, throwing out "suspect" and "ongoing investigation" and "federal offenses" as he'd heard them do a million times before, in other people's worlds, fixing other people's problems. This newest arrest, at least, Kane could almost understand. He was local and had been fired from a lumber yard not far from the Vermont border. He'd been caught stealing food at a gas station in Canada. Apparently, he'd been trying to live off the land and had nearly starved for two weeks. He had been the one, in between cursing out the police, the government, and the Mexicans, to confirm that the leader of this sick little crew was Henry Tennant.

Someone put a poster up of the three mugshots, and then enlarged pictures of Tennant—found God knew where, maybe his driver's license—on easels on either side of the podium. Tennant was... unremarkable. Somewhere around sixty, balding, gray hair, small blue eyes, pouchy cheeks. Just another guy, doing his forty-hour week, his life blown to pieces when Kane's was.

Kane scrubbed his hand through his hair. He should be feeling better: Ellen was safe in his apartment. Besides, Tennant couldn't do any more harm without his team, could he? But not knowing where he was, was worse almost, than not knowing where any of them were. Tennant had gotten this far in destroying his company; maybe he wasn't done yet.

He caught his name; the superintendent was introducing him. He walked in front of the half dozen or so people who for some reason needed to be behind the podium, and automatically fell into his habitual nonchalant pose: standing back a little, one hand on the podium, the other in a pocket. He thought of the bullet points that Leo wanted him to remember.

Then the poster of Tennant caught his eye. He turned to look at it. Ignoring how he was supposed to stand, and the list of platitudes in his head, he leaned his elbows on the podium, shoulders hunched, and with no preamble said, "This man."

He paused for a long moment. "I can't think what hell he went through, being in that fire."

Absolutely nothing and no one moved. He hadn't talked about *that fire* in a decade. "They've told me about his injuries, the rehab," he continued. "You and I have no idea how painful, how hard that must have been." He searched the crowd, following protocol enough to catch individual reporter's eyes, to look into the cameras one at a time. "It changed both of our lives, that fire. And the lives of others; don't anyone think I've forgotten the families who lost men.

"So I don't know why he's doing this, in this way. I've done everything I can for thirteen years to stop anyone else from going through what I—what *we*—went through. I'm proud of our company, of the products we sell, but I'm most proud of our safety record. And this guy... well, he's trying to make history repeat itself." He couldn't look at anyone now; he fixed his gaze on the double doors at the back of the room. "I really don't want that to happen."

He swallowed. He realized his fist was clenched, and as he flexed it, he hoped it was hidden behind the podium. Going back to the script a little, he thanked the local police departments in the towns and cities that had Fielding buildings in them. "I know how important these mills are in some towns," he said. "I appreciate how hard you've all been working to keep them running, and all those who've been disrupted, with extra shifts coming in and the added security. No one can want to get back to normal on this more than me, I can tell you. So please, anyone who recognizes this guy"—he threw a hand out toward the poster—"don't give him another chance to destroy what you're all working so hard to keep."

He leaned back, indicating that he was done and they could ask questions. But instead of the usual cacophony of voices, it seemed to be a few seconds before someone had something to ask. Most of the questions went to the investigators, so Kane just stayed hovering, going over what he'd said, hoping he hadn't totally messed up.

"Mr. Fielding?" he heard and moved up to the microphone. "How's Ellen?"

There it was. But it was asked in a diffident, almost apologetic tone, and he found himself able to say, "She's doing okay, thanks. Better."

But when some cocky journalist started asking more searching questions, Kane just stepped back and was grateful when the commissioner came forward to tell the reporters to read the press release about the mugging, and if they didn't have any more questions about the arsonists, thanks very much and the conference was over.

◆

Kane didn't wait to get a debriefing from Leo. For the first time he hadn't followed any of the rules, and he didn't feel like getting a ticking off. He was even impatient in the elevator. What had Ellen been thinking and doing in his absence?

Penny had gone, which was a blessing. She'd made it pretty clear she still wasn't on his side. If he'd had more time, he could have convinced her too...

Ellen was showering again. He was going to have to go out for more bandages if she kept this up, but he understood.

"Hey," said Carl from where he sat at the window, reading. "How did it go?"

Kane went to the refrigerator for a beer. Leaning back against the closed door, he took a grateful swig. "I don't know," he said, and honestly, he didn't care right now. "How's Ellen?"

"Okay," said Carl. "Kind of quiet."

Kane stayed where he was. Thinking. She was thinking her way out of his life, he knew it. She hadn't told him what her parents had said, but if he'd been them, he would have told her to go back home. And in any case, as far as he knew her visa was still up in three months. He didn't think he had that long.

"You were right," he said to Carl. "I shouldn't have left."

"Do me a favor," said Carl, coming over for a beer of his own.

"What?" said Kane. He was exhausted; the only person he wanted to help right now was Ellen.

"Fight for her."

Kane's eyes flew to his friend's. "What do you think I've been doing?" he said. "Any more fighting and someone's going to get a camera up his ass."

"Not them," said Carl, nodding at the windows, at the outside world. "Fight *her* for her."

Kane scrubbed a hand through his hair. "I was hoping I was imagining it."

"She's just scared. Don't let her give in to it. Don't *you* give in to it. Remember it was you she came to last night. That counts for a lot more than she realizes."

Kane looked bleakly at him. "Did she say anything to you?"

"No. But she made me take her to the police station. They'd picked up two guys."

Kane came away from the refrigerator. "Was it them?"

"Yes."

"Shit." And she hadn't wanted Kane with her. "Goddammit!" He heard the shower turn off. "I don't have any *time*," he said desperately to Carl.

"Fight anyway. Don't let her run away."

"God, it sucks when I'm the one you're giving relationship advice to."

Carl grinned. "This'll be the last time, I hope."

It might be, Kane thought despondently, but not for the reason Carl hoped.

He went to his bedroom.

"Hi," Ellen said a little breathlessly, seeing him. She was mostly dressed in one of the outfits she'd left at his apartment. He'd loved that sign of permanence a week ago. Everything she'd brought to his house was laid out on the bed, and his heart dived into his stomach. He stayed near the door.

"Where are you going?" he said.

She swallowed. "Home."

His hands clenched into fists. "Home, your apartment? Or home, England?"

"My apartment. I got my keys back." Her eyes slid away from his.

"Carl told me. You really want to go back there?"

"Yes," she said and made an attempt to smile. "You know me, need my stuff around me to feel better."

Your stuff would look fine right here. But at least she wasn't saying she was leaving for good. "Okay. You want some dinner first?"

"Oh, no," she said quickly, as if she couldn't stand one more minute in his company. "I'm not hungry," she covered. Kane folded his arms. "Do you think we could go now?"

He looked at her as he'd looked at her weeks ago, when he hadn't expected to see her again. How much more precious was she to him now? Her wet hair, neatly combed but dripping a damp patch onto her blouse. Her blue eyes, that had been so cold at first, and then flashed such fire at him. Her natural passion when she'd been shouting at him and later, when they'd made love.

Maybe he'd mistaken passion for love. That was what he might have to accept.

"Sure," he said past the lump in his throat. "I'll get a case for your things."

He watched with the intensity of a hawk as she put on her coat and said goodbye to Carl, whom she allowed to hug her, Kane noticed. Carl opened his eyes very wide to Kane over her shoulder, but Kane shrugged.

"Thanks for all your help," she said to Carl.

"So long, sweetheart," Carl said. Kane could have hit him then. *Give me the words*, he begged silently. *Don't just let me let her go.*

The weight over the two of them lasted all the way to her front door, Kane saying nothing, Ellen opening her mouth a few times, but apparently also not finding the words.

When she got her keys out and made to open the door, Kane put his hand over hers. It seemed to be the signal she'd been waiting for. "They're transferring me," she said in a rush.

He was standing very close to her. He could smell his shampoo in her hair. A single bulb illuminated them from above. "When?" he said.

"After Christmas. I'm going home for Christmas and then... wherever I choose."

Kane slumped against the doorframe. "Ellen," he began.

"I wanted to say thank you," she said over him, her voice tight. "I've had such... such a good time. Thank your family, too, will you?"

"No, I won't thank my goddamn family," he growled. Angry felt a lot better than the black fist crushing his heart. "Why? Why are you leaving?"

"Because I'm being transferred."

"So ask to stay."

"I can't. If I want to move up the ladder—"

"Bullshit, Ellen. You love what you do now. You really want to run a whole hotel? You really want to move all over the world? You love it *here*. You really want to start again?"

She pressed her lips together; her face had gone white. "What if I say yes?"

"Then I'll know you're lying, because it's me you want to get away from."

Her jaw worked for a moment. "Kane," she said, as if she had to explain something simple, but her eyes were miserable, "it was always a dream. We knew I would have to leave."

"Ask to stay," he said again. "Change your mind. It's permitted, you know."

"I don't want to stay," she whispered, again unable to look at him.

"Because of last night? You can't make a life-changing decision like this right now. I know it was devastating. I know it reminded you of... before. But don't leave. Give yourself some time." His throat closed over. "Give *me* some time."

The tears that were burning in his chest started in her eyes. "I can't," she whispered. "I can't. I have to go home."

"Make your home here. Stay." He mustered the bravery to say it. "Stay with me. Please."

Ellen closed her eyes. "I can't," she said again. "It's too much. I don't know how to... I thought I was better, but I let down my guard and look what happened. I'm no good at being... with someone."

"The mugging didn't happen because you let down your guard!" he exclaimed. "Are you blaming yourself again? Fuck, Ellen, I thought we'd been over this."

She shook her head. "I know. And I don't think I'm going to change. That's why I'm going. You deserve better."

"Better? Jesus." She turned the key in the lock, and the door opened, but he put out an arm to stop her going in. "Don't," he begged. "Don't give up on us."

She shook her head again. "Not on you. Just me. You can find someone else." She pressed a hand to her cheek as the tears spilled over.

His heart was being ripped out of his chest, but he had to say it. "I'm not in love with someone else."

"Don't say that!" Her tear-filled eyes met his. She sagged against the door. "Don't say that."

"Too late."

"I'm sorry," she said, crying hard now. "I love you too. Don't," she said when he moved closer. "It doesn't matter. I don't think I love you enough, because I can't do this."

He hadn't realized until now that he had tears on his own face. "How can you think of going back?"

"It's the only way I can stay sane."

He didn't have the words to make her stay. The breath he took got caught in his throat. He was really going to lose her. The only woman he couldn't stand to lose, and he was going to let her go.

When he lowered his head to kiss her, she sobbed deep in her chest, and her lips trembled against his. "I'm sorry," she whispered. "I wish I'd never met you."

"Me too," he murmured back. "I love you."

She mouthed the words back at him, unable to speak, and closed the door.

Chapter 27

Ellen was sitting on the edge of her bed, looking at her hands. Sometimes she lifted one to wipe at the tears that ran down her face; otherwise, she just let them flow. Her hand was already healing. She could see that the smaller scratches were less red. It was a betrayal, almost, because she'd just torn everything inside her wide open.

The sun hadn't yet risen when she decided that whatever the state of her visa, the Boston Rosette had a conference starting in two weeks, and she'd missed two days of planning already. Perhaps the ethereal silence of the office and the hum of her computer would be soothing.

Her skittishness about taking the stairs from the parking garage was back, so she waved at the night guard at the gate and walked through the front doors of the hotel. She figured there was about a one-in-twenty chance that someone she cared about would be on duty.

Just her luck: it was Francesca. The lobby was deserted, so she was spotted right away. "Elena!" Francesca called, hurrying out from behind the counter. Ellen flinched and then covered it up with as much of a smile as she could muster.

"*Ciao*, cara," she said, ready to submit to Francesca's usual big hugs and European cheek-kisses.

But Francesca pulled up short when she was five feet from her. Ellen had forgotten about her face; her hair was in a ponytail, and she hadn't replaced her bandages. The bruising was probably quite spectacular. Francesca's eyes immediately filled up. "Oh my shit," she breathed, covering her mouth with one hand and reaching out the other to Ellen. "It is terrible."

Ellen let her touch her cheek. Her touch was cool and

uncomplicated, and Ellen was grateful for it. "It looks worse than it is. It doesn't even really hurt now. I'm sorry, I forgot to–"

"*You* are sorry! Ellen, always with the sorry!" Francesca's tears were falling onto her blouse.

"Honey, stop, please; you're going to get yourself all messed up, and you've got four hours of your shift to go." Ellen brushed at the wet patches on Francesca's shirt. She also wanted her to stop because it made Ellen want to cry again.

Francesca made a half-hearted attempt to stem the flow, mopping her face the way Ellen had been doing earlier. "But why are you here? It is so early!"

"I..." This was what she didn't want to have to explain. "I didn't have a good night. I thought I could start making up the days I missed in peace and quiet."

Francesca fixed her with a hard stare. "Your eyes are red also; not from the attack, I think."

Ellen looked over at the reception desk. Right now, a nice shift-work job, with no need to make plans for the future, just figuring out what hours you'd be working this week or next, sounded so good she could have put her head down next to the phones and wept. "No," she admitted, unable to look at her friend. "But not now, okay, please?"

"Okay," Francesca said slowly. "It is very bad, then?"

"It was... inevitable." That was what she kept telling herself.

"Now *I* am sorry, cara." Francesca did hug her then, her small frame somehow enveloping Ellen's tall angles. Ellen gave in to it for a long moment, then gently pushed her away.

"All right, enough with the pity party," she said, sniffing. "Can I grab some tissues?"

She was almost at the elevators when Francesca called, "I have not heard you say 'honey' before."

Ellen closed her eyes. He'd been right: how could she go back?

◆

A stack of messages sat on her desk, and her voicemail light was blinking. Dropping her purse under the desk, Ellen picked up the top message.

It was addressed to Jon and was from a big client. "Stephen Oakes says if Ellen doesn't have a visa, you'd better get her one quick."

The next one said, "Trainor Electronics says if Ellen goes, so does he."

"Barton Laing says he'll hire Ellen if you don't want her."

And so on. Still reading them, but unable to believe her eyes, she pressed the button on her phone to retrieve her voicemail. Lucía's voice, from late on Thursday night, came out loud and clear. "Ellen, I'm sorry. I was really pissed today, and this just took me by surprise. Let's not let business mess up our friendship. Call me, okay? Let's go punch something." Then from the following morning, high-pitched, frantic: "Is this you? On the TV? They're saying your name but I can't– Why aren't you answering your cell phone? It is you! Oh *God*, Ellen! Are you okay? Where are you? Call me!"

Then there were messages from other clients, some about the article, some checking on her after the mugging. Some were forwarded from Jon's voicemail.

And then she heard Claire's bare, clipped tones. "Yes, hello, Ellen," she began. "Well, obviously we're all very sorry about what happened last night. We're... very, very sorry." It was about as human as Claire had ever sounded. "So, obviously, take your time coming back to work. The CIS only made us go back four years, and they're satisfied we're not breaking any rules. And Jon's put in a request to get you on the list for a green card. If you want it. So... feel better. Give me a ring when you get back."

It was Claire's stiff, impersonal voice that finally made Ellen believe that she really wasn't being thrown out of the country. But the next message was even better. It was Tony Stephanopoulos, the chairman of the hotel chain and one of the people at her table at the Queen's Ball. "Ellen, my dear," he said in his Greek accent, "I am in Bangkok, and I just heard. We will fix this. You are a credit to this hotel, and I have told Jon that I will make you hotel manager myself if this is what it takes to get you to stay. Do not worry. And next year may I suggest stuffed grape leaves for an appetizer?"

Ellen put the phone down carefully, got up on rather shaky legs, and went into the kitchen. She picked up the kettle, took a step to the sink to fill it, and then sank into the nearest chair, the kettle still in her hands, crying with relief.

She thought of the night before, and her sleepless night, and that Kane had said all sorts of things she'd been hoping he would say, right up until she rejected him for saying them. She cried harder. She felt almost churlish for crying over her breakup with Kane, which was her fault, when the visa issue, which wasn't, had been solved. But she cried anyway because so much could have been different if she'd known she could stay. Perhaps that would have given her the bravery to flip the bird at Edward and the muggers and embrace the life Kane had given her.

She went home feeling exhausted but restless. Maybe eating might help pass the time. But she'd been at Kane's for so long that her fridge was almost bare. Just a cup of tea, then.

It was a couple of steps from the kettle to find the remote and turn on the television. With the weekend came a new news cycle; it seemed that discussion of her and women's safety was no longer a talking point. She made the tea and looked around the room, trying to think of something to do. What had she done with all her weekends up till now? Maybe she should get a dog. She went over to her bookshelf and stared blankly at the titles, pulled out a well-thumbed Joanna Trollope, and sank onto the couch.

The nine o'clock summary came on. The first shot was of a building in an industrial park, with smoke billowing out of one side. The usual fire trucks and vans surrounded it. Later Ellen could swear that she'd begun to tense up before the newscaster even read the headline. "Yet another fire at Fielding Paper," he said, somehow sounding both serious and gleeful at the same time. "The firm's warehouse in the Inner Belt Park has been blazing for the past two hours. We'll have our correspondent, Shari Jones, on the scene after the day's other headlines."

Ellen wasn't sure when she stood up, but by the time Shari came on, she was close enough to the TV to see the pixels on the reporter's face. The fire seemed to have started at around seven that morning. The shift workers, brought in from other locations to help with Fielding Paper's increasing distribution problem, were just turning over from the night shift.

The parking lot was packed. The fire chief gave the details he had while the pictures alternated between fire coming out of the warehouse's small upper windows, the hoses of the fire trucks, an aerial shot, and the reporter with her microphone. An old-model Audi was parked haphazardly between a fire truck and a police car. The ticker at the bottom of the screen gave doom-laden information like, "this fire fourth in six weeks" and "1,500 Fielding workers now displaced by arsonists."

With Kane and the workers nowhere in sight, the reporter ran out of report, so the studio put on the press conference Kane had given on Friday. Ellen put her hand to her mouth. She could immediately tell that he wasn't putting on the act he usually did. His voice was even different, more like the way he talked with her and Carl, not like he was reading from a script. She kept her hand at her mouth, lips trembling under her fingers. The way he'd been before was all an act, one he'd gotten so good at it was easy to mistake that Kane for the real one. But she'd been given the real one. And she'd handed him back.

The image on the screen switched back to Shari Jones, the reporter onsite. She'd gotten ahold of the police captain. He said that the workers were all being questioned in the smaller office building across the street, and they would be released when the police were good and ready to release them. She asked him if he knew if Kane was with them. He said he thought he was. The fire chief came back into shot at that point and said, "Well, can you ask 'em to get him out here and move his car? He's blocking the trucks."

Ms. Jones looked ecstatic. She thanked the captain and planted herself firmly behind the Audi.

Things were winding down. They cut back to the studio for a

recap of the other fires, then went back to her, because Leo Palmer had just shown up. In the slick, media-savvy language that Kane had used before, he answered her questions, seeming to be very helpful while giving away nothing at all. Yes, there had been security guards at all the entrances, but he wasn't about to get into a discussion about how the arsonist had been able to get inside. When she asked how Kane was holding up, considering his family history, Leo just smiled blandly at her and didn't say anything.

Then the building behind them, the one with everyone in it, exploded.

The blast had them both ducking behind Kane's car and then running to the more substantial cover of the fire truck. The camera pointed down, showing running feet before peering down the length of the truck to the auxiliary building, which had disappeared in a storm of smoke and debris. "Oh my God," the reporter said, and Ellen didn't need to hear Leo's horrified yells to know. "They're in there! He's in there! They're all in there!"

Ellen's book and mug fell to the floor, the tea spreading over the cover and onto her rug. Terror like she'd never known propelled her to her feet. She didn't stop to change or put on a coat or turn off the TV. The only thought her horrified mind could process was *go*. Keys, purse, and she was out the door.

Chapter 28

The secretaries and foremen answered phones and Kane's questions from the offices on the second floor, while the police got statements from all the workers in the cafeteria. Kane was kept well supplied with coffee and cigarettes, but he couldn't even summon up a smile of thanks for the mousy little woman who timidly handed him another cup every twenty minutes. He knew he looked frightening, but that was how he felt.

He'd been sitting on the side of his bed, staring into space, when the call had come in. He hadn't even noticed that day was breaking, that he'd been sitting there all night. He couldn't lie down without smelling her on the other pillow, and he didn't have the energy to change the sheets.

When his cell phone rang, the hope that it was her leaped into his mind one last time. But no; she wouldn't change her mind, and he wouldn't blame her. As sickening as it was to hear that another building was on fire, he honestly welcomed the distraction.

Coming out of his room, he went into the kitchen to see if he could grab something to eat before leaving. Food was hard to get hold of at these things, he'd learned. He must have disturbed Carl with the opening and closing of cabinets because when he turned around, Carl was at his own bedroom door. "What's up?"

"Another fire. Inner Belt." Kane pulled out a leftover carton of takeout from the night before. He didn't remember eating it the first time.

"Damn," Carl said. "I have no idea where that is, but anyway. You were right."

"Yay for me," Kane said. He seriously contemplated having a slug of scotch. But then he remembered the hot toddies Ellen had plied him with, and his stomach turned over.

"I have to go." He reached for his jacket and keys, then grabbed a scarf and gloves. Freezing rain was coming down, and he didn't know how long he'd have to stand outside. The weather matched his mood perfectly anyway; ice sat in his chest, and it wasn't because Tennant was obviously still active.

Carl came over to him. "I'm sorry, man," Kane said. "This wasn't how I imagined this weekend would go."

"Don't be an ass. Did you sleep at all?" Kane had given him the barest facts about the breakup, and Carl had done what he did best: sat with him, watched a movie where a lot of people got shot, and drunk a six-pack. Realizing that he couldn't remember how many beers he'd drunk, Kane was even more glad he hadn't had the scotch. He did remember feeling nothing but sober when he'd finally gone to bed.

The roads were terrible. He'd have done ninety if he could, but black ice lay all over the place. When he finally got to the address, he skidded on a patch right in front of the building, sliding to a halt between the fire truck and the police car. The water coming from the hoses was already freezing on the sidewalks and roads. He couldn't even run over to the first official he saw without losing his footing.

He spent most of an hour sitting in the cafeteria with the workers, on the first floor of the auxiliary building. He'd had opportunities to talk to his employees at the other mills and warehouses, but most of these people had grown up where he had, and it was restful to sit and let his vowels broaden, to joke about the roads and the Bruins.

Not that they let him get away with small talk. Half the men were done with their shift and wanted to go home; the other half were pissed because they obviously weren't going to get to work today. He was asked point blank if they were getting paid for their lost shifts.

Before, he'd been able to continue to pay the workers who could travel to other buildings—most of the night shift were from the New Hampshire building. The secretaries were working overtime to get the paperwork sorted. He'd even asked the cafeteria staff to come in this morning. But he was straining the company's reserves to a breaking point. And the police hadn't told him anything about where Tennant might be now. He figured the man had done his usual trick of orchestrating from afar and was long gone.

Finally, the foreman and building manager were done with their statements, and they came to bring him upstairs to the offices. They all looked worried. Everyone looked like that when it was their hometown that had been hit. No one believed it would happen to them until it did. But they'd all counted on being so close to Boston to keep them safe. Everyone knew this was a home-grown business, that no one would help someone destroy that.

At least this time the damage was minimal, only really affecting one side of the building. Of course, the inventory was ruined, between the sprinklers—which had worked, for once, as had the security cameras, but they were still going through those—and the quick arrival of the fire department and their hoses. The fire had really only caught in the lobby and the supervisors' offices that lined one wall. He was told that it was out now. There had been two minor injuries, from guys slipping on the ice as they ran out of the building, but that was it. If it weren't for the idea of Tennant still out there and perhaps ready to do this again another day, he might have relaxed.

He was rolling his neck on his shoulders, trying to tell his muscles to chill, when the explosion came. It sent the doors to the stairwell on the second floor bursting into the office area and knocked Kane and everyone else to the ground. He fell to his knees, caught himself on a desk, and then had to use his arms to cover his face as the windows, including the one he'd been smoking at two minutes before, shattered, scattering safety glass over their heads.

Kane, shedding the glass, managed to stand. He could feel heat through his boots and hear people screaming downstairs, smashing through doors and windows to get out. Three others were with him in the open cubicle space on the second floor, down the hall from the conference room where the police were conducting interviews. The two officers ran out of the conference room with one of the workers, toward Kane and the others. But smoke from the stairwell was already coming into the room through the blasted doors. Kane helped the mousy woman to stand; her eyes were enormous, but she had set her jaw and suddenly didn't look so timid anymore.

"Where's the other fire exit?" shouted one of the policemen.

The building manager, who was just getting to his feet, waved back the way they'd come. "Through my office," he said, beginning to cough as the smoke thickened.

"I'm an EMT," the not-so-mousy woman said clearly to the officer. "I can help." He nodded, and they turned back to the other end of the hall.

But as Kane passed the last cubicle, he saw another woman, crouched down between her chair and desk, whimpering, gripping the chair as if it would protect her from the smoke that was starting to gather on the ceiling. "Hey!" he shouted and tried to fold himself into the tiny space left in her cubicle. "Come on, now," he tried to say calmly, but panic made him harsh, and she stared at him and keened and held on tighter. "Come *on*," he insisted, but she shrank back at the edge to his voice.

He was going to get her killed if he kept this up. "Help!" he yelled down the hall. Thankfully the EMT came back; Kane extricated himself and let the expert soothe the secretary and ease her out of the space.

While he was listening to her, cursing his own uselessness, he heard another voice, another frantic plea. It was coming from the damaged staircase. A corridor on the other side of the stairs led to offices that he'd assumed were empty.

So maybe he could be useful after all.

He ran to the water cooler in the corner, heaved the bottle out from the base, ripped out the cap, and let the cold water pour over him, soaking his shirt and jeans. He gritted his teeth against the shivering his body immediately started up. Then he pulled off his shirt and wrapped it around his mouth and nose, tying the sleeves as best he could behind his head. When he ran back past the cubicle, the EMT and the frightened woman he hadn't been able to help were gone.

He had just forced his way through the doors to the stairwell when another explosion came from the fire escape end of the building, knocking him backward into the stair rail and making him yell out at the hit to his back.

For a moment there was just noise, a roar and screaming and shouting. Kane swore and pulled himself upright. He hoped the others had made it out before the second blast.

In here a sour, chemical odor threatened to knock him back again. He held his shirt more closely to his mouth and shouted as loudly as he could, "Is someone here?"

In the lull after the cacophony of the explosion he heard, "Yes! Help us! Help!" from below him. The concrete stairs weren't burning, but the acrid chemical smoke was being dislodged around Kane's head, and he knew he barely had a minute to help them.

Somehow, despite the cold water dousing him, he was sweating. Looking down the stairwell, at first he just saw gray: gray stairs, gray railings, gray smoke. He ran down the first flight of stairs, calling out all the way, and being answered. The ground-level exit doors at one end of the stairwell were blown inward and the outer wall had collapsed on top of them. The stairs leading to them were buckled, pieces of rebar sticking out where some of the stairs should have been. A woman, whom he only saw because she was wearing some kind of festive necklace and, ludicrously, it was flashing red and green at him, was crouched next to an unconscious figure who appeared to have just one leg sticking out in front of him.

"He's stuck!" the woman moaned. "I'm stuck! His leg…"

The man, who must have weighed upwards of three hundred pounds, was slumped over one of the holes in the stairs. Kane got to them as quickly as he could while trying not to break his own neck. The man's leg was stuck in the hole; when he'd fallen through, he must have hit his head on something and passed out. The woman's arm was pinned between him and the wall.

The acrid smell was making Kane cough. The woman's breath was coming in short, terrified sobs. He tried to roll the man's shoulder away from the wall, but the dead weight slipped out of his hands. He had to kneel down in the rubble and use all his strength to pull the man away from her. She gasped in pain but was finally able to get her arm out. She stood up at once and began to run down the stairs.

"Stop!" he shouted. She kept running. He couldn't blame her, but he couldn't move the man by himself, and he could tell he was losing lung capacity by the second. "Wait!" he pleaded.

The woman looked at the doors at the other side of the stairwell that weren't damaged, that led to safety. She looked back at Kane, wasting seconds in indecision. He tried to get his arms under the man's shoulders to pull him out, but he was too heavy and his leg was too wedged in the hole. Kane tried again; his hands slipped again.

He couldn't do it, he thought frantically. Couldn't save him. He met the woman's eyes. She was feet from the door, waiting for him, and any moment there could be another explosion or the chemical fog above them would lower and kill them both.

He couldn't do this.

He didn't need to.

"Go!" he yelled and let go of the man. He stood up, dislodging the fog, setting himself coughing so hard he almost fell down the rest of the crumbled stairs. Bent double, he used the last of his energy to run to the woman and barrel his way out of the doors.

"My boss is there!" the woman shouted, pointing behind them; Kane couldn't speak. Two firefighters, wearing breathing apparatus, pushed past them through the doors, and he was finally able to sink to the icy ground and let everything swim to blackness.

Chapter 29

Ellen's wasn't the only car racing to the industrial park. She had to fight through TV trucks, SUVs, and sedans, all coming to a screeching halt the second they saw the buildings she'd seen on TV. She wanted to throw herself out of her car, too, not caring where it came to a stop, but made herself pull into the nearest parking lot.

The other drivers ran to the crowd still milling about, now far away from any building, surrounded by ambulances and police cars and fire trucks. But Ellen ran the other way, straight to a fire truck which stood in front of the larger warehouse. A man who looked to be a reporter was leaning on it, his notepad in hand, a tall hunting cap on his head that hid his eyes from her.

"Did you see where Kane Fielding is?" she asked him, in no mood for preliminary politeness. "Did he get out?"

The man opened and closed his mouth. So much for a reporter's way with words. Finally, he said, "Uh-huh."

Ellen sagged against the fire truck, much of the terror that had chased her to the site lifting. "So where is he?" she said.

"Hospital," he said. He was staring at her, his head raising enough that she could see his whole face. Nondescript, late-middle-aged. Saggy cheeks that suggested he'd recently lost weight.

"Which *one*? Is he okay?" she said, reaching out to grip his arm.

"He coughed a lot," he said. "Didn't burn though."

Ellen frowned. "What?"

"Uh. Nothing."

She still had her hand on his arm. The man gave his placid smile and went to pull away.

"Wait a minute," she said. "I know you."

He kept pulling, and Ellen hung on. He went with a jerking movement instead, and as her hand lifted, his knocked his cap off his head.

Time telescoped as they stared at each other.

"You're the one on TV," Henry Tennant said. "Fought off two men."

Ellen snaked her foot around his ankle and buckled his knee with one step backward. Henry went down without a sound, but when she twisted his arm behind his back, he screamed, and she remembered that he'd damaged his back in that first fire. Funny how little she cared.

"Did you come to watch your handiwork?" she asked in a voice she didn't recognize. She'd never been more furious in her life. Blood had rushed to her face, making her bruise throb. "Did you come to see if you'd killed him?"

But Henry just yelled. Ellen had never pretended she was a perfect human being, and today she was all out of fucks for predators. She used her other hand to push his face into the ground, not bothering to keep his face free of the patches of water from the hoses, already freezing in the winter air.

Chapter 30

Instead of the hazy gray world of rubble and smoke and fumes, Kane woke up to the clean whites and shiny metals of a hospital room. His chest hurt every time he took a breath. His skin hurt. His back hurt. He lifted his arm; there were scratches all down it. Something rested against his cheeks, leading to his nose, sending a trickle of air into him that was drying out his throat. He put his hand to it.

Cat came into focus, sitting on a hard chair next to his bed. She caught hold of his hand and put it back by his side where she continued to hold it while she glared at him.

"Hey, Cat," he said, or tried to say, but the words got stuck in his throat. It felt as though he'd swallowed sand.

"Don't talk," she said. Her eyes were suspiciously shiny. "Your vocal chords might be damaged." Her own voice cracked on the last word; she was twisting the IV in his hand, from holding on to him so hard. "Because," she went on, her voice getting higher, "because you're a stupid fucking idiot whose sole purpose in life is to scare the shit out of me!" And she let go of him to hide her face in her hands and burst into loud and uncontrollable weeping.

"Cat," he whispered, putting out a hand but only able to brush her hair back. She batted him away angrily, but the next second was bent over his chest, her weight pulling on the sensors stuck to him, crying as he hadn't seen her cry since Robert had died.

At least from there he could hug her, but tears came into his own eyes at leading her to this state. "I'm sorry," he said, but not much came out except the S sound.

"Sorry, he says!" she snapped. "You think I don't remember? You think I didn't lose Dad that day too? That we all didn't?" She was gasping the words out between sobs. "You think you can just play with your life? When you're *needed* just as much as he was, you fucking asshole!"

"You're right," he said hoarsely. "I'm so sorry, Cat. I've been–"

"Will you stop talking?" she interrupted. "You want to lose your voice for good?"

She sat up. It looked as if the storm was over, but it had changed everything.

Cat reached for the box of tissues on his bedside table to mop herself up. With an almighty sniff, she was almost back to herself. She held up a small whiteboard. "You have to write it down."

Damn, he thought. "I can't write it all down," he whispered.

"You think your thoughts are that complicated?" she said grimly, but she might have almost smiled. "Whisper, then."

They had so many things to say to each other, maybe should have said them years ago, but he couldn't start there now. "What time is it?" he said instead.

"It's–" She looked at her watch. "Eight o'clock. You don't remember coming in?"

He looked away from her, at the dark sky outside. He hoped it was still Saturday. He didn't remember much after he'd gotten out of that stairwell, apart from a lot of coughing and needles and tubes, and–he lifted the front of his gown and looked down at his chest. Crap. He looked like a badly shaved monkey.

Cat did smile now. "Yeah. Well, you try getting sensors through that rug you call chest hair."

He let his head fall back, felt again for the tube going into his nose. "Oxygen therapy," Cat explained. She went for a pitcher of water next to the bed. "They said it'll make your throat dry." He nodded and happily took a cup from her, but he was too sore to drink much.

"I didn't mean to scare you," he said, trying to keep his voice as quiet as possible. It was easier to talk this way. "I don't know what the hell I was thinking."

"Megan says you were trying to save the world, as usual." Cat looked away and swallowed. "Although you did save that woman."

But what she didn't say hung in the air. "Not the man?" he said.

She didn't answer for a second, but she squeezed his hand. So he wasn't surprised when she said, "He'd had a heart attack. You couldn't have done anything."

Kane took that in for a moment. He remembered being in the stairwell, his instinct to make the woman stay there with him to help a man he obviously couldn't help. And he remembered accepting that he was helpless and that he had made the situation better by admitting that and getting himself and the woman out.

Something loosened in his chest. *Enough.*

"When can I leave?" he asked after a minute.

"Not for a few days. They're monitoring your oxygen levels." She gestured to the clip on his forefinger. "Apparently the lungs can react to chemicals a day or more after exposure, and they don't know what you were exposed to yet." She made to stand up. "I'm starving. You want me to get you some shitty little cup of tapioca pudding or something?"

"No," he said, reaching up for her hand again. "Don't go yet."

Cat settled back onto the edge of his bed. "I'm still pissed at you," she said, but she smiled.

"You've always been pissed at me," he said.

She sobered. "It's hard, sometimes, knowing that Dad loved you more than the rest of us."

Kane's jaw dropped. "No, he—"

"Yes, he did. Don't deny it," Cat said impatiently. "Even Megan knew it. You were always the one prepped to take over the company. He never asked me if I might be interested in it."

Kane's eyes bore into her. Cat glared right back at him. "Were you?" he said.

"Yes. Don't you remember? I would ask him about it, and he'd just brush me off, like nothing I said ever counted."

Kane sat back and reached up to scrub his hand through his hair, which pulled on his IV. "The recycling. It was your idea."

"I was interested in it, anyway. I might have gone to California. We could have talked about converting the other plants. Then he died, and you didn't ask anyone for help, either. And I'd done the research. But you didn't ask, so I got pissed and wouldn't tell you. Then Mom got sick and that took all my time anyway." She gave a one-sided grin that was just like Kane's. "I could have saved you some work, you stubborn ass."

"I didn't know," he said. "I'm sorry, Cat. I never realized."

She shrugged. "Well, we both know I'm a stubborn ass, too. We get it from Dad, I guess."

He nodded. How many people had told Robert to modernize?

"You're wrong, though," said Kane. "He didn't love me more than any of you. Don't you see? I was just the workhorse. You were who it was all *for*."

It was a long speech for his vocal chords, and the last words were barely audible, but Cat was crying again. "I told you not to talk," she said in a choked voice.

"Okay," he said and accepted another drink. "I love you, you bossy pain in the ass."

She stood up. "Love you too, you constant thorn in my side. I'll go tell the others you're awake."

"Who's here?"

"Oh, it's a regular Fielding invasion. Plus Carl and—"

"Carl?"

"Well, duh. You think he'd hang out at your place with you all over the news? He and that little friend of Ellen's went to get you some clothes and things. And if anyone asks, he's our brother. Adopted."

He laughed, but it came out as a wheeze.

"Oh, and Ellen's your fiancée."

His heart leaped into his throat so fast it made him cough. He sat up and groaned when his back complained. "What?"

"She wouldn't leave," Cat said. "Even when I was mean to her for knowing where you were before we did."

Kane opened and closed his mouth a couple of times. Finally, he got out, "Where is she?"

"She and Antonio took the boys to the cafeteria." Cat stood up and stretched. She didn't seem to notice that Kane had stopped breathing.

After a few steps toward the door, she turned back. "We'll get the boiler and the painting done. I only said I wouldn't to piss you off. I love that house as much as you do. More."

"I only started smoking to piss *you* off," he said, grinning.

She shook her head, but she was smiling. At the door she turned around again. "Oh, and Ellen caught Tennant."

"*What?* Ow." He put his hand to his throat.

"Yep. Sat on him until the cops came, or something. Maybe I should be nicer to her, huh? Seems like a bit of a badass."

"Shit." He went to scrape his hand through his hair again, but the IV pulled too much. "Any more revelations?"

"No." Cat opened the door but still wasn't quite done. "Don't ever do that to me again," she said fiercely.

"Okay," he promised. "Quiet life for me from now on."

Cat disappeared. Kane tried to sit up a little more and look and feel a little less sick. The ten minutes he had to wait felt like hours.

Ellen pushed the door open and padded over to him. Half her hair had fallen out of its ponytail and was tucked behind her ear instead. She was wearing yoga pants and a gigantic BC sweatshirt that might have been Antonio's. Her eyes looked huge, her skin very pale.

She stood a couple of feet away from the side of the bed. If he'd reached out his hand, he couldn't have touched her.

For a long moment they looked at each other. She wasn't smiling, but Kane knew he had a big stupid grin on his face.

She said, "How are you feeling?"

"I'm great," he said.

"Really?"

"Oh, yeah." Apart from not being able to breathe or talk, he'd never been happier in his life. "Bit of razor burn on my chest," he joked weakly.

"Good."

Suddenly she rushed forward and hit him, hard, on the shoulder. "You stupid bloody jackass!" she shouted, hitting him anywhere that didn't have a sensor or a tube attached to it. "What the *hell* were you thinking? *Must* you always play the bloody hero? God, when you get better I am going to *kill* you!"

"You're right," he said, contrite, but he was grinning fit to crack his cheeks.

"Don't talk! Quit agreeing with me!" She hit the top of his head. "You scared Carl so bad his eyes nearly turned blue!" More blows on his arms and legs.

He caught one of her hands and held it, pulling her so she had to sit on the bed next to him. "I was doing *fine* before I met you!" she said, not as loudly but still very angry. "You make me want you, God, like water and food, and you make me fall in love with you, and your family, and then you scare me sideways—"

"Ellen," he interrupted. "Don't leave. I love you. Don't leave."

"Me leave?" she almost shouted. "I'm not the one running into burning buildings! Don't *you* leave *me*!"

Kane's grin hurt his face. "Okay."

"Don't look so damn smug!" And for the second time in an hour, a woman he loved burst into tears.

Kane ignored the IV pulling on his hand and the crush of the sensors on him and pulled Ellen onto his chest. Burying his face in her hair was like coming home.

Against his neck, she said, "You were right. I was running away. I was so afraid of you because I loved you so badly."

"You scared me too," he whispered into her hair. "But that's the way it works. That's how I knew it was real."

She stayed in his arms for a few more moments. Then she sat up, pressing one hand into his chest. "You didn't have to run into a burning building to teach me that, you know," she said, one side of her mouth tilting up.

She kept saying that. "Technically," he pointed out, "it wasn't burning, and I was already in it."

"Don't be pedantic." She was recovering, swiping the moisture from her cheeks. Again, she had that fire in her eyes that meant she was determined on something. "Let me tell you how this is going to go." She counted on her fingers. "First, you're going to quit smoking. Which, if you haven't noticed, you already have done, as of twelve hours or so ago. I want you around for a long time, and you trying to get a rise out of Cat is not a good enough reason for me to lose you before I'm good and ready."

"Okay," he said.

"Then," she went on, "you're going to sell that ridiculous apartment that has absolutely none of your personality in it. We are going to buy a proper home." She grimaced. "Maybe even near Cat. And you will come to England and meet *my* family, and they'll love you, and I'll try and see things from their side more often."

"Okay," he agreed.

"And then, we are going to date, for a while."

"But—"

"And we'll be so boring no one will take our photograph."

"But... your transfer..."

"Withdrawn," she said. "Thanks to Lucía and a few of my closest clients."

Kane wanted to shout from the rooftops. Instead, he whispered, "You could have said that first!" She glared at him and pointed at the whiteboard. "Okay," he conceded. "Boring dates."

"Right. And then," she finished, fixing him with her hardest stare, "we are going to get married. And you'd better be on board with that because it's..."

Her voice had been commanding, but her cheeks betrayed her; they flushed pink, got pinker the longer he looked at her, and she faltered. "Nonnegotiable," she finished in a whisper.

Kane folded his arms—then unfolded them again when his IV pulled on his hand—and shook his head.

"No?" She looked horrified.

Kane could have prolonged the moment, given what she'd put him through the day before, but he took the whiteboard from her and wrote something on it.

He turned it around for her.

Marry.

Me.

Now.

Her eyes spilled over with tears, and she pressed her hand to her mouth the way he loved, as if she'd ever been able to hide her emotions from him.

◆

Ellen was finally allowed to take him home on Christmas Eve. His lungs would still take some time to heal. His voice might always have the slight crack he'd acquired, and his back would need anti-inflammatories for a few days yet at least. But he was better and sick of hospital food, and Cat had threatened them both with coal in their stockings if they didn't make it over to her house for Christmas.

Ellen was so worried about his back that night that she put just about every cushion he owned behind him as he sat in bed. They drank champagne and fell asleep watching *It's a Wonderful Life*, and on Christmas morning Ellen woke up at six o'clock to call her parents.

She'd spoken to them, of course, when Kane had gone into the hospital, when it had become clear she wasn't going to be home for Christmas. But she hadn't shared their other news.

Kane was still blinking the sleep out of his eyes when she fired up the computer. "Merry Christmas," he said, kissing her. "Can we go back to bed now?"

"You'll be fine," she said, patting his leg under the covers. To her, he looked fantastic, with his hair rumpled and his eyes darker than usual with sleep. He'd lost some weight in the hospital, so that his cheekbones were more prominent than usual, but generally he looked good enough to eat, which she was going to take care of as soon as they were done with this phone call.

Kane pushed the computer so it didn't face him anymore and disappeared into the bathroom. When her mother answered, Andrew wasn't the only one with her. Her brother, sister-in-law, and nephews were all beaming through the screen as well. "Happy Christmas!" they all yelled, or at least all but Charlotte.

"Happy Christmas," Ellen echoed back, astonished at how being so content in her own life made her so much fonder of everyone else. "I'm sorry we're not there," she said and meant it. "Hi, boys! Wow, you're so big! What did Father Christmas bring you?"

"You sound different," said Oliver, while his brother Rhys began a detailed explanation of his Lego hoard.

"That's 'cause I haven't had enough Olly and Rhys time," she assured them. "I miss you!" And again, she meant it.

"How's the Yank?" asked Adam.

"Much better, thanks," she said. "He just got out of hospital yesterday."

"Good; that's good to hear," said Andrew. He was wearing a joyfully hideous green jumper with red bobbles all over it. "So what are your plans today, darling?"

She gave him a clean version. Kane came back into the room just as Jen, Adam's wife, said, "So, come on, where is he?"

"Right here," Kane said, sitting down next to Ellen. The lock of hair that fell into his eyes was wet. He gave her family the hundred-kilowatt Fielding smile. "Nice to meet you all."

Ellen looked at him, felt the heat of his shoulder and arm against hers as he leaned in to get in the shot, and had never been prouder of him in her life. Even more so when there was a tiny moment of stunned silence, and Charlotte put her hand to her throat and cleared it ever so slightly.

"At last," said Andrew, recovering first. "A face to match the name. How are you feeling?"

"Good, but I think you and everyone else have seen too much of my face the past few weeks."

Lord, was he going to go there right away? Hadn't she told him to let her warm them up first? Didn't he know that her family eased around elephants in rooms? For years if necessary?

"I want to apologize for the publicity," Kane went on. Ellen felt faint. "Ellen hated it." He looked at her, his smile turning warmer, more intimate. "I guess if she hadn't been so beautiful, it wouldn't have been a problem."

Her cheeks immediately flushed scarlet. She risked a look back at her parents. Charlotte's mouth was open. Andrew's eyes were wide in his broad face. "Well," Andrew stammered, "well, of course, we're glad you think so."

"Who wouldn't think so?" Kane said, still looking at her in that blazing, intimate way. Ellen wanted to put her hand in front of his face, to hide him from them. But she was too mesmerized to move.

Kane finally looked back at the camera. "So, Mr. Hunter, I want to ask you if you will allow me to marry Ellen." Charlotte gave a little gasp. "But I have to tell you that possession is nine-tenths of the law, and I really can't let her go, so I'm counting on you saying yes."

Andrew's mouth was working, but no sound came out. Ellen had forgotten how to breathe. Charlotte, who hadn't said a word the entire call, found her voice at last. "But we don't know you! And you've only known each other a few weeks!"

"I know," Kane said. "I wouldn't believe it myself, except that it's happened."

"We don't plan on getting married right away," Ellen said quickly, her voice sounding high and unnatural.

"*She* doesn't plan on it," Kane said. He squeezed her to him for a second. "I plan on wearing her down."

Oh my God. All this public display of affection! Ellen closed her eyes and then squinted at her family. Adam had gone sideways out of the shot; Jen had a silly dippy smile on her face that Ellen hadn't seen since her wedding; Charlotte and Andrew looked as though they didn't have the software to respond.

"The bottom line," said Kane, "is that for some reason Ellen loves me." Ellen closed her eyes again and blushed, if possible, even more. "And God knows I love her, and it would be the greatest achievement of my life to make her happy for the rest of hers."

"Oh God," Ellen said weakly, putting her hands to her cheeks. She dared one last look at her parents before she melted into a puddle of embarrassment.

But Charlotte's cheeks, that ordinarily betrayed nary a crease or even a dusting of emotional pink, were as red as Ellen's. Ellen had never seen her like this. "Well," Charlotte said, putting one hand to them as Ellen was. "Well, of course we love her too."

Ellen's mouth fell open. All embarrassment was forgotten in the shock of hearing her mother say that word. "*Mum.*"

"Yes, dear?"

"I... I just... nothing. I love you back."

Kane beamed at her. Ellen put her hand over his face and pushed gently. "Shut up," she muttered, though she couldn't help but smile too.

Charlotte gave an almighty sniff and patted her cheeks with her hands. "Right, then," she said, already arranging her face back to its usual serene expression. "So when can we expect a visit?"

♦

Ellen closed the laptop. "So, what, you thought you'd get all the embarrassment out of the way at once?" she said to Kane, who had a very self-satisfied grin on his face as he leaned back against the pillows.

"Yep," he said, taking her hands and pulling her so she was lying on top of him. "That was fun."

"I can't look my dad in the face ever again."

"It's just love, Ellen," he said, his voice lowering again. "Not the plague. You'll survive."

She blushed, for the fiftieth time that morning, and kissed him. "How's your back?"

His eyes crinkled up at the corners. "Just fine." They kissed again, for a long time, loving the freedom of knowing that they had the rest of their lives.

But when Ellen pulled away and went to unbutton her pajama top, Kane took hold of her hands and stopped her. Surprised, she looked up.

He kissed the palms of both hands. "Let me," he said.

And she did.

Preview of Hold

Want to know how Thea gets her HEA? Enjoy a sneak peak at the next book in the Fieldings series, HOLD.

♦

Being Audrey Hepburn sucked.

"Cat!" Thea Fielding shouted from the back porch, into the pouring rain. "Caaat!"

The gutter leaked a steady sheet of rain onto her head. She almost welcomed it for its cooling effect on her headache, but it was sending icy drops down the back of her neck, making her shiver and curse.

"Cat!" she yelled again. "Goddamn, flea-bitten, ratty old caaaat!"

Through the back door behind her, an unholy wail started up. For a few seconds, three-year-old Benji had forgotten his tantrum in his shock that his mother had turned her back on him, walked out of the kitchen, and slammed the door, leaving him alone. But apparently he'd remembered his grievance.

"Shut up!" another voice called down the stairs, breaking into a squeak on the last word. "Shut up shut up shut up!"

"Nooooooo!" Benji wailed at his brother, Jake. "Youuuuuu shut uuuuup!"

"God, Benji, quit it!" She could imagine Jake's angular body bending down the narrow staircase to shout through the railings. "You're so stupid!"

"Cat!" Thea called, hoping she could drown them out. What did she care if the damn cat didn't come in, if it got soaked and lost and run over by a car? They hadn't even named the thing. It would be one less thing for her to have to take care of.

Benji was thumping something, or maybe hammering his heels

against the kitchen floor. Jake echoed the sound with his feet running back upstairs, no doubt to jam his earbuds into his head so he could tell the truth later when he said he couldn't hear her. Thea put one hand on the peeling porch post, which moved a little, and leaned farther out into the rain.

Now she really was Audrey Hepburn, crying and yelling at the end of *Breakfast at Tiffany's*. If Audrey had had Thea's dull brown hair, awkward height, and exhausted, dark eyes, that is. And if she'd had two boys and a useless ex who'd left them all with no warning, left *her* with nothing but what she'd scrounged and kept for herself for fifteen years. Which, from this end of a leaning porch at the wrong end of this Boston suburb, didn't look like a whole hell of a lot.

She scrunched her hand into a fist as Benji's yelling passed beyond misery and into anger. He was probably rubbing his head into the macaroni and cheese he'd just thrown on the floor. Which she would now have to clean up. Benji *and* the floor.

Dammit, this was not how her life was supposed to go! She was the smart one! She was going to beat them all! All her teachers had said so. So how did she end up with two kids and a crappy job and–

"Mooooommmmm!" Benji's voice had transcended anger; now it was hitting her where it really hurt: her heart. He sounded lost and pathetic, his sobs body-shaking to both of them. Thea knew how he felt.

She turned back to the house. As she opened the back door, a black streak of matted fur dashed past her into the house, smearing a wet line along her calf. But Benji was crying too hard to touch the cat as it went past.

Thea sat down on the floor, picked Benji up, and deposited him in her lap.

"Okay, buddy," she murmured, wrapping him up as tight as she could in her arms, mac and cheese be damned. His hot, wet face leaned into her chest, and she felt a juddering sigh escape him. "It's okay."

"I want Daddy," he said.

Thea squeezed her eyes shut, more of her own tears falling down her cheeks. "I know, sweetie."

Jake didn't say these things. He didn't ask for his father. He knew Gabriel wasn't coming back, and that broke Thea's spirit more than Benji's endless hoping.

They'd been like this for a month: the shock of Gabe's final voicemail, sent from his mother's home in Ireland because he was too chicken to call her until he was well out of reach. The three of them held in this limbo, waiting for something to happen, for something to get better.

Benji's head got heavier against her, his sobs subsiding into gulps. She loved him fiercely, and her love for Jake bordered on obsession. He suffered more, and would suffer more, from his father's desertion. Thea sighed, her fists clenching on Benji's back.

This has to stop. We have to change. I have to change.

The solution came to her between one heartbeat and the next. As soon as her mind formed the words, she felt the change in her. A thrill of energy that wasn't anger or fear or panic. She pulled Benji away from her so he was facing her, and began wiping his wet cheeks. His birthmark, which spread down his cheek and would probably need surgery one day, was even darker against his red face.

"Ben-ben," she said, giving him a big smile that made his eyes widen, "Mommy's going back to school."

♦

Liam McConnell stood in the vestry of St. Barnabas's church, running his hand over his close-shaven chin and feeling at once sick and elated. His father, next to him, was dressed in the same morning suit as Liam but with a more subdued waistcoat—Avery had put Liam in a lavender vest because it and ivory were her colors. He had a suspicion the purple clashed with his hair, but he wasn't about to say anything.

"I don't have any great speech for you," his father said. Like Liam, Pat McConnell had red hair, but his had turned white over the last few years. Dad always said he'd gotten it watching his only son swan off to college when he had a perfectly good job waiting for him at home.

"You don't need a speech, Dad." They didn't see eye to eye on much, but today Liam loved everyone. He had exactly what he wanted: Avery, a career in teaching despite his dad's best efforts, and a house that would pretty soon be worthy of his new wife. A future doing what he loved, with the woman he loved by his side. "I just hope I'm as happy as you and Mom."

His father scrubbed his chin the same way Liam did. "What your mom and I have doesn't come along very often."

Huh. But Liam was sure his dad didn't mean that the way it had sounded. "I know it's a lot of work, keeping a marriage going."

"You got that right. And your Avery here, she's used to the finer things." Dad waved a hand at their boutonnieres, which were sharply sculpted calla lilies in a darker purple than Liam's waistcoat.

Liam ignored the uncertainty in his voice and the implied criticism of his fiancée's style. He was more a wildflowers and straw kind of guy, but wasn't every man? "She's the same as me, Dad. We'll be working for those things together. She knows two teachers' salaries won't stretch to fancy cars or exotic vacations. We talked about it."

Pat grunted. "Good. Well, I hope you're right, son. 'Course, if you'd stayed with the business, you'd have—"

"Dad." Liam scrubbed his chin again. "Not today, okay?"

His chin was cold. And it *itched.* But Avery had asked him to shave his beard, just for today.

"You don't like the beard?" he'd replied. "You could have said something sooner!" They'd been together for three years.

"I love you, hon, and the beard is...well, part of you, I guess, but I just thought for the wedding you could, you know, be kind of a little...groomed."

It wasn't like you could nest birds in his beard; he kept it cut pretty close. But if it was what she wanted for the wedding, who cared? He only had to look at Avery's perfect Cupid-bow mouth and big blue eyes, fringed as they always were by impossibly long, dark lashes, and he knew he'd give her anything she wanted.

Because she was giving him everything he wanted.

Want more? Get HOLD at your favourite bookstore! books2read.com/u/m2dZV1

Acknowledgements

Too many people to name here have helped me get this book to this place, so I must be picky. I give effusive thanks and gratitude to you all, but especially:

To my agent, Veronica Park, whose boundless enthusiasm and support sustained me through the rollercoaster ride of being a writer on submission.

To my original editors at Crimson, Tara Gelsomino, Jess Verdi, and Julie Sturgeon, who helped me birth this book baby.

To the first ever readers of this story, Asabe and Bea, who knew Kane and Ellen way back when. I hope you like how they turned out. And to my first editor, Ella Slayne, who made me believe I wasn't totally crap at this.

To the ladies of New Jersey Romance Writers, without whose love and support I might have given up on this game fifteen different times. Michelle Joyce Bond, I really lucked out to get you as my critique partner! Thank you ever so for your clarity and encouragement.

And finally to my family, and most especially to my mother, whose love of language I inherited. Hello up there, Mummy, and don't read the rude bits.

Other Books by Kimberley Ash

The Fieldings

Hold

Stand

Rise

The Van Allen Brothers:

Forgive Me

Forget Me

Free Me

Standalones:

Champion

Connect with Kimberley!

I hope you loved Kane and Ellen and *Breathe!* Join my Facebook Group, Read Your Ash Off, sign up for my newsletter, and follow me to get the latest info on my new releases and events. I look forward to meeting you!

Website: www.kimberleyash.com
Bookbub: @KimberleyAsh
Instagram: @KAshAuthor
Goodreads: Kimberley Ash
Facebook Page: Kimberley Ash Books
Twitter: @KAshAuthor